Alan Scholefiel
His first novel,
immediate success, enabling him to give up
journalism and become a full time writer.

He now lives in Hampshire with his wife and
three daughters.

Alan Scholefield's many books include: *Great
Elephant, Lion in the Evening, Point of Honour,
The Stone Flower, Venom* (which was filmed in
1982 starring Nicol Williamson, Sarah Miles,
Oliver Reed and Susan George) and *The Sea
Cave.*

Also by Alan Scholefield in Sphere Books:

THE STONE FLOWER

GREAT ELEPHANT

THE SEA CAVE

The Eagles of Malice

Alan Scholefield

SPHERE BOOKS LIMITED
London and Sydney

First published in Great Britain by
William Heinemann Ltd 1968
Copyright © 1968 Alan Scholefield
Published by Sphere Books Ltd 1984
30–32 Gray's Inn Road, London WC1X 8JL

For my daughter
NICOLA
with love

TRADE
MARK

Printed and bound in Great Britain by
Cox & Wyman Ltd, Reading

AUTHOR'S NOTE

There is no such place as Falkenberg, either the village or the castle, in South West Africa, so that none of its inhabitants ever existed other than in the author's imagination. Thus any similarity between Falkenberg and those German castles that still stand with Gothic splendour among the dunes of the Namib Desert is purely coincidental.

The description of the Herero Rising (1904-05) in Book III and the consequences of General von Trotha's brutal Extermination Policy are taken largely from the 'Report on the Natives of South West Africa and their treatment by Germany' (Command Paper No. 9146 of 1918 presented jointly to the British and South African Parliaments); *Peter Moor's Fahrt nach Sudwestafrika* by Gustav Frenssen; and *Strategie des Allemands dans leur guerre contre les Hereros* by A. Kerremans.

BOOK ONE

The Mendicants

We all sense that in the distant future humanity must
be faced by problems which only a highest race,
having become master people and supported by the
means and possibilities of an entire globe, will be
equipped to overcome.

Adolf Hitler, Mein Kampf

It was a strange, freakish dawn of high, striated cirrus clouds, some already an angry red where the sun was catching the high-flown desert dust, some pale pink, some slate grey. If he turned his head there were other clouds, fleecy cumulus lying beneath the cirrus, heavy and mouse-coloured in the early light. And if he turned again there was nothing but a blue-grey vacuum stretching as far as his eyes were able to comprehend. Here, in the Kalahari Desert, the empty heart of Africa, the sky was total.

Red clouds in the morning; shepherds' warning. Red clouds at night; shepherds' delight.

Andrew Black gazed briefly up at the sky then clamped the prismatic glasses to his eyes once more and let the 6×30 lenses bring the desert closer. He could remember his father repeating the old saying to him when he was a child. It might have worked in the Cape; it had no meaning whatsoever in the Kalahari.

No rain had fallen in this part of the desert since December 1901—more than a year before—and no aphorism, however well it rhymed, was going to make a jot of difference. It was now winter. No rain fell in the Kalahari in winter. That was that.

Had he been a different sort of person Andrew might have studied the dawn for its own sake, wondering at its ominous Wagnerian beauty; but neither had he heard of Wagner nor had he time for aesthetic appreciation. Sunrise was sunrise; the start of another day.

By comparison with the sky the desert was a two-dimensional sepia monochrome that gradually changed as the light strengthened. The sepia became reddish-brown and shadows added the necessary dimension, bringing limestone outcrops, boulders and the occasional acacia tree up out of the flat landscape.

He lowered the glasses and wiped his eyes with the back of his hand. Already he could feel the sun striking on his right cheek,

3

sending a spasm of warmth through his chilled body. It was at rare moments like these that he felt anything but hatred for the Kalahari's sun : that was how he thought of it. In reality, of course, if it was anyone's sun it belonged to the British Government, out of whose protectorate of Bechuanaland it was presently rising. Later, as it swung westwards across its zenith, it would become the Kaiser's sun, in the wastes of whose colony, German South-West Africa, it would sink to rest.

But Sub-Inspector Black of the Bechuanaland Protectorate Police had not considered these fancies either. At present he was an agent of His Majesty's Imperial Government and as such it was his duty to collect the hut tax in an area three times the size of the land which employed him. This he had signally failed to do. There had been no mistaking the tone of the letter. Unconsciously his fingers went to the breast-pocket of his tunic. He withdrew his hand sharply. It was time to forget the letter.

Chik, the Bushman tracker, who lay at his left side, and Trooper Jonathan, his Basuto orderly, who lay at his right, both pretended not to notice the gesture. They knew there was a piece of paper in his pocket for they had seen him read it many times and each time they had seen his face. Neither knew what the letter contained; neither wished to know.

Andrew shifted his elbows to a more comfortable position on the iron-hard ground and brought up the glasses, this time focusing directly on the village. It lay still and deserted as it had done all through the long cold night and the longer day before. The word village hardly defined the collection of a dozen or so huts that crouched against the southern slope of a slight rise, although the huts were of a more solid construction than the average Kalahari *pondok*, which was of skins over a wooden framework. Andrew had once seen some in the Bushman country that were little more than lairs, tufts of grass tied together to act as windbreaks.

Here in Seitsang's village, however, the roofs were thatched and the walls were of mud. Mud. That was the significant factor. Where there was mud there was water. He swung the glasses past the last of the huts and picked up the well-worn track—darker than the surrounding area—that led to the water-pit. It was the only water for a sixty-mile thirst in any direction. That's why he was waiting. Seitsang would have to bring the people back.

He remembered the first time; this was where it had started,

4

more than a year ago, on his first trek to collect hut tax. He was green then, unsure of himself. He was also afraid of the desert and, being afraid, was in sympathy with the pathetic groups of desert people who fought to survive in such a terrible place. So when Seitsang had pleaded poverty Andrew had believed him. They had eaten a *makatane* melon or two between them and old Seitsang had promised that better times would come and that he would surely pay his due to the king across the water and Andrew had gone on his way filled with pity for the old man and his handful of people and filled too with a noble satisfaction at his own magnanimity that did much to raise his flagging spirits.

At first the fact that so many other villages also pleaded desperate poverty—had not the drought been crippling?—did not seem significant. But slowly, as his newness wore off, as his own spirit hardened to the harshness of the country, he began to realize that somehow the word had gone before him, until he could almost see the contempt in a headman's eyes as he said he could not pay the hut tax that year. Could not? In some cases the inflection of the translated words almost became *would* not.

And then the letter had come from Headquarter House, Mafeking, signed by the Resident Commissioner. Although it was couched in the remote phraseology of the Colonial Service its meaning was clear. In effect it said: 'You have made a fool of yourself, and therefore you have made a fool of the Bechuanaland Protectorate Police and therefore you have made a fool of your superiors, the British Government and the King himself. But above all you have made a fool of me.'

The next village headman who pleaded poverty was tied to the wheel of Andrew's Scotch-cart and left without water for a day and a half. The letter he kept as a reminder.

Now he was here again and it was Seitsang's turn. But the wily old Kalahari must have had a good communications system for he and his people were gone. It would have been possible to track them down but that would have been exhausting and perhaps dangerous. Andrew had learnt many things since his last visit and the most important was never to fight the desert; let it fight for you. He waited.

The sun had cleared the horizon and already the brief lavender beauty of the early morning had vanished. The desert revealed itself in all its harshness. It was a red desert of endlessly similar vistas ending always in a horizon of low scrub-covered hills, already twisting and writhing as the heatwaves rippled on their surface. He changed the water-bottle from his right to his left side where he could shade it with his body. He was tempted to take a mouthful, but only briefly. He had drunk once in the night and would wait now—unless something happened—until sunset, when the evaporation from his body would be less. He had learnt to play a game with himself in which he was conscious of his own limits. When he was thirsty he would postpone a drink for one hour. When that time was up he would set himself another hour. In this way he usually arrived at sunset. Even when water was plentiful he drank sparingly. He had early learnt that self-discipline in the Kalahari was more than a moral philosophy; it could be the difference between living and dying.

On his very first trek, on the long, sandy thirst between Kokong and Lehututu, he had come across the body of a white man, already half eaten by jackals and hyenas. Somewhere along the way the man had discarded his shoes—or perhaps worn them through—for he was in his stockinged feet. Near the body was an empty water-bottle, in the neck of which had been placed a note. It read simply :

9.30

Dear S.,

Last night the cattle ran away. I have no more water. I despair. I left the wagon on foot in the hope of reaching Kokong, but my strength fails. My private papers and stamps send to my children in Bulawayo, and inform them that I have died of fever in the desert and am buried. The thirst kills me. These are the last words of a dying man.

Your true friend,

M.

P.S. A little water would have saved me.

Andrew had held an inquiry on the spot and discovered that M. was a trader called Meyer. The letter was to his partner, Silver. He must have been new to the Kalahari for he had left

Lehututu on the 100-mile thirst to Kokong with a fifty-gallon drum of water; more than enough for his needs. It was obvious that he had been recklessly extravagant with it, using it for cooking, washing and watering some of his stock. When the drum gave out his drovers deserted and he was left to his own resources. What had affected Andrew most deeply was that Meyer's body had been discovered less than a thousand yards from the Kokong pits. The postscript to the letter was cut into his mind.

But water was not his problem now. If the water in Seitsang's pit was too foul there was always Watch with the Scotch-cart. By Andrew's estimate Watch was about two days behind. Later, if necessary, he could send Chik out to warn him. He didn't want the old fool blundering into Seitsang's people and losing both water *and* supplies. If he did he'd have his head on a plate. No matter how carefully he briefed Watch the old Nyasa always gave the impression of knowing better. One day . . . Andrew shrugged with irritation, more at himself than anyone else. One day . . . one day. . . . He had been saying that from the very start. One day he'd get rid of Watch. But he knew he wouldn't. From the first day the Nyasa had walked into his camp near Lake Ngami and pronounced himself the best cook and camp boy in the whole of the Protectorate Andrew had been lost, seduced by a meal of succulent ant-heap mushrooms stewed with venison. Watch claimed to have been camp boy to Selous himself on his crossing of the Great Thirst in 1878 and it might have been true. One thing Andrew did know was that he could no longer live with his own cooking. Watch was his one luxury.

The first time Andrew had gone to Bulawayo to sit for his law examinations, on which all promotion depended, he had taken Watch with him on the long trek past the southern fringe of the great Makarikari salt pan and left him at Francistown while he, Andrew, boarded the Northbound Mail. He had returned to find Watch the centre of a conspiracy in which at least two brother officers were trying to bribe the old man into their service. He had hurriedly loaded him into the Scotch-cart and rumbled away into the interior, putting as much distance as possible between Watch and temptation. His saving of Watch for himself had in some way mitigated against his total failure in the law papers. The second time he sat the examination, only a month ago, he had left Watch more than 200 miles from the nearest outpost of civilization.

Now, as he thought of the hushed room, the scratching of steel-nibbed pens, the impersonal, almost cold, air of the examiners, he could feel a tightening of his stomach muscles. How the hell was one supposed to study law in the middle of a desert? He thought of the books: *Native Law and Administration, Constitutional Law, Criminal Law, The Law of Evidence*—all neatly packed away in their box on the Scotch-cart. He thought of the endless evenings when, his own supper over, Watch would light the lantern and bring out the books with all the fussiness and concern of a parent. And he would have to sit there, his head ringing with tiredness, reading and memorizing cases and precedents and tribal customs of the Bakalahadis and the Barolongs, the Bangwaketsis and the Batlhwaris, the Bakwenas and the Bakhatlas, the Batawanas and the Bamangwatos, the Mancal Bushmen and the Magon Bushmen—when it was taking him all his time just to learn their dialects. Often he would fall asleep over the pages and wake to find Watch shaking him crossly and he would raise the wick in the lantern and try to see the pages through the blur of insects that were attracted to the light.

If it hadn't been for Watch he would have done very little reading indeed. As it was he might not have done enough. The results would be out in a few weeks at most; again he experienced a cold feeling at the thought of a second failure.

There was no question in his mind : if he failed again he'd get out. He wasn't going to spend the rest of his life as the oldest sub-inspector in the force, condemned to wander the burning desolation of the Great Thirst, his only company an illiterate Bushman, a slow-thinking orderly and a nagging cook. Yet what else was he to do, where else was he to go?

He felt a touch on his leg and came abruptly out of his reverie. It was Chik. Andrew swung the glasses up to his eyes and followed the Bushman's small and very dirty finger.

At first he could see nothing except the heatwaves which rose and fell like a ground swell. Then he made out the faint movements of people, like darker dots on a dark background.

He had been watching the moving specks for perhaps five minutes before he heard Trooper Jonathan clear his throat and announce in his sonorous basso voice : 'Something move far away, Morena.' He shifted ponderously and pointed in the direction Andrew was already looking.

8

'Thank you,' Andrew said coldly. 'You have wonderful eyes.'

'It may be they are Seitsang's people, Morena,' the Basuto continued.

Andrew ignored him.

'They will be dry,' Jonathan said.

The group appeared to be thirty to forty strong. They straggled over the desert singly or in pairs, making a long, broken line half a mile in length. In front came the men, hurrying now as they approached the water, at the back came the women who were carrying babies, and the old people. Andrew noted that except for one or two of the younger men all were shuffling along, heads bowed with weakness. In the centre of the group he could see a party of five or six. That would be Seitsang and his wives. He wondered how many had died in the desert. Almost certainly some of the older people would have perished. Well, these were desert people and they knew the penalties of fighting the desert. It was their own damn fault.

'They come for the water,' Jonathan continued remorselessly.

Andrew touched Chik on the shoulder. The Bushman quivered like an alert hunting dog. 'You go over there,' Andrew said, pointing to an outcrop above the water-pit. 'If you have to shoot, for Christ's sake be careful where you point that thing.' The Bushman smiled a curiously childlike grin and glided away from them, swiftly merging with the landscape. He was a young boy, and now that he was eating regularly his skin had a sleek, oily sheen. He wore a torn khaki shirt and an old pair of Andrew's shorts which came down past his knees, for although Andrew was not above medium height Chik only came to his shoulder. In his hand he carried an old and violent muzzle-loader, down the barrel of which he stuffed an assortment of ironmongery, and which, when fired, sprayed a forty-five-degree segment with the ferocity of a carronade. In the eight months Chik had been with him, Andrew had tried to instil into his head a spit-and-polish philosophy. The Bushman looked untidy and Andrew did not care for untidiness in people.

Once, when Chik was upwind of him, he had been conscious of an unpleasant smell. At first he thought an animal had died nearby, then he realized that the smell was emanating from Chik. It transpired that the Bushman had got his hands on some eland

9

fat the day before and had smeared his entire body. They had a reasonable supply of water at the time and Andrew had instructed Jonathan to make sure Chik was cleaned up by supper. He was just sitting down to his meal when he heard a scuffling noise from behind the cart, then a yell and the sound of a bucket being thrown. He found Jonathan on his back, the bucket jammed securely on his head. Chik was perched on his chest beating a rapid tattoo on the bucket with a piece of wood, the Bushman's shrieks of anger mingling with the yells of fear which emerged hollowly from the bucket.

Later Andrew asked Chik if he ever washed. The Bushman had looked innocently puzzled. Then he asked: 'Why?' After that Andrew left him alone.

Trooper Jonathan was different. Even in the middle of the desert his boots were always gleaming, his buttons highly polished, saddle and bridle glistening. Unlike most black skins his did not seem to be affected by the desert dust and shone as though it was newly waxed every morning. On parade at the Gaberones base camp he had even been known to blacken the soles of his boots below the instep. Andrew thoroughly approved of his dedication, for he himself was painstakingly neat, and had his examinations been based on turn-out he would already have been a senior inspector. The last time he had been down to the German border for an evening or two of Lieutenant von Steinberg's company he had been very pleased with Jonathan. The Basuto had made the German's Hottentot orderly look like a scarecrow. Still, that was hardly to be wondered at; for trustworthiness and general bearing a Basuto was worth ten Hottentots any day of the week, which was why they were brought all this long way from their homeland. Andrew liked to think that wherever they were the Resident Commissioner himself could step out suddenly from behind a mopane tree, and find him and his small company—with the exception of Chik, who hardly counted—present and ready for inspection.

'You stay here,' Andrew said to the Trooper. 'If you see me wave my hat thus'—he removed the wide-brimmed veld hat and waved it in front of Jonathan's nose—'stand up and let yourself be seen. Don't fire unless it's necessary. D'you follow?'

'When the hat is shaken I stand up, Morena.' Jonathan took hold of the issue .303 and began to scramble to his feet.

'Not now!' He waited until the Basuto had subsided. 'Let them see the gun.'

'I will hold up the gun, Morena,' Jonathan said doggedly.

Andrew picked up his own rifle, a .404 Jeffries and slowly made his way down the side of the outcrop. Then he remembered the ropes. He turned and scrambled back. It was no use leaving things in the air with Jonathan; he didn't have Chik's imagination. 'If I wave my hand thus, bring the ropes down. Follow?'

'Yes, Morena.'

Seitsang's people were now about 500 yards from the village. Several, trying to put more speed into their steps, had stumbled, fallen, picked themselves up and were coming forward at a slower pace. Andrew sat down in the slight shade of an acacia tree that grew near the lip of the water-pit, and with great deliberation began to fill his pipe with tobacco that was so dry even the slightest pressure caused it to crumble into powder.

The Kalaharis stumbled towards the water-pit like the tattered remnants of a defeated army, carrying their household goods on their backs. They passed a few feet from Andrew, ignoring him completely in their extremity. Those who first reached the pit looked down the sheer limestone sides of the natural well at the dark water lying twenty feet or more below. As the women and children who had been near the back came up, the press of people completely encircled it. They stood there, dusty and wretched in their skin wraps, as though stunned by the vision of cool oblivion. But Andrew knew the reason for their confusion. Someone began to whimper; it could have been a child or an old man. He was unable to see. In spite of himself he felt pity for them but even as it grew on him he pushed it aside. It was their own bloody fault. They should have stayed where they were and paid the hut tax and not gone off into the desert hoping he would think the village was abandoned.

At last someone said what was in everyone's thoughts. 'The ropes. Where are the ropes?'

As though the spoken words had finally communicated their terrible predicament the sun-stricken rabble began to search feverishly among the boulders and wait-a-bit thorn that grew near the pit. Abruptly, Seitsang broke away and called one or two young men to his side; they turned in Andrew's direction; cause and effect had finally sunk in.

11

'Greetings, Seitsang,' Andrew said as the old headman approached him. 'I hope you have had a good journey.'

The Kalahari, dressed in long brown worsted trousers, a torn and dusty black jacket and what had once been a pair of Oxford brogues, stared at him with hatred. In his hand he carried an ancient muzzle-loader. He looked twenty years older than the last time Andrew had seen him and even then he had been an old man. Now his eyes were sunken in his head and his cheeks were hollow. He was flanked by two of the young tribesmen. Each carried a gun of similar age and pattern.

At last Seitsang spoke. 'You have the ropes,' he said. 'And the buckets.' It was a simple statement of fact and was made in a voice that grated with dryness.

Andrew nodded. 'That is so.'

'We cannot get to the water. My people are dying.'

'I can see that. You have taken them on too long a thirst.'

'We must have the ropes.'

'Of course you must. And the Government must have its taxes.'

The remainder of those who could still stand had gathered around their chief. The enormity of Andrew's action—so alien to a desert people—had not yet been taken in. They looked hurt and bewildered.

First one, then a second, seemed to grasp the significance of the dialogue. They shuffled forward, muttering angrily. Andrew guessed there might be a dozen old muzzle-loaders among them. He stood up casually and shifted the rifle to the crook of his right arm. There was a slight ripple among the tribesmen as some took a backward pace.

'Let us drink,' Seitsang said, 'and then you shall have your taxes.'

'Doubtless that is the manner in which you would like to conduct the affair. But what then, Seitsang? You would become a poor man again; too poor to pay. I think it will have to be the other way.'

Several of the women had stretched out on the ground regardless of the sun. One, holding her infant under her left arm, was allowing it to suck at a withered, dried-up breast. Their faces bore expressions of complete resignation.

Suddenly, as though he had made up his mind, Seitsang spoke

quickly to one of the young men at his side. Andrew, whose attention had been diverted for the moment by the woman and her baby, missed what had been said and was only aware of the young Kalahari moving towards him. Automatically he stepped backward. His foot turned on a loose stone and he fell. In that instant the roar of Chik's firelock broke the desert silence, followed a split second later by a rushing noise as the assorted missiles from its barrel flew overhead.

The villagers made no move to run. They stood fearfully where they were, too exhausted, too far gone to make the effort.

Andrew, on his back in the dust, found himself looking up into Seitsang's eyes. There was a curious mixture of contempt and satisfaction on the old man's face. 'Be not afraid,' he said. 'I had merely ordered that the taxes be paid. The young man will take you to the hut.' With that he turned away and seated himself beneath the acacia tree.

Andrew picked himself up and dusted his uniform. He grabbed for the rifle which had been knocked from his hand by the fall. He stood for a moment, trying to regain his former stature but he could see nothing in their eyes at all; there was neither respect nor elation, only indifference. He turned and followed the young Kalahari into the village.

He was seething with rage but knew enough not to show it. To be made a fool of twice by the same native was almost more than he could bear. Consciously he tried to calm himself down, tried to relax his arms and legs, which seemed to jerk rigidly as he walked.

They entered the third hut. The interior was completely bare, the same as all the other huts—as he knew from his search of the day before. In the centre of the hut the young Kalahari went down on his knees and with his hands scraped away the ash and coals of the old fires. Soon he came to a large flat stone buried under the mud floor. With Andrew's help he raised it and laid it on its side. Andrew found himself looking down at a chamber about three feet deep. It was filled to the brim with skins—silver jackal, clousie, sepa, lynx—and, better still, ostrich feathers.

As the young man brought up the bundles, Andrew slit the leather binding-thongs with his O.I.O. knife and examined each pelt. All were excellent winter skins. He stepped to the hut doorway and called Chik to collect the horses, then went back in. He

13

counted each skin before he finally signalled to Jonathan for the ropes.

He ordered the Kalahari to fasten the skins into bundles again, and in the half light of the hut he consulted the figures in his diary : 31 silver jackal, 75 clousie, 12 sepa, 8 lynx. He could only estimate the weight of the ostrich feathers but he was certain it was over 20 lb. He decided to take everything.

When they were tied he watched the Kalahari struggling with the stone and unwillingly moved to help. In doing so he looked down into the darkness of the chamber. Something in one of the corners seemed to shine dully. He went down on his knees but couldn't make out what it was. He dropped into the hole, holding his breath against the feral, musty smell that rose to his face, and groped with his fingers. He brought up a cigarette case.

He examined it in the light of the doorway. By its weight he guessed it to be silver. He could distinguish the initials M.E.S. on the engraving plate. He pressed the catch and the case sprang open. The elastic straps were perished and loose. A few grains of tobacco still clung to the hinges. He closed the case and looked at it thoughtfully, then, hearing the horses, dropped it into his pocket and stepped outside.

When the skins had been loaded to his satisfaction he caught up the bridle of his own stallion, Duke, and told Chik to bring the other horse. In the distance he could hear the dull thud and splash as the hide buckets hit the surface of the water. Everyone with any strength left would be pulling on the long leather ropes.

The Bushman moved to the head of Jonathan's mare, carefully avoiding Andrew's eyes. When they reached the pit Andrew noticed that Jonathan was exhibiting the same unwillingness. The Trooper was absolutely correct in manner when Andrew ordered the horses watered but there was some indefinable change that he could not place : was it in his eyes? The stiffness of his back? Whatever it was, both Chik and Jonathan were displaying subtle though unmistakable signs of reproof.

He strolled over to where Seitsang still sat under the acacia tree. There were runnels of water on the front of his black coat. But if the water had refreshed him, he was showing little sign of it. His eyes were closed and his breathing was slow.

Andrew leant forward on one knee and stared into the wrinkled,

14

dusty face. He's more like an animal than a human, he thought, yet no animal he knew of would live on like this. Among animals the fight was to the strong and old Seitsang would long ago have had to battle for his leadership with younger and stronger contenders.

'Seitsang,' he said softly. The old Kalahari did not move. 'Seitsang!'

The eyelids fluttered and opened, revealing whites that had long since become a cloudy yellow-brown and irises that were purple with age. He looked up bleakly and slowly turned away, facing into the shadow.

'I'm talking to you!' Andrew touched one of Seitsang's legs with the toe of his boot. 'Look at me.' But the headman could have been asleep for all the notice he took. Andrew was forced to walk round the other side of the tree to bring himself into Seitsang's vision. He took the cigarette case from his pocket and held it under the headman's nose. 'I want to know where you came by this.'

He could tell by the way Seitsang's eyes moved and slid away that he had focused on the case. Then once more he gathered what strength he had left and shifted his body so he would not have to look at Andrew.

'All right!' Andrew glanced around quickly for Jonathan but the Basuto was on the far side of the pit, pulling water for the horses. He bent down and grabbed Seitsang by his coat lapels and hoisted him to his feet. He was so light it was as though the clothes were loosely stuffed with rags. Andrew was able to prop him against the tree trunk with one hand while he drew handcuffs from his belt. He fastened one to Seitsang's left wrist and the other to a branch above the Kalahari's head. The headman stood, swaying slightly as his legs tried to take the strain of his body. He looked down at the ground. He had made no move to resist.

'You can stay there until you find your tongue,' Andrew said. And he meant it. He was prepared to sit out the day if necessary. Something was going on, something he did not know about. He reached into a pocket and drew out the watch. It was an old hunter. The back had been ripped off, the glass and hands were gone. The face was so scratched that not even the maker's name was clear. A week ago a Bushman woman had walked into his

15

camp and offered it to him in return for tobacco. He had given her a six-inch length and questioned her briefly. She said she had found it in the desert somewhere to the north. He had not been greatly interested. It could have been in her possession for years. It was the sort of object, however valueless, that a Bushman might carry about, hoping some day to find a use for it. Now a cigarette case. . . .

'Master.' He looked up and saw one of Seitsang's wives. She must have been nearly as old as the headman himself. 'Master, you will kill him.' She was standing in such a way that Seitsang was able to lean most of his weight on her.

'It is with him,' Andrew said shortly. 'As soon as he tells me where he got this I'll release him.'

The old woman glanced at the case. He could see her mind working.

'If you lie to me,' he said, 'I will find you out.'

She looked at him uncertainly. Then she said, 'You take all our skins. How many will you leave if I tell you?'

He smiled a thin, hostile smile. 'None. Nor do I care whether you tell me or not. Eventually he will speak.'

'It was found,' she muttered.

'Where, when, who found it?'

She nodded in the direction of the pit where water was still being drawn. 'A man found it.'

'Bring him to me.'

She tried to move away but Seitsang fell forward, hanging from his wrist.

Andrew unlocked the cuffs and allowed him to slide onto the ground.

At the end of another hour he knew a little more about the cigarette case. It had been found by a young man doing the rounds of his game traps more than a week before. He had simply seen it lying on the desert floor and had picked it up. Was there any harm in that? Yes, there had been three cigarettes in the case and these he had shared with his brother. The place where he had found the case was six days north-east of the village. No, he had seen nothing else. No tracks, no spoor, nothing.

By this time the villagers had drunk their fill and drifted back to where their chief lay. Andrew looked at their faces. The indifference was gone. They were looking at the skins and looking

16

at Seitsang, and they were remembering. He knew it was time to leave.

Andrew looked down at the nasty congealing mess on the tin plate in front of him. Usually he loved fried kidneys but these might have been done in axle-grease and then dipped in sand. Also, his coffee was cold. He pushed the plate away. Instantly he heard Watch's step.

'Captain not like breakfast?'

It was on the tip of his tongue to say what he really thought of the food but he held back the words, knowing that days, even a week, might be made miserable by Watch's irritation.

'I'm not hungry.'

'Too much. Too much.' Watch muttered mysteriously to himself in his high-pitched and rather querulous voice as he scraped the wasted food onto the sand and banged the knife and fork against the plate.

Watch must have been nearly sixty and the peppercorns of hair which showed on the sides of the white cook's hat were a uniform grey. He was dressed as always in a white top and white shorts, with white canvas shoes on his feet. He was a slight man with more of a Hamitic than Bantu cast to his face, giving him thin lips and a thin nose. His movements, as he cleared the box top which Andrew used as a table, were fussy.

'Too much,' he muttered again and marched away to clean the plate and cutlery with a handful of dry grass and sand. Water was getting low in the drums and this was what had started the present domestic row.

It had occurred the day before when Andrew had discovered a slight cut just above Duke's fetlock. He had long since learnt that no trouble was too great when it came to caring for the horses, especially when they might be fifty miles from the nearest pit. So he had sent Jonathan to fetch a cup of water and the first-aid tin from the Scotch-cart. But water was Watch's province. It was he who had to check the levels and make certain there was always an emergency supply in the drums; in fact it was Watch who determined whether or not Andrew could wash or shave. Normal procedure, which Andrew had laid down, was that no one could draw water without Watch knowing; in this way he could calculate what the losses were. But either Jonathan had forgotten or Watch had not been at hand, and there had been the most stupid and noisy row. As he waited for the water he heard raised voices and when he went to discover the reason he found Watch waving a kitchen knife in Jonathan's face and calling him 'Basuto!'

Watch had never called Jonathan by his correct name. Whenever he referred to him it was by the name 'Yackson', possibly for the same obscure reason he referred to Andrew as 'Captain'. He didn't refer to Chik at all, pretending he didn't exist. In moments of deep anger he called Jonathan 'Basuto', investing it not only with loathing but extreme derogation. It was the one thing that broke through Jonathan's cast-iron demeanour and several times he had been on the verge of removing Watch's head for it.

Since leaving Seitsang's village they had been going hard for more than a week and Andrew was tired.

'Don't be such a bloody old woman!' he shouted at Watch. 'Can't you see I told him to fetch it? Now look what you've done.' In the confusion Jonathan had spilt the water. It lay at their feet, a dark stain on the reddish sand, rapidly disappearing as it dried. .

Later, when he thought about it, he knew he should have taken Watch's side—the procedural—but the one thing you didn't do with natives was to switch sides in an argument, it only confused them. Now Watch was paying him back in the simplest and most effective way, by cooking badly. Well, he'd have to make his peace some time but he felt disinclined to do so at the moment. He lit his pipe, took one or two pulls at the dry tobacco, knocked it out on the heel of his boot before it burnt his mouth, and pushed himself upright. 'Jonathan!'

'Morena.'

'Come on, let's get going.'

The Trooper led Duke from the other side of the Scotch-cart, where he had been feeding him cut-up *kgeñwe* melons, and handed Andrew the reins.

'I will look for you in five hours,' Andrew told Watch as he swung himself into the saddle. Watch muttered an incomprehensible reply.

Already the winter sun was hot on their bodies as they rode.

18

They were well north of the dry bed of the Okwa now and the country was empty of all human life. Further north, at Kela Pan near Ghanzi, they might come across the Mancal Bushmen and a few Kalaharis. North-east of Kela was the southern tip of Lake Ngami, north-west was the dreadful expanse of the Sand Veld, where little could survive. Nothing would have induced Andrew to go into the Sand Veld and he was thankful that most of it lay in German territory. No, he'd continue the search for two more days and then they'd make for the nearest water and let the animals rest up for a few days before trekking to the border and a reunion with von Steinberg. There'd be cigars and schnapps and good talk. He'd been looking forward to it for weeks.

But first he had to finish what he was doing and he wasn't quite sure *what* that was. A broken watch; a silver cigarette case with the initials M.E.S.; who in God's name would carry things like that in the centre of the Great Thirst? And what had happened? He remembered the note written by the dying trader. Is that what he would find? Just a skeleton, picked clean by the vultures and jackals, lying in the shade of a boulder? That is, if he found anything at all, which was unlikely. But an effort had to be made, a report written. What if news had already reached Francistown or even Mafeking? What if the only man in the Protectorate who should have known what was happening didn't?

He pulled Duke to a halt and let the glasses range over 180 degrees. Nothing except the shimmering scrub, the endless lime-stone outcrops, the occasional tree and always the stony red floor of the desert. But then he had not expected to see anything else, since he did not know what he was looking for.

Two hours later, when the sun was like a burning shield in the cobalt sky and he could feel the sweat gathering in his crutch and soaking onto the saddle, Jonathan's cry came as a sudden shock.

'Morena!'

He followed the Basuto's outstretched arm and found himself looking at what appeared to be a black hump some twenty yards away. He urged Duke forward until he was almost above it. He stared at it in disbelief. It was a large steamer trunk with a brass padlock and it lay on its side, abandoned and eerily lonely in the centre of Africa. Jonathan kept well away as though at any moment it might suddenly spring up and bite him. Even Andrew found himself momentarily apprehensive. Then he swung down and bent to inspect it.

It was japanned tin and on the lid in gilt lettering were the initials M.E.S. At one end was a Castle Line label. Half had been torn away to show other torn labels underneath. On the part that remained Andrew could just make out writing. He dropped to his knees. The ink was very faint but the words 'Trinity Hall' were legible.

'It is a black box, Morena,' Jonathan said with absolute certainty.

Andrew took hold of a handle and tried to turn the trunk the right way up, but it was surprisingly heavy.

'Come down off that bloody horse and give me a hand.'

Between them they managed to right the trunk but there were no further labels.

Andrew stared at the squat and strangely malevolent object in front of him, then he leant forward and rattled the padlock. It was large and strong. Lettering stamped into it stated that it had been made by Alfred Dobie & Sons, Wolverhampton, England. It was burning hot to the touch.

'It is fast,' said Jonathan.

Andrew was experiencing conflicting emotions, which was uncharacteristic of him; one part of him wanted the trunk open, the other was strangely uneasy at what he might find. The whole situation was disquieting, but he couldn't go on sitting in front of it as though it were some pagan altar. Abruptly he straightened. 'My gun,' he said. Jonathan pulled the Jeffries from the leather saddle-bucket. Andrew placed the muzzle at the point where the staple joined the tin and pulled the trigger. The heavy-grained solid blew the staple from its moorings. Still holding the rifle, he pushed back the lid with one foot. It started slowly, then crashed open. The trunk was filled with books.

Both men stood for a long moment staring at the neat piles of reading material and then Andrew gave a short barking laugh and handed Jonathan the rifle. The Basuto's eyes were wide with wonder and then, as Andrew laughed, he joined in, giggling softly behind his hand and shaking his head.

'Books,' he said.

'Yes. Books.' Andrew felt the tension melt away. 'Just the

20

very thing we need—a couple of hundred pounds of books.' He squatted down again and began to pull them from the trunk, glancing as he did so at the titles. They all seemed to be about Africa, and this part in particular. There was Andersson's *Lake Ngami*, and Alexander's *An Expedition of Discovery into the Interior of Africa*, Galton's *Narrative of an Explorer*, Campbell's *Travels* and Baines's *Explorations in South West Africa*, Carl Buttner's *Das Hinterland von Walfischbai und Angra Pequena* and *Nama und Damara* by von François, and Ebner's *Reise nach Südafrika* and several by Dr Fabri.

There were almost as many books in German as in English and Andrew picked one up and flicked over the pages, gratified that he could read the language as easily as he had when, as a child, he had spoken it with his mother.

Under the books was a large wooden box containing water colours and brushes and a quire of heavy white paper, none of which had been used. That was all. He went back to the books, this time looking at the title pages. The first one he opened was inscribed 'Matthew Southgate, Cape Town, '99'. Another read 'M. E. Southgate, Trinity Hall, Cambridge, Oct. '97'. Near the bottom of the trunk he came across an old, tattered and obviously well-loved copy of *Through the Looking-glass*. In a childish hand was written 'Matthew Edward Southgate, "Morgenster", Rondebosch, Cape Town, Cape of Good Hope, Cape Colony, South Africa, Southern Hemisphere, the Earth, the Universe.'

He stared at the book for a long time. Something was stirring in his mind but refused to emerge. Southgate. M.E.S. These were the names to fit the initials all right, but it was something else. . . . He shook his head as though to clear it, but nothing came.

He stood up, still clutching the book, and in doing so seemed to leave behind a strange and intimate world into which he had stepped for a short time, just like Alice. Now he was back in the Kalahari and the books were piled in the dust at his feet. 'Put them back,' he said to Jonathan. For a reason that was not even clear to himself he walked over to Duke and carefully placed the book he held in one of his saddle-bags.

All through the hot noon they searched for tracks, starting with the steamer trunk as a central point then working around it in increasing circles. Andrew did not expect to cut a spoor in the soft sand because the wind was constantly smoothing it over.

What he was searching for was a newly crushed rock or dung pats, and it was an hour before he found the first mark. It was faint, the line an iron tyre-band makes on hard-top.

Just then he heard Jonathan call. The Basuto was crouching over a pat of bullock dung. Andrew broke a twig and pushed it into the pat, breaking it up. It was brittle but it had not shrunk into a hard flat cake as usually happened after long exposure to dry hot weather. It could have been recent, but the point was: in which direction had the wagon been travelling? He wished he had Chik with him; this was the sort of problem for a Bushman.

He tried to put himself into a map position. The tracks were at a tangent to his own line of trek, which meant that the wagon had either been travelling north-east or south-west. If he was accurately assessing his own position he would put Kela Pan about three days' trek to the north. Due west of him, about six days away, was the German border and beyond that he had heard of water at a place called Rietfontein. So it was likely that Matthew Edward Southgate was travelling either from Rietfontein to Kela, or vice versa; that is if there were such a man and if he were still alive.

But which way? If Andrew chose the wrong direction it could mean travelling away from someone obviously in grave trouble —you didn't begin to jettison things unless you had to, especially silver cigarette cases.

He squatted down and turned the dung pat over as though a message might be written on its base. He broke off a piece and rubbed it between his fingers, letting it powder. If he sent Jonathan for Chik he would waste half a day, and half a day, even an hour, might make all the difference to the sort of man who took a steamer trunk full of books into the desert.

Jonathan, who had been quartering the ground nearby, called: 'Morena.'

Andrew dusted his fingers and looked up. 'Another?'

'Yes, Morena.'

The dung pat was about three yards away on the other side of a small bush, and about the same size as the first. They found a third and fourth. Yes, the line was right, but the question of which way the wagon had been travelling along it remained unanswered.

22

'It is an ox, Morena,' Jonathan said.

'I know it's a bloody ox. What did you think it was, a locust?' He took out a large khaki handkerchief and wiped the sweat from his face and neck. The sun's heat was like a forge. 'What I want to know is which way the damn thing went.'

'That way, Morena,' said Jonathan mildly, pointing to the north-east.

'How d'you know?'

'Look, Morena.' He took Andrew back to the first pat and together they marched up the line. The first pats were large with a similar circumference but then they quickly diminished in size until there were no more. Jonathan smiled and pointed to the last small droppings. 'He finish here, Morena. No more inside.'

Andrew looked at the Basuto with astonishment. It had been so simple. The line of droppings was pointing like an arrow in the direction the wagon had taken. 'You're a bloody marvel, Jonathan,' he said.

It was late in the evening before they saw the lights of Watch's fire. All afternoon they had followed a north-east compass bearing and at intervals they had seen evidence of the wagon's passing. Then as it grew dusk and the temperature dropped to the low forties they had turned east-north-east and within a few miles had cut the track of the Scotch-cart. Both men were exhausted and it was then that Watch had proved his worth. Like a wife who knows when to stop nagging he took one look at his master and began to work. He built up the fire, brought out a kaross made of jackal skins and wrapped it around Andrew's shoulders against the bitter night wind that had sprung up. He found Jonathan's black-and-orange Basuto blanket and brought it as well. He fetched drinking water for both men and then he appeared with an almost unheard-of luxury, small pans of warm water. Andrew washed his face and neck and placed his feet in what remained. Jonathan, crouched close to the second fire, was making an even more elaborate toilet. Then came food, great steaming plates of eland stew into which Watch had dropped pieces of fat bacon and wild herbs. As he ate Andrew felt warmth and strength returning to his muscles. He finished the meal and

23

sat sipping a large enamel mug of scalding black coffee pungent with wood ash. He had not spoken a single word since entering camp. Now his mind became active again.

By his reckoning they were about three days from Kela Pan; three days in a direct line—but he knew he couldn't follow a direct line. He would have to pick up Southgate's spoor again and follow it because there was a very good chance that Southgate had not reached Kela.

He called Watch over and told him briefly what they had found. The Nyasa stood in silence, his lips pressed primly together. Finally he said, 'He a German, Captain?'

'No, I don't think so. He's got an English name.'

'He sound too foolish.'

'He's a bloody fool, all right.'

'Like Germans.' White people whom Watch found wanting were all classed as Germans, the legacy of brutal treatment he had received on a plantation in German East Africa.

Andrew outlined his plan for the following day. He and Chik would take up the wagon spoor again. He would leave Jonathan with Watch. This he always did when he was going to be away from the Scotch-cart for more than a couple of days. He never liked to take both horses in case something happened to the bullocks.

He instructed Watch to fill extra water bags and a sack with melons which he could carry on the crupper. Then, telling Chik to be ready at dawn, he rolled up in his kaross near the fire. What he had in mind would be simple and, he hoped, effective. He and the Bushman would track the wagon as fast as they could and hope that Watch and Jonathan would not be more than a day behind in the Scotch-cart. Just before he slept he wondered again if Southgate was alive or dead or, at that very moment, dying. And he felt anger rise. How many men, he wondered, policemen like himself, had lost their lives trying to save fools like Southgate who didn't deserve to be saved.

The wind strengthened in the night and by dawn the whole surface of the desert seemed to be on the move. The sand was sliding and slithering in eddies. The sky was overcast and the wind itself, blowing in from the frost-bound High Veld, was bit-

24

terly cold. Andrew hunched himself low on Duke's back, holding his hand before his face. By his side trotted Chik, his eyes closed to thin slits. In the grey morning light the desert was featureless, drained of life and colour.

Andrew knew there was little point in searching for tracks. He timed himself on a north-west bearing and when he estimated that he was bisecting Southgate's line he turned northwards. For hours they fought the wind until he wondered if what he was doing wasn't hopeless. It might have been better to stay with the Scotch-cart in spite of its more leisurely progress. Then, about mid-afternoon, he saw something white flapping on a bush. At first from a distance he thought the movement might be the wings of a hawk as it settled on its prey, but as they drew nearer he could see it was an article of clothing. He leant down from the saddle and pulled it off the thorny spines. It was a shirt. He heard Chik calling. The Bushman had found a heavy leather suitcase. It had burst open and clothing had spilled out onto the sand.

They didn't stop for more than a few moments. Andrew hurriedly went through the suitcase but it contained nothing more than shirts and underwear. He left it, knowing that in the months to come he would see some of the items again in villages perhaps a hundred miles from this spot. Nothing lay unnoticed for ever in the Kalahari unless it was buried.

In mid-afternoon they found the first dead bullock. It was already badly blown. When the wind dropped the vultures would find it. By nightfall they had come across three more. They rested for six hours and went on after midnight. The wind still blew hard but the sky had cleared and Andrew fixed their line on the Pole star.

At dawn they stopped again, cutting up melons and feeding them to the horse. Andrew and Chik ate a little biltong. Throughout the morning the trail was marked by abandoned utensils and trade goods and even, at one point, eight boxes of rifle ammunition and a side of bacon which must have weighed nearly 20 lb. They found four more dead bullocks. As they pushed their way through the tearing wind Andrew felt he was entering someone's life by a strangely circuitous path. It was like visiting an unfamiliar house and going through all its drawers and cupboards long before he met its owner.

After three hours the country began to change. There were more trees, thicker patches of wait-a-bit thorn and yellow winter-grass bending and shining in the wind. They breasted a small rise and came immediately upon the wagon. Its tent was ripped and large patches of torn canvas were flapping and cracking. It, too, had been abandoned.

They moved now into heavier and thicker thorn-bush and Andrew wondered what had happened to the bullocks. They had counted eight corpses along the way and Southgate would have needed a minimum of sixteen to pull a large Cape wagon through drift sand, especially the way he had loaded it. He must have outspanned when he abandoned the wagon. Which meant . . . Andrew kicked Duke into a gallop, swinging him left and right through the trees, feeling the thorns catch and rip at his breeches and tunic. Suddenly the timber gave out and he was looking at Kela Pan. It was an enormous shallow depression covered with small stones. A limestone wall at one end formed a natural dam. It was completely surrounded by thorn-coppices, intersected by thousands of game trails. It was a place of infinite dreariness and seemed quite devoid of water.

But in the centre of the pan, about 400 yards from where he had stopped, he could make out several dark shapes. He examined them through the glasses : they were the bullocks. As Chik came up Andrew motioned him forward and they moved onto the pan. The dry crust was hard and brittle and broke crisply under Duke's hooves. As they drew up with the bullocks Andrew noted that they stood with heads bowed, listless, almost dead on their feet. Behind them was a black scar of mud perhaps twenty yards long and ten yards wide. Lying next to it was the body of a man. He lay on his side with one arm covering his head as though for shade. The upper part of his body was naked and already burnt red. His hair, which was long and unkempt, was the same colour as the waving grass.

As he squatted down, Andrew's first reaction was that they had come a long way to find a corpse, but, looking more closely, he could see the faint flutterings of a pulse on the neck. He un-stoppered the water bottle and wet his handkerchief. Southgate's mouth—if this was indeed Southgate—was gummed up with black scum and blown sand and his lips were cracked and oozing bloody matter. Gently Andrew softened the dry mucous and, as

26

the water slowly soaked it away, he was able to peel the lips apart. The mouth cavity was almost completely filled by a swollen tongue and now Chik carefully inserted a hollow reed, pressing down the tongue and working the reed towards the back of the mouth. With equal care Andrew began to pour small quantities of water into the top of the reed. At first the mouth simply filled up and liquid trickled out of one corner and dripped down onto the sand. But gradually, as the cool water softened the tissues, Chik was able to move the tongue and at last water dripped down into the man's throat. He coughed immediately and then, as the passage to the lungs closed, he began to take water as an unconscious infant will suck at a teat.

Andrew gave it to him little by little, stopping every now and then to wipe his face with a wet handkerchief and remove the scum that still rimmed his mouth and tongue. At first he wondered why the face, mouth and hands were blackened by mud and when he saw the reason the whole picture of Southgate's arrival at Kela was plain. About five yards from his body was what had once been a khaki shirt. It was filled with mud. It was as Andrew had feared when he realized that Southgate had outspanned the bullocks. They would have been smelling the water for the best part of an hour and when Southgate unyoked them it had obviously become a race which they had won. Andrew could visualize the small pan of water being churned into mud by the hooves of the frantic beasts long before Southgate had even reached it. He would have had to dig out handfuls of mud, put them in his shirt, and try to wring out the water, sucking at the cloth as he did so.

For two hours Andrew and Chik worked on him, alternately dripping water into his mouth and wiping his body with wet cloths. Eventually, when the terrible flayed appearance of his facial skin was beginning to take on a more normal appearance, Andrew mixed a little salt with the water and managed to get him to take it from a tin mug.

It was evening before the man regained consciousness. His eyes opened and he looked up into Andrew's face. He tried to speak but the thickness of his tongue produced only a mumble.

'Are you Matthew Southgate?' Andrew asked.

He nodded.

'You've led us a bloody dance!'

27

It was said with the brusqueness of relief but its effect on Matthew was immediate. His eyes seemed to fill with a deep personal hurt and he turned his head to one side.

Andrew sat in a camp chair in the shade of a flamboyant tree and started to re-read the letter for the third time. It had come, as all his post did, by runner across the empty desert. At first the maintenance of this tenuous link with civilization had caused him no little wonder. It had seemed almost beyond comprehension how anyone could find him in so great an area but then, as he had built up his own lines of communication, he'd realized how quickly news of his presence spread through the desert, like dry tumbleweed on the wind.

He was now at Tsau on the edge of the great Okavango marshes and in the long thirst from Kela they had moved from winter in the desert to early summer and the damp heat of the swamps. The difference was dramatic; from a land of aching dryness he had only to raise his eyes to the bottom of the magistrate's garden to see lily-covered creeks, banks of green grass, spreading acacia, flame flowers and the still waters of the Taokhe River, one of the two arms that surrounded the marsh. There was bird life everywhere, fish eagles, herons, crested water birds, hammerkops, kingfishers, crimson bee-eaters, royal Barotse egrets and an occasional sky-blue African roller.

Tsau was the capital village of the Batawana people and the oasis of every desert traveller's dreams.

Five days ago he had brought Southgate out of the desert with the object of handing him over, for recuperation, and the solution of his future, to the magistrate, only to find that Mr Williams was on tour of the district and had taken with him the N.C.O. and troopers from the police post. Except for one or two servants his house, built away from the thatched huts of the Batawanas, was closed and deserted. So Andrew had camped in his spacious garden and settled down to wait. For five days he had existed in a state of suspended animation, eating, sleeping, sitting in the shade, fishing every evening for Okavango bream, and allowing the infinite variety of green to seep into his brain. Now the letter had come. It was from the Resident Commissioner in Mafeking and read :

Sub-Inspector Black, B.P.P.,

This will inform you that the political situation in German South-West Africa vis-à-vis the natives has worsened in the past few months.

As you are aware the Germans are now engaged in putting down a rising of the Bondelswart Hottentots and are having to keep the peace in the whole of Damaraland.

Information reaching me from German territory convinces me that this is the opportunity for which the Herero people have been waiting and that they will soon attempt to rebel against their German masters. There have already been incidents between German settlers and Hereros north of the capital, Windhuk.

Reports further state that refugees are beginning to move eastwards towards the Protectorate border. As to this you will endeavour to obtain as much information as possible and pass it on to me.

If refugees cross into the Protectorate you will first direct them to hand over to you all guns, rifles and ammunition and you will send such guns, rifles and ammunition to Gaberones, by any reasonable opportunity, giving the carrier a special permit to proceed with them.

I do not anticipate any difficulty in disarmament, but if there is you will send to me for necessary assistance.

You will note, as far as practicable, all stock of every kind which may have been brought across the border, warning the persons in charge that they are only allowed to hold such stock pending any claim which may be made by any lawful owner.

You will warn refugees that they must not return to German South-West Africa as long as hostilities continue.

You will make the best arrangements you can for placing the refugees where they can exist. You will warn them that they must not steal from the local natives, or cause them annoyance, and you will instruct the local headmen that the refugees must not be molested.

You will, *if absolutely necessary for the preservation of life, but not otherwise*, issue necessary food to refugees who are in a starving condition, but this point I leave to your discretion.

You will impress upon the refugees the necessity of supporting themselves, and inform them of the facilities for obtaining work which are afforded by the agents in the Protectorate of the Witwatersrand Native Labour Association.

You will act within your own discretion on all matters generally, and go to such places as you may think desirable, not running any unnecessary risks.

You will keep me frequently informed of all that you do by reliable special runners, who will be paid such reward as you may arrange.

You will always bear in mind that economy, so long as it is consistent with thorough efficiency, is essential.

(Signed) Ralph Howland
Resident Commissioner

Refugees! What refugees? And who were the Bondelswarts? 'As you are aware . . .' the letter had said. Aware of what? How could he be aware of something in German territory when it took him all his time to keep up with what was going on in his own—and read for law examinations as well? He knew of the Hereros, just as he knew of all great Southern African tribes, but what was this about the possibility of rebellion? Against the Germans? You had only to talk to von Steinberg for five minutes to realize the Germans aimed to be masters in their own colony. They had the right idea: strength and discipline, the one dependent upon the other.

He looked at the letter again. 'You will make the best arrangements you can for placing the refugees. . . .' Christ! That could only have been written by a man who had never set foot in the Kalahari. 'You will impress upon the refugees the necessity of supporting themselves. . . .' How? With what? '. . . and inform them of the facilities for obtaining work which are afforded by the agents in the Protectorate of the Witwatersrand Native Labour Association.'

Why the hell didn't he just say what he meant? The whole letter could have been summed up in one sentence: 'If you find any natives crossing the border send them down to the mines in Johannesburg.' That would have been clear. As it was. . . .

First he needed some background. Southgate had just come in from German territory. He should know what was going on there.

'Jonathan!'

'Morena?'

'Fetch Baas Southgate.'

He folded the letter and placed it in his pocket, then he mopped at the sweat on his face and neck with a handkerchief. It wasn't noon yet but the damp heat had almost wet him through. He stared out across the grass and trees to the river but some of the magic had gone out of the scene.

He turned impatiently in his chair and looked for Matthew Southgate but the garden, his own camp and the magistrate's house, with its black corrugated iron roof and netted verandah, were deserted. He supposed that Southgate would be off sketching somewhere with the paper and pencil he had borrowed. Ever since they'd arrived at Tsau he had been wandering off by himself. Not that Andrew particularly wanted to accompany him, but he should have asked permission. In a sense he was Andrew's prisoner, though naturally this had not been pointed out. But on paper it was true. Southgate had entered the Protectorate without permission and without a pass; if Andrew had wanted to exercise his authority he could have dumped him across the border and simply left him to get on with it.

There were moments when he wished he had. Perhaps not quite that—you wouldn't do that even to a native—but certainly he wished he'd never come across Southgate at all. He wasn't very keen on people like Southgate.

For the first week or so after he had found him at Kela Pan things had gone well enough. As far as he was concerned his interest had been in fighting for Southgate's life. He'd enjoyed that, in a way, because the odds were against him and he'd won. It wasn't only thirst that had been affecting Southgate but sunstroke as well and a tremendous loss of body-fluid. But they'd gradually brought him round. Watch had taken him over as though he were a child. If Andrew could ever place his finger on the start of his irritation with the man it would probably have dated from this period. The way Watch carried on you'd have thought Southgate was the only one of them who needed any attention at all. Everything was 'Master Matthew this . . .' or 'Master Matthew that . . .' and if meals were late or cold or inedible it was because Watch had been 'seeing to Master Matthew', and if he couldn't get enough shaving water it was because

31

'Master Matthew must wash, Captain'. Still, he had accepted it because deep inside him was the knowledge of his own success. There weren't too many white people who could have tracked Southgate through the wilderness and not only have found him but saved him from death.

They'd camped in the timber near Kela Pan, sending Chik on with both their own bullocks and those of Southgate's that remained, to water at Ghanzi. When he returned several days later the bullocks were in greatly improved condition and they began the long thirst to Tsau past Camel Pan and Gray's Pan and Kobe until they reached the southern tip of Lake Ngami.

Until then Southgate had remained for much of the time lying on a kaross in the Scotch-cart, too weak for any but the simplest statement of his needs. As they began to approach Ngami he seemed to grow more and more nervous, asking over and over again when they would reach the Lake and making Andrew promise that he would not pass it by without allowing him to see it.

'You'll see it all right,' Andrew reassured him. 'We'll be camping on the western edge.' He was puzzled about Southgate. There was nothing particularly fascinating about Ngami, unless you found blackwater fever fascinating. He himself had no interest in the Lake whatsoever.

They reached the south-western tip after an exhausting trek through a kind of demented parkland of camelthorn and mopane trees, with here and there an occasional baobab. Between the trees was thick secondary bush that in places had to be cut down to allow the Scotch-cart passage. There was game everywhere: roan, sable, hartebeest, even an odd gemsbok. Watch had been feeding Southgate on rich venison soups and pungent stews and he must have gained a certain strength from them because when Andrew put his head in through the rear flap and said matter-of-factly, 'Well, here's the lake. You wanted to see it,' he was able to climb down for the first time and take a few steps on the sandy ground. Andrew stepped forward to take his arm but was anticipated by Watch.

'Master Matthew not strong,' Watch said severely, as though it was Andrew's fault. The Nyasa encircled Matthew's waist with one arm and helped him through the last of the trees to the edge of the lake.

'Just reeds,' Andrew said, looking out over the enormous yellow-green depressions. 'Not a lake at all, really.'

They were standing on an eminence which formed the southern and western wall of the lake. As far as they could see was a great reedy marsh intersected by small streams. There was no sheet of water visible at all.

'I thought I'd never see it,' Matthew said, and his eyes were bright with tears.

Embarrassed, Andrew turned away. If Southgate was going to get upset by looking at nothing but a couple of hundred square miles of reeds what the hell was he going to be like when they reached the marshes proper?

That night, for the first time since Kela Pan, Southgate was strong enough to take his meal with Andrew. It was as though the very sight of this dreary moonscape of feathery reeds and reddish mud had dissipated the last of his weakness.

They sat in camp chairs a few feet apart drinking coffee by the light of an acacia-wood fire, watching the flames leap up each time a globule of gum dropped hissing into the embers. The two men were dissimilar. Andrew, with black hair and light brown eyes which gave a curiously feline look to his face, sat upright in his chair, neat, alert, the picture of someone used to being in command, ready at a moment's notice to leap out of his chair and rattle off a series of orders. Matthew was tall and thin with sandy hair, and in the clothes which Andrew had lent him and which were several sizes too small he looked bony. Andrew supposed him good-looking—or supposed anyway that women might find his soft blue eyes attractive—but his face was too pretty, and prettiness in men meant weakness. However, it wasn't easy to tell what he did look like under normal circumstances because areas of his face were still blotched red and peeling from his exposure to the sun at Kela. Where Andrew sat compact and watchful he was hunched forward on his elbows, all curves and angles, as he stared into the depths of the fire.

'This business about Ngami,' Andrew said, breaking a longish silence. 'It seems—it seemed important to you.'

'It was.' Matthew threw the dregs of his coffee into the fire and placed the tin mug next to his chair. Then he turned, smiling. 'Did I embarrass you?'

'Not at all. No, no. I just wondered, that's all. Couldn't imagine

33

why an Englishman would come all this way just to see a dried-up lake.'

'It wasn't always dry, you know. And anyway, I'm not English.'

'You talk like an Englishman.'

'I suppose I do. Must have been a bad habit I picked up at Cambridge. You'll have to forgive me.' Andrew listened carefully for sarcasm but Southgate seemed quite sincere. 'No. I'm from the Cape, born and bred there. But my mother was English. My father's always been more English than the English, too, though he was able to turn it on and off whenever he pleased. I remember as a small boy watching him in court and one moment he would be rattling along in colloquial Dutch and the next you'd have thought he was an English aristocrat. It was all a pretence, really.'

Court. That was the clue. And the name Southgate. Suddenly Andrew remembered the book in his saddle-bag with Matthew's name inscribed in the cover. 'Morgenster' the house had been called. His mind went whirling back to his own boyhood. Of course. Morgenster. He could remember it now, a great gabled house on the Main Road at Rondebosch, set back in a huge overgrown garden and shaded by towering oaks. He would have been ten or eleven then and his father would still have been alive. They had lived near Morgenster in an old semi-detached bunga-low with an Adam fig-tree in the back garden and a corrugated iron coal-shed. Their neighbours had been Cape Coloured people. He could see himself now, on hot, empty Sunday afternoons, trying to peer through the thick Australian myrtle hedge that en-circled Morgenster, trying to identify himself with the tennis parties and the croquet parties, trying to enjoy vicariously plea-sures that were so remote from his own life that they could have been taking place on the far side of the moon.

And other memories. Grey winter mornings, with the rain lash-ing out of the north-west, striking him on his bare legs, drumming on the school-bag he carried on his back. And then seeing the landaulette come out of the big wrought-iron gates, and a flash of fair hair and a pale face and the superior expression on the Coloured coachman's face as he drove the young master off to his private school.

Here was the pale face again, only this time there were no

34

tennis parties and no warm carriage. Andrew was in no doubt. He hadn't known the name then, or couldn't be certain that he had, but later he had learnt that Morgenster was the home of Mr Justice Southgate. He could remember Sir George Southgate quite well, though they had only met once. Andrew had been walking back from playing in the Liesbeek River near Westerford Bridge when he'd seen Matthew on the other side of the road, about to enter Morgenster. Without thinking he had scooped up a stone from the unmade road and thrown it. He could still remember its parabolic flight in the dimming light of early evening. It had struck Matthew behind the ear. He had given a slight cry and dropped down on his hands and knees with the blood pouring across his chin. Andrew had stood transfixed and suddenly there were lights and voices and someone had grabbed him by the arm and was hauling him forward and he was looking up into a face that filled him with terror. It was angry and red and was framed by mutton-chop whiskers and as it leant towards him it seemed to grow bigger and bigger and then the mouth opened and Andrew thought he was going to be swallowed and the last thing he heard was an enraged voice shouting: 'Why, you young tramp. . . !' and then, mercifully, he had fainted.

His father and mother were told, and the following day he was sent to apologize. Matthew's mother met him at the door. 'I've sent my husband away,' she said, smiling at his relief. 'I think we can manage better without him.'

She had taken him to a bedroom where a young boy lay wanly on the pillows, his head encased in bandages. 'I'm sorry,' Andrew had mumbled. 'I only meant to give you a fright.'

'It's all right,' the boy had said. 'It doesn't really matter.' But in his hurt eyes there seemed to be the question mark—why?

Lady Southgate had given them home-made lemonade and slices of dark fruit cake and then he'd gone home. At the door she had said: 'You must come round often. I'm sure you and Matthew will get along quite famously.'

But he never did go again because his father died soon after and then they could not afford the rent of even the semi-detached bungalow with its shrunken fig tree and its rusted coal-shed.

Now, sitting around a camp fire near the south-western tip of

35

Lake Ngami, Andrew forced his attention back to what South-gate was saying about Cambridge.

'. . . my father's idea. I hated it. I hated the people and I hated the place. You weren't up, were you?' Andrew shook his head. 'Flat,' Southgate went on. 'No mountains, not even a hill to break the monotony. God, it was awful. I remember one winter weekend I walked to Southwold and stood there on the edge of the North Sea and looked out over the water. There was an icy wind blowing and the sea was churning and brown and there was a line of dirty foam all along the pebble beach. I don't think I've yearned for anything as much as I yearned just then for the heat and colour of Africa. I wanted to sweat again, not the dirty, muggy sweat of an English summer but. . . .' He stopped and laughed abruptly. 'Good Lord, I'm carrying on! Put it down to the fact that you're the first person I've spoken to for weeks.'

'What were you studying?' Andrew asked, his tone carefully neutral.

'Law; but after that weekend I didn't bother. I decided that I was doing something I didn't want to do in a place I didn't want to be, so for the rest of the term I read everything I could about Africa. Did you know that Livingstone was the first white man to see Lake Ngami? It was enormous then. A huge sheet of water. You've read Andersson and Green?'

Once again Andrew shook his head. 'Marvellous stuff. You should try them. I could have let you have a copy of Andersson except it's lying out there in the desert somewhere. But what I'm saying is that Ngami seemed to take hold of me. So many men had tried to reach it and failed—Galton, for instance—that the idea of trying to reach it myself began to grow. I wanted to do it like Andersson, by wagon through South-West and then up past Ghanzi. . . .'

He was talking rapidly now and Andrew had the impression that it was more an explanation for Southgate himself than a narrative produced to interest someone else. He formed a picture in his mind of Southgate, alone and lonely in a country he disliked, feverishly planning something totally opposite to his Cambridge environment.

'Of course my father was furious,' he was saying. 'I hadn't told him I was coming back and he threatened all sorts of things, but my mother had died some years before and I'd come into her money when I was twenty-one so it didn't much matter how angry he was. I bought the wagon and bullocks in Windhuk and hired three Hottentots but they left me after we'd passed Rietfontein. I don't blame them. It wasn't much fun for them. I mean, they didn't care about Ngami or anything like that, and the water was getting low. Well . . . you know the rest. If it hadn't been for you I'd never have got here, never have got anywhere at all, for that matter.' He paused for a long time as though exhausted by the effort of so much speech and then said : 'You know, I've a curious feeling we've met somewhere. You weren't up at Oxford, were you? I met one or two South Africans there.'

'No, I wasn't at Oxford either.'

'Perhaps I'm thinking of someone else.'

'You might have seen me at the Cape.'

'You're not related to Duncan Black, are you?'

'Shouldn't I be?'

'I didn't mean it that way. What I meant was—well, are you? He was a friend of my father's. I used to go out to Drakenstein quite often. I thought if you *were* we might have met there.'

'He's my uncle,' Andrew said, the old lie coming easily to his lips.

'There you are, then. We probably knew each other as children.'

'Yes, there we are.' Andrew threw his cold coffee dregs into the fire and stood up.

'It's odd that we should meet up here. I mean our families have always been pioneers of one sort or another. There was your great-grandfather coming out from Scotland and my people coming from England with the settlers in 1820.'

Andrew was suddenly sick of hearing his voice. 'I think it's time we turned in,' he said.

It took him a long time to sleep. It seemed that almost everything he had heard that evening had left a sour taste in his mouth. Here he was trying to pass a series of examinations on which his future depended and men like Southgate, with enough money and influence to go to Cambridge, simply didn't bother to try. God, if he'd only had the same chances : private schools, wealthy parents, pampered, coddled, spoiled no doubt—and where had it all ended? On a mud-churned pan in the middle of the Kalahari where he'd no bloody business in the first place. And all this mystical nonsense about Ngami. Livingstone, Galton, Andersson; they meant less than nothing to Andrew. Ngami was Ngami, a pestilential mud-hole in the middle of nowhere.

He turned over angrily on his kaross. And Duncan Fraser Black. 'Fraser,' he thought, bitterly. Only those with the blood royal had 'Fraser' in their names. And Drakenstein. Yes, he could imagine those other tennis parties and picnic parties and the drinks on the verandah in the evenings. It would all have been a bit different from the only time he had visited the place.

It was after the death of his father, when they'd moved to the rotting boarding-house near the railway line at Salt River. He remembered the journey by train to Stellenbosch and the liveried servant who had met them with the trap. And he remembered the long dusty drive through the vineyards and the huge white colonial Dutch house with the name 'Drakenstein' inscribed on the front gable. He remembered the red-flagged verandah and the room in which they had waited, with its gloomy oil paintings and glowing yellow-wood furniture, and how his mother had sat in her dusty black dress, fingers plucking nervously at the hand-kerchief on her lap. She had looked precisely what she was, the daughter of a poor German immigrant, the widow of an insignificant clerk.

The silence in the room had been punctuated by her instructions. 'Sit up straight, Andrew. . . . Your shoes are dusty, wipe them please. . . . Your uncle is a great man, please to remember that. . . . Are your fingernails clean? . . . Did you wash your ears? . . .' And all spoken in a thick German accent. For a moment then, when she had succeeded in communicating her nervousness to him, he had hated her; hated the square peasant body and the stupid accent and above all hated her for being in such a subservient position. There was no question but that they had come cap in hand.

After a while she was called away. 'Sit still now,' she warned. 'Touch nothing.'

She'd returned about an hour later with a tall, grey-haired man. Andrew remembered that his face resembled a hawk's; his eyes were cold and contemptuous. 'This is the boy?' he said.

Andrew's mother had bobbed her reply, then she turned on Andrew. 'Stand up when Mr Black speaks,' she hissed. He had been momentarily too nervous to remember his manners and now he stumbled to his feet, knocking over a small coffee table on which a cigarette box had been standing. In a flash his mother was down on her knees gathering together the cigarettes. 'So sorry,' she said. 'Most clumsy of my boy.'

'Please,' said Mr Black, taking her by the arm and helping her to her feet. 'There are servants for that.'

On the verandah he turned to Andrew and looked him up and down. 'You are being given an opportunity in life; see that you make the most of it.'

'Oh, he will, sir, he will,' his mother said fervently. 'Say thank you to Mr Black.'

As they were getting into the trap Mr Black had said : 'There's no need to be in touch with me again, the allowance will come directly from my solicitors. When the boy has finished school let them know and other arrangements will be made. Is that understood?'

'Yes, sir, I understand well. And may Our Lord watch you, sir.'

'You are very kind,' Mr Black said dryly.

They had not even been invited to luncheon but he had hardly expected that. Years before he had been taught his place in the scheme of things. He hadn't been too sure why he had a place and had to keep it until he understood what the word illegitimate meant and what that one word had done to his father. Later, he had heard someone say, laughing, 'Why, there are as many Blacks as blacks at the Cape.' He had asked questions and, bit by bit, they had been answered. His grandfather, he discovered, had been Donald Fraser Black, one of whose sons had been born in scandal and secrecy out of wedlock. That son, Arthur, was Andrew's father. From the moment of his birth to the day of his death he had never been acknowledged as a member of the Fraser Black clan; Andrew had never been able to establish whether his grandmother had been paid off as he had been paid off by Duncan Fraser Black.

Now, thinking about it, he felt a hot flush of shame. Duncan Fraser Black : industrialist, financier, gentleman wine-farmer— how Andrew would have liked to get him out here in the Kalahari where money meant less than nothing. He was the other branch of the family, the son of Donald's half-brother, Robert, and although Andrew called him 'uncle' he was, in reality, not an uncle at all but a cousin. And yet, in spite of himself, he knew that whatever he did have he owed in great measure to Duncan.

The allowance which arrived punctually on the first day of each month had meant they were able to move from the boarding-house to a two-room apartment in Observatory. It meant, too, that with the sewing his mother took in they had just enough left over to pay the fees at the South African College School. When he was finished with school there had been four years on one of Mr Black's farms; four back-breaking years in the heat and dust of the vineyard when he earned less than three pounds a month and slept in a shed like a Coloured. And then had come the letter from the solicitors. The Bechuanaland Protectorate Police were in need of recruits and it was understood that if Andrew applied there would be no obstacle in the way of a sub-inspectorate. Sub-Inspector! It had sounded magnificent. Inherent in the phrase was cachet and dash and best of all the very fact that it was a title. He accepted immediately. On the train from Cape Town, as he watched Table Mountain recede in the summer haze, it was as though he were leaving behind not only his past, but all its socially restricting by-products, of which his mother was a part. He had felt no pang whatsoever.

'Oh, certainly,' Matthew was saying. 'I'm quite sure they will. You can't go on persecuting a whole race as the Germans are the Hereros and expect nothing to happen. When I was in Windhuk there were rumours that something of the sort was beginning to happen even then.'

'But they'll be slaughtered,' Andrew said impatiently.

They had been discussing the letter in the shade of the flamboyant tree for nearly half an hour and nothing he had heard had made him any happier. Just the contrary, Matthew spoke with a calm certainty that both irritated him and made him apprehensive. He had visions of thousands of starving Hereros moving across the border into his territory. 'You will make the best arrangements for placing the refugees. . . .' He stared at the letter again, then flung it down on the grass.

'How many Hereros are there?' Andrew asked.

'About a hundred thousand.'

'Christ, what a bloody mess. Still, it hasn't happened yet.'

'It will.'

'What makes you so damn sure?'

'Well, look at the situation: the Germans began to colonize the territory twenty years ago. At that time all the land was already owned. To the south of Windhuk you had the Hottentot tribes like the Rehoboth Bastards, the Bondelswarts, Paul Goliath's People, the Velskoendraers, the Orlams, the Red Nation, the Witboois and several more, all pastoralists and hunters. North of Windhuk lay Hereroland with its capital at Okahandja. You know about the Hereros, of course?'

'That's what I was hoping you'd tell me.'

'No one knows for certain where they came from. Somewhere to the north, obviously, but they settled Hereroland hundreds of years ago with their cattle. *They* say that in the very beginning they came out of an Umborongbonga tree. The important thing to remember is the cattle. They're probably the greatest cattle owners in the whole of Africa. Cattle are something special to them, they love them like other people love children. Always stroking and fondling them. . . .'

'Where did you get this?' Andrew interrupted. 'From books?'

'Some of it. But I spent months travelling in Hereroland before leaving for Ngami.'

'Go on.'

'It's quite simple: the Germans came into the South-West with nothing but guns and land-hunger. Now the Hereros find themselves trespassers in their own territory. Every day more and more land is confiscated. Traders rob them of cattle. Even the burial ground of the Herero chiefs at Okahandja has been occupied by the Germans. The sacred trees have been cut down and the place is now a vegetable garden. In twenty years the Germans have just about got the lot.'

'I can't believe they simply *took* everything. It doesn't work like that.'

'Listen, the Germans have passed a law forbidding the Hereros to possess large stock. I'll give you one guess why.'

'Yes, but. . . . Look, the place was absolutely virgin territory before the Germans moved in. I mean, no one *owned* it.'

'Except the various Hottentot races and the Hereros and the Bergdamas and the Saan and the Ovambos and the Heikom

Bushmen and the Tjimbas. It was owned all right. What you're saying is that it wasn't owned by a European power.'

'Christ, you don't call a few huts *owning*, do you? What I mean is that it wasn't civilized. It's people like you who are in the way of progress.'

'I'd like to see the country civilized, too. Just compare German territory with the Protectorate. You're trying to bring civilization here, but you're not depriving the people of their land and possessions to do it. That's the difference.'

'Morena!' Andrew saw Jonathan hurrying into the garden.

'Yes, what is it?'

'There is a man, Morena.'

'What man?'

'To see you.'

'A native?'

'Yes, Morena.'

'What does he want?'

'I don't know, Morena.'

'Well, find out, damn it. I don't want to see every bloody native that's got an hour to waste. Find out what he wants.'

Jonathan shifted feet and looked embarrassed.

'I gave you an order, Trooper!'

'Morena, we do not speak his tongue.'

Andrew frowned. 'All right, bring him.'

They waited in silence for Jonathan's return. Suddenly Matthew pushed himself to his feet. 'Oh, my God!' he said. He stared in horror and sympathy at the apparition that was making its way through the garden towards them. Then he ran five paces and took hold of one of the native's arms. 'Have you given him food and water?' he asked Jonathan.

'We have given him water, Morena, but no food yet.'

Matthew was about to open his mouth when Andrew cut in, 'I'll give the orders here. Jonathan, tell Watch to prepare food.'

Matthew said, 'Don't you think he should eat and rest first?'

Andrew turned slowly. 'Isn't there something you want to sketch?' he asked, coldly.

Matthew flushed. 'I'm sorry.'

The native sat in the grass at their feet as though he was already dead. His head hung forward, his arms were slack and rested on his drawn-up knees, his long fingers dangled in the air like

42

bunches of thin black twigs. He was grotesquely thin. The muscles in his calves and thighs had melted away, leaving only the long bones to stretch the skin. His cheeks were sunken and his skull was strangely large. It was possible to count each rib. His only clothing was a piece of tattered skin around his waist.

'Where do you come from?' Andrew asked in one of the local Batawana dialects. The native did not even raise his head. Andrew touched him with the toe of a boot and he looked up. For the first time they were able to see his face. He was a young man, between twenty and thirty, and yet the sagging skin of his cheeks and jowls made him look much older. But it was his eyes that held them. They stared hopelessly out of separate dark caves: huge, melancholy eyes, imprinted with anguish and suffering. Andrew tried again, this time in a different dialect.

Slowly the native raised and lowered his hands in a gesture of despair. He said a few words in a language Andrew did not understand and then his head dropped onto his chest.

Suddenly Matthew leant forward. 'I think he's a Herero.'

'Can you speak the language?'

'Only a few words.'

'Try them.'

'I've got a better idea.' In halting German, Matthew put the same question.

This time the native's head jerked up and some of the hopelessness went out of his eyes. He answered in German.

'He says. . . . I think he says he comes from far to the west.'

'Thank you,' Andrew said. 'I'll take over now.' As the fluent and idiomatic German phrases flowed from his tongue he saw Matthew's eyes widen with surprise and a warm feeling of satisfaction rooted itself in his chest.

The native's story was pathetically brief. His name, he said, was Kaneena and he was a nephew of the great Maharero himself. He had been born in the Year of the Sacrificial Charger and was now chief of a branch of the Hereros who lived in the eastern part of Hereroland. Two months before, the Germans had taken their cattle because it was said that a law had been passed which forbade Hereros to own cattle. He, Kaneena, and two of his under-chiefs had journeyed to Okahandja to protest at the taking of the cattle but they had been arrested and flogged and the two under-chiefs had died of the floggings. When Kaneena had returned to his people he had told them of the floggings and how the Germans had said to him that sooner or later they would finally deal with the Hereros and he knew this to be true because the Germans had field guns and machine-guns and with these they could kill many Hereros. And so he had taken his people further into the desert because he knew that deep inside the desert were the English who had been much spoken of by his uncle and also by his great-uncle Tjamuaha, the greatest Herero king of all.

They had journeyed for many weeks with their goats and other small stock until they had nothing to eat and no water and the stock had died and they had killed the rest and drunk the blood. Then he had found a patch of melons and he had left his people there and journeyed in search of the English and within a day had come upon a pan where there were wagon tracks and recent fires and he had followed the tracks to a pit of fresh water and past a great reed bed and along a river until he had finally found the English.

Matthew, who had only followed one word in three, turned to Andrew.

'Just a pack of bloody lies,' Andrew said, and briefly sketched the story.

'I don't think he's lying.'

'Of course he is. You don't get flogged for nothing. They probably stole the cattle in the first place. Anyway, this chap's a rabbit. Scared stiff of something or other. He says it's the Germans, but I don't believe it. But the point is his people are waiting somewhere near Ghanzi—'

'You say someone who walked this incredible distance just to save his people is a *rabbit*?' Matthew's tone was incredulous. 'You know nothing of the situation in German territory and yet you disbelieve his story!' His underlip began to tremble with emotion. 'What sort of man *are* you?'

'Jonathan! Take this native and feed him,' Andrew said.

Matthew sprang to his feet. 'I'll go with him.' The tremble of his underlip was more pronounced. Between them he and Jonathan lifted Kaneena to his feet.

'Southgate!' The voice cracked like a cartridge. Matthew stopped and turned. 'You ask what sort of man I am? Let me tell you: while you're mooning about holding his hand I'll be trying

44

to shoot enough game to feed about 200 people. Then I'll see that the meat is smoked and packed in the wagon. Then I'll trek back along the thirst to Ghanzi taking food and water and once I've fed them and watered them and wiped their arses for them I'll have to think of what I'm going to do with them and then I'll have to do it. Does that answer your question?'

'You won't be alone. I'll be helping.'

'For Christ's sake, what do you think you can do?'

They were late. They should have reached the river while it was still dark. Chik had located the herd of buffalo the day before and Andrew had questioned the local hunters. The movements of the herd had been much the same for the past few days: they would come out of the reed-bed at night, drink at the river, feed on the new grass and then, as darkness gave way to dawn, they would be grazing their way back towards the reeds and by full light would have disappeared.

It was full light now and all that remained of the buffalo were the mud scars on the river bank and the new wet droppings.

Andrew's idea had been simple and expedient: they would lie up in the timber between the river and the reed-bed and wait for the buffalo to make their stately, aldermanic progress past them. Well placed, they might have taken out three or four before the herd knew what had happened. But now . . . he rubbed hard at his chin in vexation. Now they'd have to go into the reed-bed after them and it wasn't the sort of job he relished at all. He'd no doubt that the local hunters had been savaging the herd with their muzzle-loaders so it was quite possible that each animal was carrying a piece of lead or iron somewhere in its body, and nothing made a buffalo more irritable than that.

When it came to hunting, the natives had no honour at all: fire off at anything, but only follow if it was something harmless like a lechwe or an oribi. He wondered how many lions and buffalos were wandering the Protectorate carrying festering lumps of iron inside them. Normally the buffalo was stolid enough, just like a domestic cow; he'd rather get out of your way than face you. But blow a lump of metal into him and leave it there and see how his mood changed. The old-timers always used to say:

45

'Once you hit a buffalo he starts to think.' Well, Andrew thought, if that was so, there might be upwards of 150 buffalo in the reed-bed, all in some degree of pain, all *thinking*.

What made things even worse was that it was Southgate's bloody fault they were late. Just as they were leaving he'd come along with his pretty face and his saintly air and said how sorry he was he'd spoken like that and how he wanted to help. What had annoyed him even further was that he, Andrew, had been put in a false position. The apology had been so sincere, so warmly expressed, that he could do nothing but mutter some phrases of acceptance and once he'd done that his own position was weakened and it hadn't been possible to refuse Southgate's offer. So he had had to dig out the old double-barrelled Rigby and find cartridges for it and then they had to find another horse and there had been trouble about the saddle girths. This was the result. . . .

They stood on the edge of the reeds. Andrew had sent Chik up a tree to see if there were any movements, but not even the Bushman's eyes could detect the presence of the buffalo, which wasn't surprising since they were probably lying down anyway. Andrew felt the sweat break out on his body. If there hadn't been an urgent need for meat nothing would have induced him to go after buffalo in thick reeds.

The reed-bed was about 1,000 yards wide and perhaps two or three miles long. In one or two parts, he understood, there were small mud wallows but mainly the floor of the bed was dry, and remained dry unless the flooding of the Okavango was exceptional.

'All right,' Andrew said, 'we'll divide this in two. We'll go in about the middle, you'll work your way west and I'll go east. That way we'll be moving outwards from each other towards the ends. And listen, I don't want a bloody bullet in the back so watch the sun. Keep it behind you all the time, if you can, and I'll keep it in front of me. That way we'll be firing away from each other. Understand?'

Matthew nodded. His face was pale and drawn by tension. For a second Andrew was tempted to go in alone with Chik or Jonathan and order him to remain where he was, but he'd said he'd done some shooting in German territory and they *did* need the meat.

'You take Chik,' Andrew said. 'He's had more experience of this sort of thing. He's got a .303 and he'll be backing you. He knows where to stand so don't worry about him. And remember, you must get a side shot. It's no bloody good shooting at it straight on unless you're a marksman. The boss of the horns will turn the bullet and you might just as well have saved yourself the trouble of pulling the trigger. You've got to get a side shot. All right?'

'Yes.'

'And don't worry. They're just cows, you know. Just bloody domestic cows. It's a pity to shoot them in a way; too easy.'

Matthew tried to smile but it didn't come out very well.

'Let's go, then,' Andrew said.

They moved into the reeds and almost immediately lost sight of everything else. The trees that fringed the bed were no longer visible after a few steps. Andrew touched Matthew on the shoulder and pointed his direction. The other nodded and turned away. In seconds he and Chik were lost to view and in a few more even their rustling passage could no longer be heard.

It was stiflingly hot. The reeds grew to a height of eleven or twelve feet and above him Andrew could see their feathery tops moving gently in the land breeze. But no breeze entered the bed itself and in a short while his bush shirt was soaked black.

The reeds grew in patches, dozens of slender yellow-green arms rising from a single root-clump. Between the clumps the floor of the bed was a mass of game trails. Andrew and Jonathan moved silently into the centre of the bed, then, turning so the morning sun was ahead of them, they slowly began working towards the eastern end.

There was evidence of buffalo everywhere : droppings, spoor, regurgitated cud lying in small dry balls and always the heavy smell of animal. As the morning strengthened, the heat increased until it was like a furnace. Andrew's hands felt slippery on the rifle but his mouth was as dry as chalk.

After every ten paces or so they stopped and tried to see through the thick green curtain that surrounded them on all sides. They would pause, look, listen for some tell-tale sound, a belly rumble or a belch, and then take ten more silent paces. Each time they stopped Andrew heard the irregular thud of his own heart. What they were doing was plain unadulterated madness. Even now they might have moved unknowingly into the centre of the herd.

It would take only one frightened cow to stampede the herd. . . . He cleared his mind of the thought. They were just a bunch of cows. And even if they did panic he still had the Jeffries and Jonathan was there to back him. No, it wasn't so much a stampede that he feared, it was the individual animal, the one with a month-old slug in its body, watching, waiting, calculating. Then the sudden rush through the reeds and. . . . Once again he forced his mind clear of the images. Walk—stop—look—listen—

An hour passed. The heat was overwhelming. His neck muscles were as hard as tarred rope and the tension was beginning to give him a headache. They had seen nothing, heard nothing. And suddenly the shot came. He had no idea how far away it was because the sound was muffled by the reeds. In the distance he heard a crashing noise of heavy animals. He slipped the safety and stood back to back with Jonathan. He had no idea from which quarter the rush would come. He waited for the second shot. The crashing noise faded. There was no second shot. A great silence settled on the reed-bed.

He wasn't sure afterwards how long he stood there and it was important that he should have known because it was just possible he might have been able to avert the tragedy. But the point was he'd *had* to work things out. One shot : that could mean one of three things : a dead buffalo, a wounded buffalo, a missed buffalo. And then the crashing noise. Was that the whole herd, were all the buffalo in Matthew's section? Or were there some in his, even now standing rock-still in the reeds, waiting for a movement or a smell that would shock them into action? In his experience the herd instinct was not total. He had often noticed that some animals were more nervous than others. At first when a herd of buck went jinking away in alarm he had assumed he had lost them all, and in those early days had missed dozens of trophies by suddenly coming, unprepared, on the two or three who had stayed in their camouflage.

'Morena !' the word was a hiss in his ear.

Jonathan was pointing. He could see nothing. The Basuto's head was bent forward. And then Andrew heard it. It sounded like a faint cry. He strained his ears. It came again and this time he could just make out his own name.

'It is Baas Matthew,' Jonathan said.

Yes, Andrew thought savagely, it's Baas Matthew all right, wandering through the reeds yelling at the top of his voice. It had to be Baas Matthew; there couldn't be two such fools in the whole of Central Africa.

'Come on,' he said. 'Let's get out of this bloody place. He'll never find us here.'

They moved quickly towards the perimeter, uncaring now of the noise they made. Both knew that something had gone very wrong.

Crack! Crack! Andrew fired two shots, paused for a minute and then fired two more. He was standing on a rise overlooking the reeds; Jonathan had climbed a tree. Crack! Crack! Around his feet were a dozen gleaming brass cartridge cases. He wondered if Southgate could hear. If he couldn't they'd have to go in after him and that might take hours. Between shots he listened for the cry of his name but heard nothing.

'He comes, Morena!' Jonathan called and at that moment Andrew was able to see the abrupt swaying of the reed tops that marked Matthew's passage.

He came out of the reeds at a shambling trot. His hair was plastered down onto his face with sweat, his clothes were soaked and caked with mud. As he came towards them Andrew saw that his eyes were wild and his cheeks were wet.

'Hurry,' he shouted as soon as he saw them. 'Please hurry! Help me!'

Andrew caught him by the shoulder and held him. 'What's happened?'

'Hurry! It's Chik!'

'What *happened*?' Andrew began to shake him. 'What happened to Chik?'

'I'll tell you as we go. But we've got to hurry.'

'Where *is* Chik?'

Matthew waved vaguely towards the far end of the reed-bed. 'God, if anything's. . . .'

'Not now, not now!'

The three of them ran towards the western verge of the reeds.

'It was here,' Matthew said. 'I'm certain it was somewhere about here. Up a tree. Just like this one.' He pointed to an acacia tree. It was the exact replica of a thousand other trees that grew on the high ground around the reeds.

'Southgate!' Andrew shouted in his face. '*What happened?*'

Piecemeal, and in no coherent order, he managed to extract the facts of the past hour.

Matthew and Chik had been working their way through the reeds in exactly the same pattern as Andrew when Chik had suddenly knelt down and felt the ground at his feet. Then he'd shown Matthew a large depression in the reeds where a heavy body had been lying. Some of the young reeds had been crushed, others were slowly straightening even as they watched. Matthew had placed his hand on the leaves and they were warm to the touch.

He had realized that they were almost on top of the herd. But before he could even consult with Chik they had seen the bull. It had been standing quite still watching them, a dark shape in the darker gloom of the reeds. Matthew was appalled at its size. It seemed even larger than he had imagined a buffalo to be because its outlines were blurred. He could remember its eyes, he said. They were hot and angry and at the same time there was a frightening shrewdness in them. Without any warning the bull lowered its head and charged. In those first seconds as Matthew stood numbly, incapable of movement, he was aware that the buffalo had stretched its neck and all he could see was a wet black nose, a half-open mouth with a lolling blue-pink tongue which dripped saliva and, above the frightening eyes, the great black boss of horn which covered the forehead and behind which even the body seemed to take shelter. Matthew turned and ran.

Two things happened almost simultaneously : he felt a terrible blow in his back as the bull caught him with the flat of its horns and he heard, almost in his ear, the thunderclap of Chik's rifle. After that all was confusion. The herd must have been all around them for the reeds were suddenly a plunging mass of great black bodies. For a second he thought the whole world was collapsing in noise and fury and then they were gone and he was left alone in a bower of green.

After a few moments he picked himself up and began to force his way through the reeds, calling to Chik. As he came out of the reed-bed he'd seen the Bushman. Chik had wedged himself in the fork of a tree. Below the tree stood the old buffalo bull. Blood was pouring from a hole in its stomach.

He had called to Chik, but either the Bushman didn't hear or he was unconscious. The buffalo had shown no sign of hearing either. That was when he had decided to go back into the reeds to get Andrew's help.

Andrew had been listening with mounting rage; even Jonathan's eyes were clouded with indignation.

'Help!' Andrew shouted. 'What bloody help? You were there. And you left him!'

'But there was nothing I could do.' His voice had risen and there was an edge of hysteria in the tone.

'*You could have shot the damn thing!*'

'But—' Slowly an expression of dawning horror crept into Matthew's eyes as he looked down at the rifle in his hand. It was there, forgotten, like an extension to his arm.

'I didn't think—I didn't—'

Andrew grabbed the rifle, broke it, pulled out the two heavy-grain bullets and held them in front of Matthew's face.

'You didn't even try, you bastard.'

It was five hours before they found Chik. Matthew's sense of direction had deserted him completely. The Bushman was on the far side of the reed-bed. They found the dead buffalo first. It lay beneath an acacia tree with its nose in the ground. At first Andrew thought it had been vomiting blood, there was so much smeared around its nose, but when he saw Chik he realized what had happened and felt a queasy sickness in his stomach.

The Bushman was dead. He was wedged in the fork of the tree as Matthew had described. His rifle lay about twenty yards away, the stock smashed and splintered.

Down one side of his ribs was a long jagged wound. It was obvious that the bull had caught him just before he had reached the tree. But the wound was the least of it. It was his right foot that held their horrified attention. All the skin had gone from both the foot and ankle, leaving only the crushed white skeleton. The whole of Chik's body was etiolated and shrunken; the natural apricot-yellow of his skin was now a dirty khaki colour.

Andrew bent down at the side of the buffalo and reached for its bloodstained horn, letting his fingers rasp over the surface. He knew exactly what had happened. Chik had been bludgeoned to death. He could visualize the scene: the unconscious Bushman safe in the fork of his tree except for one dangling foot, and that foot just within stretching reach of the buffalo's head. And then the bull had begun to smash it. A hundred . . . a thousand weak blows with the boss of the horns, splintering the leg bones so that pieces were embedded in the bark of the tree, the blood flowing in rivers and then in small streams until the last drop squeezed itself from the Bushman's body and he was dead.

'What happened?' Matthew's question was no more than a whisper.

'You let him die,' Andrew said. 'That's what happened.'

'I want them in line,' Andrew was shouting. 'I've told you fifty times. Get them in line. Single file. One behind the other.'

In the centre of the milling mass of refugees Kaneena and Jonathan were trying to produce some sort of order. Earlier, when the wagons had arrived, the Hereros had been sitting in the shade of low bushes waiting, with a stunned stoicism, for whatever was their fate. But now, sensing that food was a reality after all, they had pressed forward at the wagons, frightening the bullocks and causing Watch to snatch up one of the long driving whips and send the lash hissing through the air. Andrew had fired over their heads and Jonathan and Kaneena had managed to force back the leaders. After an hour of pushing and pulling they had formed the whole company into some sort of queue and Andrew went up the line counting them like sheep. There were just over two hundred. When he had finished he walked back up the line and told Kaneena and Jonathan to collect all the firearms. Some, he noticed, were relatively new German combinations, unwieldy-looking things that fired solids from one barrel and shot from the other. But most were old Martini-Henrys, the stocks bound with copper wire where they had split with age and neglect.

Reluctantly the Hereros gave up their guns. They were carried to a pile of brushwood fifty yards away and set alight. Andrew began to breathe more freely.

'All right,' he called to Watch. 'You can feed them.'

The old Nyasa had made a table out of packing cases. Wisely he kept the food in boxes on the far side. As each Herero shuffled forward to get his rations he could only see what was put in front of him.

They were all in the last stages of starvation. Thirst had not been one of their problems because just as their supply of melons was on the point of exhaustion an early rainstorm had broken.

Andrew watched them. Under his arm he carried the Jeffries, just in case.

At that moment Matthew climbed down from the rear wagon and walked slowly across the hot sand to the shade of a bush. Apart from the line of refugees his were the only definite movements to break the pattern of stillness. And yet no one seemed aware of him. The Hereros were too intent on what was to come; the others seemed to look right through him as though he wasn't there.

It had been the same ever since Chik's death. Andrew had said nothing more about it to him and neither Watch nor Jonathan had mentioned it. The only reference had come when Andrew was writing his report and that had been as impersonal as either man could make it. Andrew had questioned him on the Magistrate's verandah: name, age, occupation, date of entry into the Protectorate, address of domicile, nationality. . . . Matthew had answered in monosyllables. For the rest he had been ignored.

The day after the tragedy Andrew had returned to the reeds, this time an hour earlier, and between them he and Jonathan had killed four buffalo. He had bartered for a further six native cows, smoked the meat, commandeered 300 lb of flour and 200 lb of rice from the magistrate's supplies, and helped himself to a second Scotch-cart and spare oxen, and they had come down in fast night treks past Ngami and Kobe, back along their own tracks to Ghanzi.

Later, when he had made some decision about the Hereros, he would take Southgate on to Kela, pick up his abandoned wagon, give him the spare span of bullocks and put him across the border. He had no doubt that this would be the best way of dealing with the situation. Southgate had not committed a criminal action, apart from entering the Protectorate, and there was no question of a prosecution. When his report went in it would be seen that he had dealt diplomatically with the whole question. After all, Southgate's father was an important man; the authorities would not want a scandal. What could be more natural than that Southgate should quietly be returned from whence he'd come? What happened to him in the sandy wastes of the southern Sand Veld was no concern of Andrew's. He'd given him food, water and fresh bullocks—which was a damn sight more than he'd had when he arrived.

He could spare a few days where they were. The food wasn't going to last forever but it would do until the Hereros were strong enough to move. Once he got them up to Ngamiland the Bata-wanas could keep them alive on fish until orders came from Mafeking.

In the meantime there was news that von Steinberg was camped on the border less than fifty miles away. If anyone should know about the troubles in German territory and whether more refugees were likely to come pouring over the border, it was he.

The Kalahari night was like soft, warm down on their faces as they sat under the raised tent awning. Away to the west the Kaiser's thunder rumbled and muttered. Occasionally the black horizon flickered faintly with sheet lightning but the storm was a long way away.

'Come,' von Steinberg said, holding up a glass of schnapps. 'What shall we drink to now?'

They had aready drunk to the King and the Emperor and to Britain and Germany, to their brother officers, even to absent friends. Andrew, who was not used to hard liquor, could feel the slight lack of co-ordination in his muscles and speech, but he was far from caring. It had been a splendid evening, one he would cherish over and over again in his own lonely camps.

'To friendship,' von Steinberg said, the light from the hanging lantern glinting on his steel-rimmed spectacles and on the high, round forehead that was running with sweat. 'To comradeship. Between ourselves, my dear Black.'

Comradeship. Friendship. What a wonderful thing comrade-ship was! He raised his glass and they clinked together. 'To com-radeship.'

At first the schnapps had taken his breath away but now the fiery, slightly oily liquor rolled over his tongue and down his throat without making him catch his breath. To comradeship. Yes, by God, that's what he missed most of all. Sometimes his yearning for it became an ache inside him. A comradeship where there were no barriers, where nothing was held back, where one could express worries and fears and doubts, unembarrassed and unashamed; a sharing, a pooling. Without any question comradeship was the finest thing in the world and it was precisely what his own life lacked.

His brother officers, on the few occasions when he ever saw them at Francistown or Gaberones, were like a race apart. All were English, all had different backgrounds from his own. To him they seemed stiff and uncommunicative. On the rare times when he had proffered friendship or sought even the barest moment of intimacy he had met a chill of unconcern and uninvolvement. And Southgate was like the rest, more English than anything else. In his case it was worse because he was masquerading as something he wasn't.

That left only the natives and there was no comradeship to be had there. Just the opposite. You had to be on the look-out all the time. One friendly act and they immediately took it for weakness. Like Seitsang, with his poor-mouth talk of drought and devastation. A moment of weakness, an extension of friendship, and what had happened? It had been flung back in his face by every bloody headman in the area.

But von Steinberg was different. Perhaps it was the German character. They were able to speak about things like comradeship and friendship as though they really meant them. When von Steinberg drank to comradeship there was nothing embarrassing about it; just the contrary, it seemed something good and warm and protective.

Andrew studied the German through eyes misty with sentiment. He did not see a squat, bespectacled lieutenant with the thin white hair and pinkish eyes of the albino, but a comrade in arms; true friend and lonely traveller like himself.

Abruptly he said : 'I would be honoured if you would call me Andrew.'

The German looked up quickly, his shrewd eyes resting for a moment on Andrew's face. 'And you will call me Kurt, ja?'

'And I will call you Kurt.'

'To that we must drink.' He refilled both glasses and they clinked again before draining them.

Andrew leant back in the canvas chair. A feeling of great happiness seemed to relax every muscle. There had been a moment, only a very brief one, when he had thought he might have gone too far, but it had passed without embarrassment. He pulled contentedly at the fat Jamaican cigar which von Steinberg had pressed on him. The Herero refugees seemed a long way away. In fact, from the moment he had reached the German's camp that afternoon he had almost forgotten them. First there had been the beer. *Beer.* After the long dusty ride it had been like a miracle. Where von Steinberg had got it he had no idea but there it was, two bottles of Löwenbräu each.

The German had been delighted at his reaction. 'My dear Black, just to see your face has made it worth while. There were many times when I was tempted. One is only human. But I thought of this moment and placed my mind on other things.'

They had drunk the beer, which had come all the thousands of miles from its brewery in Bavaria to this camp in the shade of a camelthorn tree, out of blue and white porcelain steins. Andrew had watched the froth rise to the rim, and stop there, had lowered his nose to the bursting bubbles and drawn in the bitter hop smell and felt the saliva glands in his mouth contract in orgasm. The fact that the beer was warm was of no importance.

After the beer had come dinner, a venison stew to which had been added slices of Braunschweiger and caraway seeds. With it they had drunk a bottle of Mosel—something else which had amazed him—and now schnapps with a cigar.

'Next time it will be my honour,' Andrew said, already planning how he might emulate the German's hospitality.

'I'm afraid that will not be possible,' von Steinberg said, looking down at the glowing end of his cigar. 'You see, soon I resign my commission. That is why the beer and the Mosel. One needs something special for a farewell.'

'Oh,' Andrew said, feeling a strange shock of isolation. 'Resigning?'

'It was only a temporary commission. Now my father gets old and an old man cannot manage a farm alone.'

'But I would have thought with the troubles. . . .'

'What troubles?' The shrewd eyes were once again on Andrew's face.

'The Hereros.'

'So you have heard.'

'A little.' He had not mentioned the refugees since his arrival

56

for the simple reason that he had hardly given them a thought. Now he realized that just as he had known von Steinberg's whereabouts the German would have known his. He probably knew all about the refugees. 'Some of your natives have crossed the border.'

Von Steinberg nodded. 'What will you do with them?'

Andrew decided he had said enough. 'I'm holding them until Mafeking sends instructions.'

'Naturally.'

He seemed indifferent and Andrew was puzzled until he remembered that von Steinberg was on the brink of leaving the service. Why should he care one way or the other? Suddenly he said viciously: 'They're a bloody nuisance whatever happens.'

'Precisely. And there will be many more nuisances, my dear Andrew.'

'You think so?'

Von Steinberg's eyes slid away. 'Ja, I think so.'

'What the hell's happening, anyway? One hears rumours but that's about all. What's this about a possible rebellion?'

'Why don't you come and see?'

'See? Me? I don't follow.'

'Let me give you another glass.' He poured the schnapps and they drank. This time there were no toasts. 'So you have been hearing rumours, stories about revolution. Well, maybe so. I hope so. If there is revolution it will give us a chance to solve the Herero question once and for all.'

Andrew laughed shortly. 'And you want me to pay you a visit at a time like that!'

Von Steinberg swung round to fix his strange, pink-rimmed eyes on Andrew. 'Not visit,' he said slowly. 'Stay.'

'I don't understand you.'

'You are a sub-inspector. Perhaps in time you can become an inspector. But after that? You yourself have told me that for the higher positions it depends who you know in Britain, what school you went to, who your father was. Not so?'

'I suppose so.'

'With us it doesn't matter. If a man is a man that is what counts. Now you say there may be revolution. If that is so then what happens? I will tell you. Detachments of the German Army will be sent out from the Fatherland and the revolution will be

57

crushed. But the German Army knows nothing about fighting here in Africa. The first people they will need are those who know the country. Am I clear?'

'Are you suggesting that I join the German Army?' Andrew said, laughing.

Von Steinberg shook his head. 'Why do you think I am resigning my commission?'

'Your father. . . .'

'Yes, yes,' he said impatiently. 'That is one reason. The other is that in my experience it is always better to work *with* an army rather than *in* it. Do you comprehend me?'

'Not altogether.'

'The pay of a soldier is nothing. But the pay of a civilian who works with an army—that is a different thing.' He poured them each another glass. By this time both were drenched with sweat. 'I will be plain with you. I have received permission to resign only because of family reasons. My father is an important man in the Colony and he wants me with him at home in case anything happens. Now listen carefully. Already there is talk of what the *schutztruppen* will need if they come here; of horses and supplies and this and that. Why should we let the traders skim the cream from the milk?'

'I still don't follow. I've got nothing the Army needs.'

'But I have. I have bought a herd of three hundred horses. They are waiting now in South African territory. I need someone to fetch them.'

'Me? Why not go yourself?'

Von Steinberg looked at him blankly for a moment. 'Myself? But I have just explained! If an officer resigns his commission to look after his family estate he cannot suddenly produce three hundred remounts for sale to the Army. People will talk. There will be scandal, not so?'

'You want me to act as your agent.'

'Precisely. You will fetch the horses. You will negotiate with the authorities. My name will not be mentioned. Then we come to—an arrangement. And don't worry, that is only a beginning.'

Somehow the euphoria of the evening had gone sour in Andrew's mouth. The schnapps tasted of paraffin. Was this what the toasts to comradeship had been leading to? He shook his head. 'Thanks,' he said. 'But it's not really my line of country.'

'Don't think about it now. Sleep on it. You will see more clearly in the morning.'

But he hadn't seen more clearly in the morning. Or perhaps that wasn't true, perhaps he had seen as clearly as it was possible to see and he didn't like what he saw. As he said good-bye to von Steinberg he was aware of the puzzlement, almost anger, in the other's eyes.

'You will regret your choice, my dear Black,' von Steinberg had said as he mounted.

'Perhaps,' Andrew said. 'But I will never regret the dinner.' He raised his hand in a half-salute and kicked Duke into a canter.

It was as though time had been suspended. He had been away for more than two days and yet the scene was almost exactly as he had left it. The refugees still lay or sat in what shade they could find; the Scotch-carts were standing in the same positions, the bullocks out on the pan where the last of the water was being sucked up by a greedy sun. It seemed unbelievable that only the night before he had been sitting over an excellent dinner with a bottle of wine. The only addition was Southgate's wagon which had been brought from Kela. It stood on the outskirts of the camp, tattered and sun-bleached.

And yet Andrew could feel a subtle change. As he dismounted he glanced across at the Hereros. They should, by now, have been showing some sign of recuperation and he frowned as he took in the listless, defeated figures. Whatever it was he'd find out soon enough. He handed the reins to Jonathan and took off his hat to wipe his forehead. The sun struck like a blow and he staggered slightly. He moved to the shade of the Scotch-cart and held onto the seat until the dizziness passed. That was one change he recognized, the interim period between winter and summer was over. The heat was savage.

'Anything to report?'

'There is post, Morena,' Jonathan said, and then hesitated.

'Yes?'

'Two men are sick, Morena.'

'Where?'

'By the bushes.' He pointed to an area of bush close to Southgate's wagon.

'What's the matter with them?'

'They are bad, Morena.'

'All right, show me.' As he walked through the camp he could feel depression settle on his shoulders like a cloak. Sickness. That was all they needed now.

In spite of the great heat the two men were lying on their sides in a foetal position, their knees drawn up and their heads, wrapped in torn and dusty clothing, protected by their arms and hands. Andrew looked down at them in distaste.

'When did they become sick?'

'Since one day, Morena.'

The bundle of clothing at his feet moved and uncovered its face. The man began to speak in a low pain-filled monotone. Andrew could not understand a word.

'Oh, Christ,' he began, and made to turn away when Kaneena, who had come quietly up to the group, stepped forward. 'They are sick,' he said in German.

'So I understand. What's wrong with them?'

'I don't know.'

'Well, ask them!' Andrew studied the Herero. Kaneena was a very different person from the exhausted and emaciated figure he had interviewed in the Magistrate's garden. Food and rest had given him back his body and, with that, his dignity. He was tall and good-looking with steady brown eyes and an air of quiet authority. In the talk which Andrew had had with him only a few days ago it emerged that he had had a good education at one of the Rhenish Mission Schools and had once possessed ambitions to enter the ministry.

'He says he has pains, Inspector.'

'What sort of pains?'

'In his head and back.'

Andrew squatted down and stretched out his hand to feel the man's brow for fever. His touch was perfunctory.

'What is wrong, Inspector?'

'Nothing,' Andrew said, rubbing his hand on his trousers. 'They have sunstroke. Keep them in the shade. They'll be better tomorrow.'

'But none of them has been in the sun. All day we've stayed in the shade. These men became sick in the night.'

'Heatstroke. Same thing. Can't you feel the heat?'

60

Kaneena nodded doubtfully. 'But we are used to heat, Inspector.'

Matthew had climbed down from his wagon. 'It looks like some sort of fever,' he said hesitantly, his hand touching the face and brow of one of the sick Hereros.

Andrew didn't bother to look up. 'Ask my cook-boy for more water,' he said to Kaneena. 'Jonathan, fetch the post.'

As he walked back to the Scotch-cart he rubbed his hand continually on his trousers until it began to leave a dark sweat-mark. Sunstroke. Heatstroke. Fever. It could be anything at all. What if it was infectious or even contagious? What if it was yellow fever? And he'd touched him! He called for water immediately and after scrubbing his hands in a weak solution of permanganate of potash he felt slightly better. But what if it *were* catching? He couldn't very well take them to Ngamiland and risk an epidemic. Nor could he take them south to Tsane, for the same reason, and anyway it was too far, they'd never make it. At that moment, in the midst of his depression, a feeling of utter loss swept over him. He wanted someone to turn to, not so much for orders, just someone with whom he could discuss it. But there was no one. Even von Steinberg had gone.

He took the leather post-pouch to the shady side of the Scotch-cart and sat in the canvas chair Watch had placed there. There was the usual stuff : notices about foot-and-mouth outbreaks, descriptions of natives wanted for questioning, circulars on new health regulations, a change in the law relating to grazing rights, a list of gazetted promotions, a bill from a tailor in Bulawayo. He set them to one side for further study and turned to two official envelopes marked 'Private and Confidential'.

The first was brief to the point of abruptness. It stated quite simply that he had not achieved a pass level in his examinations. The letter was only four lines long. Hardly knowing what he was doing, he put it neatly on the pile of notices and slit the second envelope with his knife. It was from Headquarter House and read :

Sub-Inspector Black, B.P.P.,

This will inform you that your presence is required as soon as possible at Gaberones. You will therefore leave immediately bringing with you all papers and possessions.

61

Sub-Inspector Creswell-Smith has already left Mafeking for Tsane where you will rendezvous with him before proceeding. You will instruct him as to the latest developments in your area with regard especially to any refugees who may have crossed the border.

I have to state that on the journey south you will not approach closer than fifteen miles to that area, or any villages in it, which was formerly ruled by the late Headman Seitsang.

I have to state further that his people have laid certain charges and made certain allegations against you, the investigating of which is the reason for the above orders.

(Signed) Ralph Howland

Resident Commissioner

'Captain,' Watch was standing silently beside the chair holding a mug of tea. 'Captain.'

Andrew allowed the letter to drop onto his lap and looked up. His face was drawn and his eyes were unnaturally bright. He stared through Watch without seeing him. In spite of the heat he felt cold; his upper arms were puckered with gooseflesh. 'Captain, tea.' There was something wary about Watch's tone and when Andrew finally noticed him and smiled his thanks the old Nyasa was glad to return hurriedly to his pots and pans. The last time he had seen a smile as dreadful as that was on the face of a skull up near the Caprivi Zipfel.

For some strange reason the smile remained on Andrew's face until the muscles of his cheeks grew tired and the expression slowly dissolved into a frown. He sipped at the tea without tasting it.

'Disasters come in threes,' his mother had always said. He could remember clearly that if she broke a plate or cup she would search the house for a box of matches, carefully break two in half and throw them away. In that way, having brought the total breakages to three, she was absolved from further accidents for that day at least.

Seitsang. The name was beginning to haunt him. He looked at the letter again. '. . . you will not approach closer than fifteen miles to that area, or any villages in it, which was formerly ruled by the late Headman Seitsang.' Charges . . . allegations . . . investigation. . . . What did it all mean? Unless. . . . But he'd a right to take the skins. There was no question about that. Anyone would have done the same thing. So it couldn't be that. Suddenly the phrase 'the late' sprang out at him; the old man was dead.

He cast his mind back to the last visit to Seitsang's village. He went through each detail as well as he could remember it. As the picture became clearer there was one image that remained most prominent of all: Seitsang lying under the tree after he had released him from the handcuffs. He could see the dusty body with the runnels of water on the jacket, he could remember the purple eyes, the exhausted face. Christ! The old man must have died soon after he'd left. They would be saying that *he* had caused his death, that he, Andrew Black, had murdered him. It was ridiculous. All he'd done was fasten him to a tree for a few minutes. It wasn't according to regulations, in fact regulations expressly forbade any such actions, but all of them bent regulations from time to time. It was known, accepted. How else could you deal with people like Seitsang, how else could you maintain law and order and discipline in a place as vast as the Protectorate?

No, he could refute those allegations anyway; he was no murderer. But there was still the water. How would it sound at a court martial if he agreed he had removed the leather ropes and buckets—especially when there were women with babies?

Andrew had learnt enough about base camp to know that things sounded very different there. The desert, with its peculiar circumstances, seemed far away when everything was being reduced to question and answer and a record kept in black and white.

He looked at the letter again. In ten years from now I'll laugh about it, he thought. It'll be a joke; something to tell in the mess. But something cold inside him told him that this would not be the case at all.

He sat as still as a rock for so long that Watch came back to peer around the tent of the Scotch-cart at him. Andrew was still holding the half-finished mug of tea. Watch slowly shook his head and retreated once more. He knew the Captain's moods as well as the Captain knew his but there was something different about this one that worried Watch. Normally he could deal with outbreaks of temper but he was helpless in the face of total withdrawal.

63

Andrew's mind had run down. There had been too much to think about, too many decisions to make. He sat there, the victim of his own spell, unwilling to move an arm or leg lest the slight safety of inaction was destroyed.

'I've got to talk to you.' Southgate was standing in front of his chair. 'It's about the sick men. I think you should know. . . .'

'Go away! Get out of my sight!' He sprang to his feet, an expression of such rage on his face that Matthew fell back several paces. For a moment it seemed Andrew might throw himself on the other man, then, scooping up the papers, he thrust them into his pocket and strode off into the desert.

Andrew was not sure how long he had walked but it was nightfall before he began to retrace his steps and by that time he had made a decision which frightened him by its very unexpectedness.

At first, after he had brushed past Southgate, his reactivated thoughts had followed a standard procedural pattern. He had been given an order and he would carry it out. He would fight Seitsang's people; he would vindicate himself. He would appear before a court martial and by his very demeanour—serious, thoughtful, hard but just—he would project an image that his senior officers would never forget; he would epitomize all that was best in the Bechuanaland Protectorate Police.

Ironically, he told himself, this might be just the very thing he needed to raise himself from the ruck of competing officers. He would be known, he would make a mark.

His mood had swung crazily from black depression to euphoria. He was convinced that what he had done was right and just and this would be seen, noted and acted upon. They would realize that he had not been responsible for Seitsang's death. When he had finished giving evidence they would know just what sort of man he had been dealing with; the worst sort of native. Yes, he would go, and go gladly. . . .

And then, like a pile of dry grass in the wind, his frenzied and confident plans blew away over the horizon. He had failed his examinations, and it said in The Book: no examinations, no promotion. And at that very moment an idea had lighted the dark places of his mind like an errant beam of sunlight.

Why go back at all?

As though his brain was released of its fetters it now began working on smooth, well-oiled lines. By the time he regained the camp he had not only made up his mind but had already decided on what action to take.

He waited until the refugees had been fed the following morning and until they had drifted back in twos and threes to the shade of the bushes. By nine o'clock the sun was already fierce. He had slept little the previous night and yet he did not feel tired; it was as though the very act of making a decision had infused his muscles and brain with new energy. That and the fact that knowing what he had to do had arbitrarily removed the pressing weight of most of his problems; they had, in fact, just disappeared. He watched the last of the Hereros take their places in the food queue. He wanted them away from the wagons. Then he went to his own Scotch-cart, loaded his shotgun with No. 5 shot and gave it to Watch. The cook-boy took it casually. He liked to affect a patronizing attitude to guns and hunters; had he not, after all, been on safari with the great Selous? Andrew checked the Jeffries, then called Jonathan. He gave him the .303 and a box of ammunition.

'Watch, I want you up on the Scotch-cart. Just hold the gun where it can be seen. You too, Jonathan. But first call Kaneena and Baas Southgate.'

During the sleepless hours of the night he had decided this would be the hardest moment. Once he got them on the move there would be little trouble. At one stage he had wondered whether it would not have been possible to hitch up his own wagon and, making some excuse, simply pull out into the desert and leave the lot of them. But he had rejected the idea. Firstly, he would want Jonathan to trek back to Ngamiland with his letter of explanation. Secondly, and perhaps this was the over-riding factor, he hated leaving loose ends. He wanted things left neatly and tidily so that when his letter of resignation was read and the explanations investigated, his superiors would be forced to the conclusion that they had lost not only a good man but one who had been defamed into the bargain. It was the death-game all over again: the game which had been born in poverty and loneliness and which always ran on similar lines. It would usually begin after some incident in which he would feel his mother or father had been unjust to him. Quickly, thoughts would accelerate into a situation in which Andrew, the dying hero of some gallant rescue at sea would hear, just before his eyes closed forever, the grief-stricken voices acknowledging that he had been right all the time. After that would come the State funeral or the burial-at-sea or whatever ending his simple imagination had created; and always his *doppelgänger* would be there to enjoy the whole procedure. How could he expect the Resident Commissioner to express grief and anger at the injustice to which he'd been subjected if he left things in their present mess?

'You wanted me?'

He looked up to see Southgate standing in front of him. He was glad to note he was unarmed, though even if he were it would have made little difference. He waited until Kaneena joined them and Jonathan had taken his place on the cart.

'I've got something to tell you both,' he began, speaking alternately in English and German for the benefit of the Herero chieftain. 'You may not like it. Orders which have reached me from Mafeking now make it imperative that you leave here at once.'

'But my people cannot travel,' Kaneena said, a frown of worry creasing his forehead. 'Another two are sick this morning.'

'I'm afraid there's no help for it.'

'It may be a good thing,' Southgate said, in a mixture of Herero and German, turning to Kaneena. 'Once we get them to Tsau the Magistrate can send for medical help.'

'You will not be going to Tsau,' Andrew said. 'None of you.'

They looked up in surprise. The only other post which could conceivably be big enough to stand the strain of sick and starving refugees was at Tsane, more than 150 miles south through the heart of the Thirst. It was apparent that none of the Hereros would ever reach there even if there was enough water, which there wasn't.

'Where to, then?' Matthew asked.

'You're going back.'

'To German territory?'

'Precisely. My orders are to return all refugees to the territory of their origin. As far as I'm concerned you originated in German territory so that's where you return.'

'I don't believe it,' Matthew said, bewildered. 'Up on the Okavango you told me your orders were just the contrary. I even read the letter.'

'They've been changed.'

'Can I see them?'

'No, you damn well can't. You forfeited any right of special consideration. I think you know how.'

'You'll never let me forget, will you?'

'No.'

Matthew nodded and there was a bitter smile on his lips. 'In a way I'm glad. I'll never forget myself but time has a way of dimming things. To know that it'll always be in the forefront of someone else's mind will help to keep it alive in mine. You see, I don't want to forget.'

He turned on his heel and walked over to his own wagon. Half-way there he stopped and faced Andrew. 'What I did,' he said, 'was the result of foolishness and cowardice, but there was no malice in it. Sending these people back is an act of murder, for if the desert doesn't claim them the Germans will.'

'Inspector,' Kaneena's voice was trembling with emotion. 'Inspector, I beg of you. . . .'

'Didn't you hear what I said? I have received orders. And just in case you doubt them, let me tell you that a detachment of police has already left Tsane on its way here. So don't let's have any trouble. Prepare your people to move out in half an hour.' He turned to the two men on the cart. 'Jonathan, I have orders for you.'

Things were going better than he'd expected. Not that he had visualized trouble from Southgate; he could handle people like him at any time. But he'd wondered about Kaneena. The Hereros were said to be a proud, touchy race. Well, not this lot. They were beaten before they started. He felt no sympathy for them.

As he was about to issue orders for the journey the thought suddenly struck him: *What if they turned back after he had left them?*

This was something he hadn't considered. It wouldn't be difficult. They could wait for a few days on the far side of the border and then begin to drift back. All his neatly tied ends would be loose again.

'Inspector.' Kaneena had returned, his face grave.

'What is it?'

'One of the men has died.'

God, he'd almost forgotten about the sick men. Without thinking, his right hand went to his trousers and he began to wipe it on the seam. Then he had an idea which would take care completely of any thoughts of returning this way.

'Show me,' he said.

Kaneena led him across to the line of bushes where the two men had lain. Andrew looked down in distaste at the dusty, dirty corpse. 'I want two men,' he said.

While he waited he called Jonathan. 'Has the stock been watered and the barrels filled?'

'Yes, Morena.'

'All right,' he said to Kaneena. 'Tell them to pick him up and follow me.' The two Hereros shuffled forward and raised the corpse, one taking it at the armpits, the other under the knees. As they walked, its hands and feet scraped along in the sand.

Andrew marched steadily out onto the pan, followed by Kaneena and the burial party. As he left the camp the Hereros, as though sensing that something important was to happen, had pushed themselves to their feet and were standing together in a group. Watch and Jonathan stood by the Scotch-cart, Matthew by the wagon.

Had he given any thought to the enormity of what he was about to do, Andrew might have faltered, stopped and changed his mind. Had he, in other circumstances, discovered a man doing a similar act he would have arrested him. Had a Bushman or a Kalahari found a native doing what Andrew was about to do they would have killed him.

The water in the pan had gradually decreased in area until there was only the pit in the centre. Here they stopped.

'Tell them to throw him in,' Andrew said.

Kaneena looked at him blankly. This was the only water between Ghanzi and the border.

'Did you hear me!'

Still the Herero stood, unable or unwilling to comprehend what was happening.

'All right, then,' Andrew said. He grabbed the legs of the

68

corpse and pulled it over the lip of the pit, hearing the splash as the body hit the surface of the black water ten feet below.

'Now you know,' he said, turning to Kaneena. 'There's no way back.'

He stood at the border beacon watching the wagon, surrounded by its cohort of Hereros, slowly disappear into the vast emptiness of the southern Sand Veld. He watched them for as long as he could with the naked eye and then followed them through the prismatic glasses until they were swallowed up in the heatwaves. Then, bending down, he carefully removed the drift-sand which was building up on the beacon, brushing it away so that the British Coat-of-Arms was visible on one side and the German Eagle on the other. When he was satisfied that the desert was as neat and tidy as he could make it he mounted Duke and waved on Watch and the Scotch-cart. He turned the stallion's head and moved into German territory. He was heading south-west and knew he should cut von Steinberg's tracks in less than a week.

BOOK TWO

The Masters

It is no accident that the first cultures arose in places where the Aryan, in his encounters with lower peoples, subjugated them and bent them to his will. . . . As long as he ruthlessly upheld the master attitude, not only did he remain master, but also the preserver and increaser of culture.

Adolf Hitler, *Mein Kampf*

At six o'clock in the afternoon on a day in early January 1904 Andrew Black felt the first faint hint of the breeze on his cheek. He had been waiting for it in the shade of a camelthorn tree on one side of the tiny village square. Near his elbow stood a litre of good Dortmund beer and now, with the coming of the breeze, he filled the tin mug and drank deeply. The sweat broke out on his forehead and chest and almost as soon it began to dry in the breeze, and for the first time on that hot, baking day he felt cool.

It was true what they said about the breeze; it never failed. Sometimes it was slightly earlier, sometimes a bit late; but always, around six o'clock, the dusty leaves of the camelthorn tree would begin to stir. It was a miraculous breeze. It started hundreds of miles to the west, far out in the Atlantic Ocean, crossed the ghostly dunes of the Namib Desert, found its way through the hot kloofs of the Erongo Mountains and across the shimmering plains until finally it arrived here at Falkenberg, to the north-west of the capital, Windhuk, still retaining some vestigial trace of the icy Benguela Current in its teeth. Without the breeze life would have taken on a much grimmer aspect; it gave each day a future. It was something more than a volume of cool air moving across the landscape, it was a watershed; it divided the day between those hours that had to be endured and those that could be enjoyed. It was a moment, if one was given to smiling, when one smiled.

Andrew settled his back more comfortably against the trunk of the tree and raised the mug to his lips again. Even the beer tasted that little bit better than it had five minutes before. His eyes, which had been closed to mere slits against the glare of the mica dust, now opened more widely as the sun poised for a moment on the tip of the Falkenberg and then vanished. With it, abruptly, went the black bar shadows cast by trees and buildings and the light became a soft pearly grey.

73

Idly he allowed his eyes to wander over the village, if such a miserable agglomeration of buildings could be described as such. On the left was the canteen—mud walls and a roof thatched with grass, its only pretension a corrugated-iron verandah supported by two slender poles. A notice in German asked patrons not to tether their horses to either one. The year before, so Andrew had been told, a stallion tied to one pole had tried to mount a mare tethered to the other, and half the building had come down on the heads of the serious drinkers within. Facing him was the police post built in the shape of a Saharan fort around an inner courtyard. Towers with embrasures dominated the four corners and the walls were broken by firing slits. The whole was painted white and normally, in the fierce heat of noon, it made the eyes ache to look at it. Now it had a quiet, functional beauty; enhanced if one knew why it had been built in that position and that shape. In the centre of the inner courtyard was a well of sweet water.

Away to Andrew's right the dun-coloured walls of Sauermann & Fricke were broken up by window-surrounds in pink wash. Andrew had spent a lot of time in the store, sometimes buying, sometimes not, depending on his mood, but always with the knowledge that he could buy almost anything he liked. It was a good feeling. He wore the marks, earned from the last horse-sale, in a soft leather money-belt and every now and then his fingers would stray to it. There was no denying the belt was hot next to his skin but he endured the discomfort with pleasure.

Often he would while away the hot hours of the day talking to old Fricke who sat perched on his high stool behind the wide wooden counter, like a small and angry lemur. Herr Fricke was a man with many dislikes: he disliked his shop, the village, the Colony, the weather, himself, and above all he disliked his former partner Sauermann who had selfishly died some years before just when Herr Fricke had been planning to sell out to him and brush the dust of South-West Africa forever from his boots.

It amused Andrew to lean against the counter and listen to Herr Fricke for although Fricke might hate everything about the Colony he had been a part of it for so many years there was almost nothing about its past or present he did not know.

'I tell you it's an outpost between nothing and nowhere,' he had said once, allowing his huge, goitrous eyes to roll around in

74

their sockets. 'What is there here? I ask you? Nothing! Sun, heat, dust. Why couldn't we leave it to the Hottentots and the Hereros and the Bushmen? I tell you, Herr Black, that these people actually *liked* living here. But no. The scramble for Africa, they called it. International politics, reputation, rubbish! The British, French, Portuguese and Belgians had cut their slices from the cake so we had to have our share, but all that was left was the crumbs. Togoland! Who wants Togoland? And the Kamerun! They tell me German East Africa is green and pleasant. But Sauer-mann said no. Too far. So we came to South-West.'

By listening to Fricke and reading one or two books in the castle, Andrew had formed a mental picture of the Colony. Its physical characteristics he had studied on various maps. Running north-west along the flank of Africa it reminded him of a gigantic sandwich. On the west its long Atlantic coastline comprised the cold and foggy dunes of the Namib Desert, their crests lashed into smoke by the icy wind which the Hottentots called the 'soo-oo-oop-wa'. Inland from the sand rose a central plateau that travelled the length of the country. This, according to several authorities, was the broad and life-supporting core. Here on the savannah, sheep, goats and cattle grew fat; here, in certain areas where water was available, vegetables and fruit could be grown; here above all was rich grazing—and Andrew could vouch for that, for Falkenberg lay on the central plateau and the horses came into condition quickly. To the east the plateau gradually lost height and faded away into the red sands of the Kalahari Desert that stretched out over the German border to cover most of the neighbouring territory of Bechuanaland.

Like Bechuanaland, he had found it a country ruled by sun, water and distance, each in its way as important as the other. In all its tremendous length there was no true river and old Fricke was never tired of saying that if a traveller washed his feet in the Orange River, which marked the Colony's southern border with South Africa, he wouldn't be able to wet them again until he reached the Kunene River, the northern border with Portuguese Angola. There were periodic watercourses called *omurambas* but they ran only after heavy rains. 'You can dive into them, Herr Black,' Fricke said with the faintest trace of humour on his face, 'and all you'll be covered with is dust.'

Apart from the small British enclave of Walfisch Bay the

Germans had built their own settlements at Windhuk, Lüderitz and Swakopmund, but Herr Fricke dismissed them as nothing more than large villages. For the rest there was a sprinkling of hamlets.

Andrew had discovered in his reading that until 1884 the country had been owned piecemeal by the Hottentots, the Hereros and the Ovambos in the north, in their various tribes and sub-tribes, and since some were pastoralists, some hunters and others freebooters there had been constant warfare.

'And then we came along, Herr Black,' Fricke said. 'The new masters, with our civilization from Europe. We brought its culture and its machinery and its commerce. We brought railways and telegraphs and heliographs, shops and banks, farm equipment and missionaries, guns and strong liquor, and don't forget the policemen and the soldiers and the prisons. For what? Just to get sunstroke!'

Most of the settlers, Andrew learnt, were much like immigrants to other lands, but some were not. There were the slow-moving peasants from Thuringia and Westphalia and Holstein. Herr Fricke could still remember some wearing the big hats of the Black Forest, the blue smocks and the top boots. They had set up skittle alleys in Windhuk and organized *gesangvereine* and slept with the official prostitutes which the government had seen fit to send out from the Fatherland for their pleasure.

'Comfort mothers, I called them,' old Fricke said acidly. 'Half an hour in bed and a pat on the head. They should have given them sweets instead.'

Then there were the remittance men, the cashiered officers, the aristocrats whose families were happy to see them settled far from their ancestral plots and who brought with them their duelling scars and their sabres and their *schloss* mentality.

'I tell you, they once filled a traction engine with pilsner and drove it down the Kaiserstrasse in Windhuk. I saw it, I was there. The whole place smelled of steaming beer for a couple of days. And gambling! You should have seen it, Herr Black! High stakes, very high. There was a time when the officers liked to play cards on the naked bellies of Herero girls but the authorities soon put a stop to it. A good thing, too. Wastrels they were.'

But the main fact which Andrew had absorbed was that

76

whether the settler was rich or poor, aristocrat or peasant, he needed stock for his cheap government farm—and the Hereros with their multitudinous herds of fine cattle owned it all.

'What can you expect now?' Fricke said with an eloquent movement of his eyes. 'Trouble. It's got to come, you know.'

When he wasn't talking to Fricke Andrew liked to wander in the store's dim and pungent interior looking at the coloured print fabrics from Leipzig and Berlin that were now, after missionary influence, being bought and worn by the Herero women instead of the leather apron and *ekori*. He liked to look at the pots and pans that hung in bunches from the roof beams, and he liked to take up a handful of mealies and let them slip back through his fingers into the top of the open sacks. Everything was so different from Bechuanaland.

The store catered mainly for Hereros with its packets of snuff and rolls of chewing tobacco, studded boots and three-legged pots, spools of copper and brass wire for bangles and necklaces, cheap combs, cotton headscarves and hairy woollens. But there was one corner kept exclusively for better-quality goods to tempt people like the sergeant in charge of the police post and the canteen owner and visiting officials, and of course, the Baron: delicacies like tinned Rhine salmon, Westphalian hams, pumpernickel and Braunschweiger, Dresden china, glassware from Prague. There was even a section containing wines and spirits that had to be brought up by ox-wagon from Collison's in Windhuk before the railway was built. Once a complete consignment of brandy and Rhine wines had been smashed on the rocky track from the south and the Baron had been somewhat annoyed. It had never been allowed to happen again.

Now, remembering the Baron, Andrew let his eyes drift up to Schloss Falkenberg, thinking—for perhaps the hundredth time —how grotesque and out of place it looked. It was built on the shoulder of the hill above yellow cliffs and the last rays of the setting sun were tinting its battlements with blood. It was a fantasy castle, a transmogrification of style, time and place. Parts of it might have looked well north of Acre, where it would have had other Crusader castles for company, other sections would have fitted more comfortably into one of the castellated *châteaux* of France. What made it even more fantastic was that the whole thing was sham. It was only a façade, for behind the walls the living quarters, although of massive proportions, were built of mud-bricks.

Staircases began where staircases normally begin but ended in blank walls of mountain stone. Corridors wound in and out, finally stopping abruptly on the edge of the cliffs, down which an unwary visitor could easily plunge. Some rooms had three doors and no windows, others had none and must be entered by stone stairs from above or below. There was not a bathroom or water closet in the whole rambling structure.

And yet, here in the middle of what had been Hereroland before the local natives were forced into a reserve, there was something magnificent about it. From the top of its battlements, built as though to withstand *ballistas* and scaling ladders, the view was spectacular. Looking down the sheer walls, one could see the soaring black wings of bateleur eagles; everywhere were unobstructed views of the great plains with their yellow *t'wa* grass; and on clear days one could see the Erongo Mountains on the one hand and the twin peaks of the Omatako on the other.

Now, at just past six o'clock, Andrew knew the Baron would have been taken to the battlements to catch the breeze, a stein of pilsner in one hand and a black cheroot in the other.

He would be helped along the tortuous corridors and up the winding staircases by Jonker and Kraai, his two villainous Orlam bodyservants, and behind, in this ritual procession, would come his daughter Eva, carrying the telescope, and Rose, his wife, carrying the damask-covered tray with the two bottles of pilsner and the great red-and-gold Munich stein which had the Imperial Eagle on one side and the Baron's own crest on the other. Rose . . . Andrew stirred slightly in his place under the camelthorn tree. What a name for her. Anyone less like a rose he had yet to meet: small, dark, with a body the colour of wild honey and eyes like treacle, always half-hidden by demurely lowered lids.

It had not taken him long to place her; she had only to open her mouth and he heard the accents of the Cape Town streets. She had obviously made an attempt at a metamorphosis to fit in with her new surroundings but her German was so dreadful it pained other members of the family to hear her, and in her presence everyone reverted to English. When she spoke she was careful to copy a middle-class Cape accent, but behind it was the whine of the gutters and Andrew would have placed her origin within half a mile of the festering boarding-house he and his mother had inhabited near the railway-line in Salt River.

They would climb the last of the many stairs to the battlements and the Baron would lean on the rough-cut stone blocks and call first for the beer and then the telescope, and if Kurt was in from the veld he would stand at his father's side and be ready to top up the stein the moment the level of beer dropped below half-way. Otherwise this duty would fall to Eva. Andrew could picture the procedure accurately because in the two months he had been at Falkenberg the daily pattern had never changed. On one occasion when Kurt had been away seeing to the horses, he had stepped forward to help the Baron to more beer. Von Steinberg had simply moved the stein a fraction and the beer had spilled on the stones. Without a word Eva had come forward and taken the bottle from his hand. Andrew's mouth turned down in irritation as he thought of the incident. It was one of many similar slights of which he had been the victim. Well, he wasn't asking the Baron to like him. As long as Kurt was able to negotiate for horses and Andrew was able to complete the sales the Baron could translate himself from King-Emperor to God himself, if he chose. And there were one or two things of which the Baron was not aware and which gave Andrew a source of continuing satisfaction; there was Rose, of course, although the satisfaction he gained there was beginning to pall slightly, but also something else. On his last trip to Windhuk he had spent two enlightening hours with a drunken ex-major in the bar of the Kaiserhof and had been more than happy to buy him one glass of Cape Brandy after another in exchange for his gossip.

It seemed that the Baron had lost an entire cavalry regiment in the Franco-Prussian War of 1870. The scandal had been so great that he had withdrawn to his estates in East Prussia and lived the life of a recluse for ten years. His wife had been unable to stand the strain and killed herself. The Baron had sold up his lands and brought his two young children out to South Africa where he had begun farming among the German settlers in Kaffraria, which had existed as a sort of buffer state between the Cape Colony and Kaffirland.

At a time when cattle-raiding across the border was common-place and when recovery commandos were frequent, the Baron always returned to his farm with more cattle than he had lost.

Soon he became the wealthiest farmer in the region, so that when, in the late 1880s, foot-and-mouth swept the region he had more to lose than anyone else. He lost everything. But unlike his neighbours he still had part of his German capital intact and, taking it with him, he moved up into the huge and almost unexplored territory of German South-West which a few years before had been proclaimed part of the Emperor's overseas dominions.

Andrew had tried to draw the bibulous ex-major out on the subject of Rose but he had leered knowingly and protested that there were things he could tell if he chose. Andrew had bought him another brandy but it was apparent that the man knew less than he pretended. The only further information he had gleaned was that the Baron had married Rose five years before when she was only sixteen, which put her, at twenty-one, six years younger than Eva, her stepdaughter, and four years younger than her stepson, Kurt.

The sun had left the battlements of Schloss Falkenberg and the castle glowed yellow in the early evening light. By this time, Andrew knew, the Baron would be well into his second litre. He would have let the telescope roam over the hills and plains of his kingdom, he would have studied the village and no doubt focused on Andrew in his place under the tree; he would have inspected the police post and the store and would have spent the longest time staring at the small white-washed mission which lay half a kilometre from the village.

Often, if he waited long enough, he would see the Reverend Kaufmann emerge to feed his chickens or, on Sundays, walk over to the great bell which had come from Cologne and now hung between two white pillars outside the church. And he would watch as the priest in his dusty black habit leant on the bell-rope, and hear the sad booming notes echo along the battlements and the high cliffs. At these times his face would become congested and he would turn to Eva and stare at her with hot, angry eyes.

Once when Andrew had been on the battlements the Baron had said to his daughter, 'They're not allowed to, you know. God said so. If they do, it shrivels up and falls off.' Watching the distaste crossing her face, he had roared with laughter, a noise so frightening that a thousand roosting rock doves had come spilling and thudding from their nests in the cliffs below.

The fact that the mission was Protestant and not Catholic, or that the Reverend Kaufmann was himself a widower, made not the slightest difference to the Baron. It was his joke and he liked it; that it continually irritated Eva gave it the more point.

The Rhenish Mission Society's presence was a blot on his landscape, and, over the years, it had goaded him ever more deeply. It was he, the Baron, who had given permission for the police post and the store and the canteen to be built on his land near the castle. The police post gave him added security, the store meant he did not have to order everything himself from Windhuk. The canteen . . . well, people needed a place to water. But the mission had been here when he arrived so there had been no question of permission. It had not existed in its present form certainly; it had been only a mud and grass hut in those days. He had never even considered the possibility that Kaufmann would stick it out, but when it became apparent that the priest was not going to leave, the Baron had forbidden his Herero labourers to attend the services and since he owned more than fifty servants, body and soul, congregations in those early days had been non-existent.

He had taken a peculiar delight in watching Herr Kaufmann toll his bell on Sundays then wait in an empty church for a flock that was never going to arrive. But slowly, over the years, first one Herero woman came forward to be baptized, then her husband, then her children, and it had spread until there were forty or fifty attending Sunday services. Not only did they attend church but the mission had brought social change as well. The women no longer wore the scanty leather apron around their loins nor the strange, Viking-like *ekori* on their heads. Now they covered themselves in long print gowns and wore cotton turbans.

Recently, however—some said because of tension between black and white—attendance had fallen off to a marked degree and Sunday services were nothing more than farcical: two or three deaf old ladies and a handful of inquisitive children all listening to the gospel according to Kaufmann. The Baron was delighted.

A day or two before, Andrew had overheard a conversation between the priest and the Baron. At first he could not imagine what business could have brought Kaufmann to the castle. It was

Eva who told him when he met her in one of the dark rambling corridors. 'Has he come to hear your father's sins?' he said, smiling.

She studied him for a few moments. He was reminded of the Baron's insolent searching gaze, except that hers was more a candid search for truth and in its way just as disquieting. Ever since he had arrived at the castle with Kurt he had sensed the barriers which cut him off from the family. The Baron had ignored him and so had Eva, but for different reasons and in different ways.

The Baron's attitude was studied, Eva's seemed unconscious, as though she were living deeply inside herself and was simply not aware of much that was happening around her. She was a tall, quiet woman with long auburn hair and a pale, almost sallow complexion. Hers was the still and serious beauty of the novice, the very antithesis of Rose. After his first few obvious attempts at warmth and intimacy had withered under her steady brown eyes, he had switched his attentions to Rose, with immediate success. Now he was beginning to wonder if he had been too abrupt. He was certain neither the Baron nor Kurt knew what was happening but there was an indefinable quality in Eva's manner to him, a veiled distaste in her eyes when they met, that made him think she might have guessed.

Now, in answer to his question, she said: 'If he listened for a week they would only be half done.'

It was the first time he had heard her say anything that could have been construed as even vaguely critical of her father, in spite of his consistent nagging at her, and Andrew realized she was not herself. A shaft of sunlight falling on her face from a high slit window showed an unnatural flush on her cheeks and he could see she was breathing rapidly.

'I'm sorry. I only wondered. It seemed strange.'

'Strange? You've only been here for two months. What do you know of our ways?' There was a bitter anger in her voice. Abruptly she seemed to take a grip on herself. 'Forgive me. You asked what the Reverend was doing here: he is here on behalf of his church. It is a regular custom in Germany, I believe, for the lord of the manor to support the local church. That is why he is here. It is the same every year. He has been coming ever since I was a young girl.'

'But does your father support the mission?' Andrew asked incredulously. 'It seemed just the. . . .'

'Of course he doesn't. He just likes to torment Herr Kaufmann. Every year it is the same; not a pfennig for the church and yet each time he says, "Come back next year, things might be different then." But they never are.'

'Why does he do it? I mean the priest. Why does he keep on coming?'

Once again, before she brushed past him, he felt himself being carefully studied and found wanting. 'I don't think you'd understand,' she said.

He moved on down the corridor, through rooms that opened one into the next, twisting and turning on themselves in crazy convolutions, and as he was mounting a short flight of stairs that led to his bedroom he heard voices. They seemed to come from the very bowels of the castle itself and yet they were clear and unmistakable. He moved along a side-landing and into a disused dressing-room which contained no furniture other than a hanging cupboard in the corner, partially covered by an old set of curtains. In the dim recess he could see half a dozen dusty uniforms. The dark green cloth was holed by a thousand moths, the silver braiding hung in rotten faded loops and the frogging was almost completely destroyed. He assumed they were relics of the Baron's inglorious military past. Here the voices were even clearer and by standing in one corner of the room he could look through a recessed arch which gave him a view down a shaft of unjoined mud walls into the Baron's private quarters. He had never been there and he stared for a few moments in amazement at the difference between the luxury of the apartment and the poverty of much of the remainder of the house. True, the castle's entrance hall behind the massive wooden doors was of a Gothic grandeur that befitted the façade of the building, and the dining-room with its enormous refectory table, said to have come from a monastery near Potsdam, and its huge chandeliers glittering with candles, was splendid. But for the rest, the parts of the castle he had seen were spartan.

The Baron's room was entirely green and black, from the deep green carpet on the floor to the ancient, smoke-black of the carved oak chairs. On the walls hung crossed lances, the regimental colours still fastened below their points. There were cuirasses from another age, and spurs, and in one corner, standing stiff and martial, a pair of black leather cavalry boots.

Between the pieces of military equipment hung dark portraits which he assumed were the Baron's forbears. Along one wall was a huge oak sideboard on which stood square-cut glass decanters, from one of which the Baron was now pouring a drink.

'Sunset, Kaufmann, never before sunset. When the sun goes down the spirits begin to rise, not so?' He held up the brandy to the light and swirled it in the big goblet. 'But this is a special occasion. Once a year. No harm can come from that. Are you certain? It's better for you than Communion wine.'

The priest shook his head. 'Thank you, no.' His voice was as dry and dusty as his habit. Looking obliquely down at him through the maze of wall angles, Andrew registered the weary face with the two incised lines down the cheeks, the high dome of the forehead and the thinning hair that allowed the sunburnt skull to show through in patches.

He had no idea how long the Baron had been toying with Kaufmann but now the priest, as though wishing to end a farce, said: 'Well, Excellency?'

'Well, Kaufmann?' The Baron limped slowly back to his chair, moving his ponderous bulk with care.

'You said this year for certain.'

'I said that?' He drank slowly, then his face set in a frown. 'You know, Kaufmann, my memory is not what it was. What is it that I said about this year?'

'The money,' the priest said. 'The money for the mission. I told you about the roof. We need a new roof.'

'A roof. Ah yes, I remember. And you want me to pay for it?'

'Excellency, you said, "Come to see me next year".'

'And you have come, as I suggested. The new year is barely a few days old and here you are.' He sipped at the drink, watching the priest over the rim of his goblet. 'You are a man of great faith, Kaufmann. Especially in your dealings with me. God and mammon! Mohammed and the Mountain!' He dropped his head back and roared with laughter. The priest regarded him patiently. 'A joke, Kaufmann! A joke! You must learn to laugh. I cannot recall a verse in the Acts of the Apostles which says a priest can't laugh. Can you recite me one?'

'No, Excellency.'

'Well, then. . . .'

'I was wondering about the. . . .'

'Don't say it!' The laughter ceased abruptly. 'Don't mention it to me again. Roofs! Roofs! What do I care about your roof. It can fall in, for all it matters. Do you hear me, Kaufmann? It can fall in on those old black whores you call a congregation. Now that *would* be a joke. But I forgot, you don't like jokes.'

The priest said something so softly that Andrew missed it. 'What was that?' the Baron asked sharply. 'What did you say?'

'I said that when you've heard the same joke once a year for fifteen years it is no longer amusing.'

'Kaufmann . . . Kaufmann . . . I think you forget yourself.'

'Perhaps,' the priest said quietly.

'Not a single pfennig! Do you follow me? Not one.'

'I didn't expect one.'

'Oh?' The Baron seemed taken aback. 'Why did you come here then, if it wasn't for your damned roof?'

'To see you.'

'What about?'

'To *see* you. To look at you. To be with you. To let you do exactly what you've been doing.'

'You're losing your reason, Kaufmann. Sad to say, but true.'

'Perhaps.'

The Baron rose from his chair and helped himself to a second drink, this one substantially larger than the first. He remained at the sideboard staring at the priest. The Reverend Kaufmann rose and crossed the room, standing close enough to the Baron to be dwarfed by the other's size.

'Let me ask you something, Excellency. Have you not wondered what sort of person I am, coming here year after year and allowing myself to be humiliated?'

'Come now, Kaufmann, don't flatter yourself. No one sits here worrying about your motives—unless it's my daughter Eva. You come, that's bad enough.'

'Yet each year you hold out hope that next year I might be rewarded.'

'Do you honestly believe that?'

'Of course not.'

'Then I think you must ask yourself the question.'

'I have. I asked it a long time ago. May I tell you the answer, Excellency?'

'Really, Kaufmann, I have many things to do. . . .'

'Wait.' The priest's voice was suddenly stern and uncompromising. The Baron blinked. 'Have you ever heard of a hair shirt, Excellency?'

The Baron put his head back and guffawed. 'Are you saying you wear one of those things? My dear Reverend, you'll be carted off with heat-stroke one of these days and then who'll look after your flock?'

'You're my hair shirt, Excellency. You're my bed of nails. Oh yes, it's true. They don't have to be made or worn—they can simply exist.' His voice had been growing stronger. 'Sometimes I waver. Sometimes, many times, I think, it's impossible. I cannot go on. And then I remember my wife. When she died I nearly gave up. You remember Elisabeth. You sent a wreath to the church. That was kind of you. Did I ever thank you for that? Perhaps I forgot. Thank you. Much appreciated. Of course, if you had lent us the wagon when she was ill I could have got her to the mission at Windhuk. They might have saved her there. But many thanks for the wreath.'

'Kaufmann!'

'No . . . no . . . hear me out. I've had to listen to you often enough. I want you to know *why* I stay, why I'll never go no matter what you do to me. Because when I look at you I find my faith becoming stronger. If I left here you would remain and I cannot allow that to happen. I cannot allow you and others like you to stand as examples for us all. I would not want the Hereros to reject our entire civilization just because of you.'

'Kaufmann, I'm warning you!'

The priest raised his hand as though in a benediction. 'Save your breath. There is nothing you can do to me that will hurt. I'm old and tired. I'm ready to go. That is power, Excellency. Do you understand? You cannot harm me. You cannot steal from me as you've stolen from the Hereros. You cannot brutalize me as you have done them. You cannot play God to me because the real God lives here.' He tapped his thin chest.

Andrew, who had been listening with a mixture of alarm and fascination, half expected the Baron to wrench one of the lances from the wall and drive it through the priest's body. He was also experiencing an emotion more difficult to define. He felt vaguely troubled, as though a mood of unease had fallen imperceptibly on him as he listened. It wasn't so much the priest's suffering; he had never cared much for churchmen. It was something else. And then he remembered: Just after they had been paid for the first herd of horses, Kurt had loaded a wagon with blankets, tobacco, bolts of cotton, brass wire, beads and other trade goods and they had moved into the north-eastern part of Hereroland. At each Herero *werft* Kurt had attempted to sell the goods, but no one had bought. The Hereros had looked at the goods with covetous eyes and silently returned to their huts. And at each village Kurt had unloaded some of the goods and left them lying in the dust before they trekked on.

'The bastards,' he had said. 'Now they'll *have* to pay.'

Andrew had discovered that this was not an uncommon form of 'trading'. Everything hinged on cattle. At first it had been an easy matter. When the Hereros, in their search for pasture, let their stock rove over what had always been Hereroland they found themselves trespassing on German-owned farms. The settlers simply confiscated the cattle they wanted.

But when the Hereros no longer trespassed and gave cause for confiscation the Germans had to go out and trade for cattle and sheep.

On another occasion Andrew had watched von Steinberg bartering with a sub-chief about forty kilometres north of Falkenberg. The Herero had ten bullocks for sale.

'How much do you want for them?' Kurt had asked.

'Fifty English pounds.'

'Good.' He had gone to the back of the wagon and pulled out a corduroy jacket and one or two other things. 'Here you have a jacket worth twenty English pounds,' he said. 'And here a pair of trousers worth ten. In these packets are coffee and tobacco worth twenty pounds. That makes fifty English pounds.'

The Herero shrugged. 'All right,' he said.

It wasn't that sort of thing Andrew minded so much; the man had been bloody stupid. But forcing them to buy stuff they didn't want; that was something else. He found that in this particular sphere of activity von Steinberg and Brock, the sergeant in charge of the police post, worked in effective partnership. When the Hereros refused to buy, goods were simply off-loaded and they were told they could pay when they liked. In a few weeks von Steinberg would return and demand payment—and payment was always made in cattle which he himself chose. If there was any trouble Brock would arrive with a couple of men. For one bag of maize meal Andrew had seen Kurt take eight cows; one cow for a pair of boots.

The priest was right. This was theft. The feeling of unease became stronger. Why? Why should he worry? What did it matter to him? He tried to shrug the feeling away but it remained.

Father Kaufmann had moved towards the door. He seemed to have shrunk slightly, as though the effort of speaking his mind had weakened him. He stopped and turned. 'I came to warn you,' he said wearily, 'and I almost forgot. It is not so much that I care what happens to *you*, though that is in itself a sin, but I care what happens to Eva. You have sown the wind, Excellency; you will reap the whirlwind. The Hereros are people, not animals. They will react like people. Soon, I think.'

'Don't talk to me of warnings! Don't drivel to me about sins; d'you think I'm not prepared? Why, I've got whole arsenals here. Guns and ammunition and. . . .' But he was talking to an empty room. The Reverend Kaufmann had walked slowly out of the door. The Baron stood uncertainly for a moment and even at that distance Andrew could hear the air whistling through his nostrils. Then he turned to the sideboard and poured a third goblet of brandy; this time the glass was nearly full.

The short twilight was almost gone and the early stars were shining. Soon a great orange moon would clear the rim of the earth and light the infinite expanse of veld that lay around Falkenberg. At his place beneath the camelthorn tree Andrew poured the last of his beer. Then, away to his right, he heard the clank of chains as Brock crossed the square with a detachment of prisoners. 'Good evening!' the police-sergeant called and Andrew looked up. Brock had stopped his little cavalcade in the middle of the square and was walking over slowly. The four Hereros, dressed in grainbags in which holes had been cut for head and arms, were joined together by six-and-a-half-foot lengths of chain attached to iron collars around their necks. They took the opportunity of raising the chains in their hands to take the fearful strain from their necks. Andrew watched Dieter Brock mince across the square. He didn't much care for him. Brock was a big man with the thick petulant lips, curly hair and generally cuddly appearance of a spoiled baby. His flesh hung on him in pink folds and he was always sweating. It was generally said in the village—though never in his hearing—that it was as well to stand upwind of him, when there was any wind. The baby look was belied by his eyes; they were small and bright and wary. Andrew had not yet been able to make his mind up about Brock. There were certain areas where he wielded a great deal of power, and until he knew exactly where the limits of that power lay Andrew, like the others in the village, would treat the sergeant with a courtesy he did not feel.

'Good evening,' he said as Brock drew up with him. There were great black patches of sweat on his tunic.

'This is better, Herr Black.' He shook out a huge red handkerchief and wiped his dripping jowls.

'It's always better when the breeze comes.'

'Ja, the breeze. A miracle, I think.'

'I'd ask you to join me in a bottle, but I see you're busy.'

'No, no. I came to invite *you*. I've been meaning to for some time.'

'I've been away.'

'Horses?'

'Something like that.'

'Ah,' he gave a gurgling chuckle. 'A man of discretion. There is something I wish to talk to you about. I've been saving a bottle of cognac. Will you join me?'

Andrew rose to his feet, standing well clear of the other's sour smell. 'Thank you.'

'Come. I'll put the animals away.' He pointed to the Hereros with a short *sjambok* made of giraffe hide.

As they passed through the main archway of the post he shouted for his orderly. The Hottentot came at the double. 'Lock them up,' Brock said, 'and bring the keys back to me.' The Hottentot saluted and began shouting at the prisoners. They held the chains in their hands and broke into a shuffling trot that would take them to the cell block on the far side.

Andrew had never been inside the police post before. He looked about him, seeing the shadowy white buildings and the roof structure of the well in the middle.

'. . . everything myself,' Brock was complaining. 'One Hottentot orderly and two Herero constables. It's not enough. Only last week my corporal was taken. Orders from Windhuk. Trouble . . . trouble . . . trouble. . . . It's this damn land. They're always expecting trouble. Now they say it's the Hereros, so they take my men. And what am I supposed to use to defend this place if there's trouble. . . ?'

Andrew was only half listening. He was looking at something chained to a stake near the well. At first he thought it was a child. Brock stopped talking and followed his glance. 'Oh, you haven't met Bismarck. Come.' As they drew nearer Andrew realized it was not a child but a half-grown male baboon hunched on a small wooden platform. It was chained by the neck with the same manacles as the prisoners wore. The baboon jerked angrily as they approached, then it jumped down from the platform and sprang at them. Andrew flung himself to one side, hearing the chain thud as it jerked the baboon back. The animal crouched, leaning forward on the palms of its hands, its great dog face towards them. The upper lip was raised in a snarl that bared the long incisor teeth; the eyes were like molten iron in the half-light.

'A pretty thing, don't you think? I've had him since he was a baby. I found him one day after a leopard had killed his mother. He was clawed badly and I nursed him. But gratitude? If that chain broke he would tear out my throat.'

Brock kicked viciously at the ground with his heavy boot, sending a shower of gravel into the baboon's eyes. It jumped back, snarled, then launched itself at him again. The chain jerked it flat on its back. Brock stood in front of it shaking with laughter, but there was little expression of amusement on his face.

'He is just like them,' he said, nodding towards the cells. 'That's why I keep him. To remind me about gratitude.'

As Andrew walked past the maddened animal he noticed that the wooden stake and platform were badly torn where the baboon's teeth had ripped and gouged them.

Andrew followed the German to a sort of ante-room where Brock returned his rifle to a wall rack. It was a small room with a mud floor and whitewashed mud walls. A hanging lantern had attracted a myriad of insects, and the bigger moths cast fluttering shadows in the corners. Against one wall was a small table on which had been placed a large china bowl and jug. Brock poured water into the bowl and held out a piece of soap.

'Go ahead,' Andrew said, his attention diverted by the racks along each wall. One of them held Brock's gun, a sporting Mauser and a shotgun, plus boxes of cartridges and a bandolier of bullets. But it was the other racks that fascinated him. They were filled, not with weapons of war or the chase, but with weapons of punishment. Brock, his face dripping water, caught up a towel and crossed the room. 'What do you think? Quite a collection, is it not?'

Andrew said nothing; there was nothing to say. He had never seen a collection like it. There were rhino hide *sjamboks*, hardwood cudgels, rope's ends and thick leather straps.

'Christ,' he said finally. 'Where did you get them all?'

'We made them,' Brock said with pride, mistaking his meaning. 'Here at the post. Not I, of course, but the prisoners. Those we call the "little sticks" '—he indicated the cudgels—'and those' —he pointed to the leather straps—'those are salted. It keeps the wounds cleaner. But I prefer the *sjambok* or the rope.'

'But good God, man,' Andrew said, 'you could kill someone with one of those things.'

'No, no, Herr Black, they are scientifically designed. I said we make them here at the post but only to the specifications laid down by the Kolonialamt in Berlin.' He threw the towel carelessly on the floor and reached for a *sjambok*. 'Feel it,' he said, holding it out. 'It must be between eighty and one hundred centimetres long and one centimetre in circumference. We can give no more than twenty-five cuts with it at one time. If a native has earned more we must wait at least a fortnight before we can give him the other twenty-five. These things are studied. The Kolonialamt knows all about them.'

Andrew handed him back the *sjambok* but Brock, caught up in the enchantment of scientific precision, failed to see the look of displeasure on his face. 'This, now. This is the best of all.' He reached for the rope's end and smacked it into his palm. 'This cures many ailments. First it is dipped in pitch, and then in sand and then the end is bound with wire. I tell you, once a native feels its touch he is very sorry for himself. Will you wash now?'

91

Andrew looked at the scummy water in the basin and shook his head. 'Thank you, I washed a little while ago.'

'Let us go in, then.'

Brock's quarters reminded him of the average police post in Bechuanaland. There were the same animal skins on the floor, the same canvas chairs, the same game heads on the walls. Where Brock's differed were in such things as the tasselled Tyrolean pipes crossed above a reproduction of the Bavarian mountains, and the beer steins on the scrubbed pine table.

'Lily!' Brock shouted. There was a noise from behind a second doorway and a native woman entered the room. She stood in the doorway swaying slightly, and Andrew was momentarily taken with her beauty. She must have been about eighteen and with her oiled skin shining in the lamplight she looked as though she had been carved in wet ebony. She wore a short bead apron around her waist that was extended in the front to drop down and hide her groin, and that was all. She came forward and at once the first impression of her was shattered. Her body was beautiful enough but the rest of her was grotesque. She had painted her cheeks and lips with rouge. In an attempt to straighten her hair she had combed out the tight peppercorns and hardened them with what looked like a mixture of mud and tar. In one hand she held a short pipe and in the other a tin mug from which emerged the strong smell of cheap schnapps. It was obvious that she was already drunk. She smiled a horrible whore's smile at Andrew and he saw that her front teeth had been filed into a V.

'We have a guest, Lily,' Brock said, smiling wetly at her. 'Bring the bottle of cognac and the glasses.'

She swayed over to a cupboard on the far side of the room and Brock watched the movements of her buttocks. 'What do you think of her, Herr Black? The best servant a man could want. Her mother died in prison at Windhuk. Lily was only twelve then and she had nowhere to go. So I took her. Like the baboon. You will think me a very soft man, but there are things one has to do and, unlike Bismarck, she does not want me dead.'

Andrew had heard rumours about Lily: rumours of drunken parties at the police post, shouting and screaming at night. The Baron had described her as 'satanic' which, from him, came with twice the force it would have from anyone else. Occasionally Kurt had gone down for an evening at the post—without the

Baron's knowledge—and returned glassy-eyed and drenched with sweat. Andrew had thought it politic not to inquire too closely into these soirées and now said carefully, 'Good servants are difficult to find.'

Brock chuckled, his fleshy jowls shaking with amusement. 'True, Herr Black, very true.'

Lily returned with the glasses and the bottle and then seated herself on the floor at the other end of the room with her back to the wall. Instead of sitting as a native woman usually did with her legs together, curving around behind her, she sat with knees bent and legs slightly apart, exposing herself. It was difficult not to look and Andrew knew that Brock's eyes were on him.

'*Prosit*!' Brock said and tossed the cognac down his throat.

'Good health.' He savoured the brandy. It was a very good bottle, much better than Cape liquor which tore at the stomach lining and exploded behind the eyes. Brock filled both their glasses again. This time, when Andrew looked, Lily was rubbing her hand up and down her thigh.

'This is very pleasant,' Brock said. 'It is something I have been meaning to do for a long time, ever since you first came to Falkenberg.'

'It's excellent brandy.'

'I'm glad you think so. There are not too many luxuries out here. Not like at the Cape, Herr Black. That is a civilized place, I think.'

'I suppose so.'

'And yet you left.'

He felt the faintest indication of a probe. Not even Kurt knew the real reason he had agreed to the partnership, but it was enough that he had entered German territory illegally and that Kurt had connived at it. He had no wish to be sent back to Bechuanaland with the possibility of a court martial and all that that involved. In any case, he was doing well. The horses were selling; he'd be a fool to be trapped by someone like Brock.

'Restlessness,' he replied shortly.

'I too.' As though sensing Andrew's suspicions he described his own departure from Hamburg and arrival in South-West, the attempt to start a guano factory north of Walfisch Bay that ended in failure, and his subsequent entry into the police. The conversation became more general and Andrew relaxed.

Lily was gently massaging her nipples between thumb and fore-finger.

'How did you meet Kurt?'

'I knew him in. . . .' Andrew stopped abruptly. The question had been put in the same easy tones, as though it were simply an extension of their conversation. '. . . in the north-western Cape,' he said finally. 'He was down on government business.'

'Ah, so. A very lucky encounter.'

'How do you mean?'

Brock smiled. 'About the horses.'

Andrew felt every sense alert. 'I suppose you could call it that, although I've been trading horses for some time.'

'But not here in the colony.'

'No. If you like to call it luck, I suppose it was. He was kind enough to give me an introduction to the Army, that's all.'

'And to bring you here.'

'What do you mean by that?'

'Come, Herr Black. . . .'

'I don't know what you're implying. The Baron owns the best horse country around here. Don't make any mistake, I pay for the privilege of grazing the herd on his land.'

'Please, my dear Herr Black, I meant nothing wrong. We shall drink to that.' He poured them each a rather bigger measure of brandy, then held his glass out. They clinked them together. 'To you! May your business prosper.'

Andrew nodded. 'Thank you.' He was beginning to feel the liquor.

Once again Brock steered the conversation into less troubled water, and then, after a while, he said : 'She likes you, Herr Black.'

'What?'

'Lily. She likes you. I can see that.'

Andrew glanced covertly at the woman. She was lying on her side cradling one breast in her hand. 'Come Lily, dance for Herr Black! He has never seen you dance.'

She smiled at him again, this time making an unmistakable gesture with her hands. Slowly she rose to her feet. Brock began to clap a rhythm and she started to dance. It was like nothing Andrew had ever seen before. It owed little to the ritual dances of Africa. Every movement of her hips, every thrust of her pubis, each straying of hands and fingers all fitted, or tried to fit, into a pattern of voluptuousness. He was at first startled by the extremity of her lasciviousness, but only for a moment. He began, instead, to feel amused and a trifle embarrassed. She was dancing as a child prostitute might who had been schooled by a clumsy voyeur. All her actions were so unsubtle that their very naïveté lost them whatever effect her naked body might have produced. He glanced at Brock. The German was transfixed. He was devouring her with his eyes as though she was Salome herself. He was holding tightly to his glass of brandy and his face was shining with sweat. His right hand thudded loudly on the coarse material of his breeches as he clapped the time. It came to Andrew then that she was Brock's creation; that this ridiculous display was, in fact, the furthest Brock's prurient imagination could take the art of choreography. Backwards and forwards, like some infant dancer at a school concert, moved the siren of German South-West, spinning her sexual web.

There was a sudden banging at the outer door. Brock, who was totally carried away by Lily's extravagances, seemed not to hear it but when it came again his rhythm-beating hand faltered and he turned to Andrew as though to apologize that their moment of entrancement should be so cruelly interrupted.

For Andrew the knock came just in time. He was already feeling rather drunk and had been about to break angrily into Brock's trance. He had had enough of the charade.

'Yes,' Brock called. 'What is it?'

There was a low mumbling at the outer door. '*Liebchen*,' he said, turning to Lily. She went out and returned a few moments later with a note. He read it and swore. 'At this time of night!' He tossed it into Andrew's lap. It was from Rose. It read simply: 'Sergeant Dieter Brock: These boys have been cheeky.' It was signed 'Baroness von Steinberg'.

'What happens now?' Andrew asked.

'They will be dealt with. It is my duty.'

Andrew looked through the doorway and was able to make out two Hereros standing in the little pool of light cast by the ante-room. One he recognized as Februarie, a gardener; the other looked vaguely familiar and he assumed he had seen him working around the castle.

'They simply bring a note asking for punishment?'

Brock nodded. 'It is customary.'

'And?'

'Oh, I think a dozen apiece with the rope. A cheeky native is a dangerous native, Herr Black, and in these times he must be dealt with severely.'

Andrew stood up. 'I must go. Thank you for the hospitality.'

'No, really, it won't take long. You can watch if you like. It is instructive.'

As Andrew moved to the door he felt Brock's hand on his sleeve and smelt the sour body odour.

'What I wanted to say,' Brock murmured, 'is that I have some sheep. Quite a few sheep. The army will need food. Perhaps if I were to tell them the sheep belong to you. . . .'

Andrew shook off the hand and went through the ante-room. Lily had already taken down a rope's end and there was an expectant look on her face. He pushed his way past the Hereros, who were waiting for their punishment with a stoicism he found irritating. As he passed the second man he slowed. There was no question but that he was familiar. Andrew stopped and looked hard at him but the bearded face was turned half away and the eyes held down. The beard only half hid the smallpox craters on his face. Andrew could never remember seeing a man with such severe scars. He went on into the courtyard, past the baboon sitting on its platform, past the well and out through the main archway. The brandy suddenly foamed in his brain, blurring his vision, and he leant against the outer wall. It seemed that only a few seconds passed before he heard the screaming, though it was more like five or ten minutes. At first he thought the screams were coming from the Hereros until he realized they were not screams of pain but of simple pagan enjoyment. The blows came regularly, dull thuds in the darkness. Automatically he counted. When the tally reached six he pushed himself away from the wall and stumbled up the hill towards the castle. Even half a mile away he could hear Lily's laughter.

The moon, which had been so overwhelming earlier in the evening, was now an opalescent disc in the night sky. The breeze had died away. The lions and leopards had fed and watered, the jackals and hyenas had cleaned the carrion and the village dogs were silent. It was just past three o'clock in the morning and the land was hushed. Andrew lay on his back trying to move as far from Rose as he could without waking her. As he moved, his flesh peeled away from hers, leaving wet areas of perspiration. With the death of the breeze the air was warm again, this time with the liquid warmth of new milk, and it caressed his naked skin, bringing out a soft dampness all over his body.

The room was one of the few which had a window looking over the cliffs from the front of the castle and the bed had been so placed that if he turned his head he could look out across the silvery veld.

He moved and Rose shifted with him, muttering slightly in her sleep. When she woke she would want him again and he wasn't ready for her yet. He lay back on the bolster and allowed his body to be overtaken by torpor. He knew it was risky lingering here in the ribbons of moonlight but his muscles seemed to have melted away and he doubted whether he would have been able to rise if the door had, at that moment, burst open. Not that he had much to fear from her husband. Rose had told him he had not been near her bed for almost a year, since he had had the stroke which had left him partially crippled.

His thoughts went back over the evening, to Brock and the ludicrous show he had put on—ludicrous until it had ended in the savage beatings. He wondered if this was the catharsis which Kurt experienced—the climactic violence—or was there something else? He wondered what obscenities had occurred between Lily and Kurt behind Brock's locked doors. He could imagine Brock looming over them like some fat salivating eunuch. . . . Andrew's mouth drew down in distaste. Not that he was immune to fantasy. Often, as he had sat with his law books in the lonely desert camps, his concentration had lapsed under pressure from his imagination. But the women had never been like Lily, nor even Rose, but more like Eva; women whom you not only took to your bed, but to whom you took your yearnings and ambitions and who understood them and helped to bring them to fruition. Women who moved through your life with kindness and understanding and who, one day when you had struck it rich, or been promoted, or achieved whatever goal the evening's thoughts had fixed upon, would be there at your side, gracious and graceful. What you did together in your bedroom was less a frantic coupling than an exchange of love and strength.

This was before he'd met Rose. Until then his experience of women had been confined to an encounter with the overseer's daughter when he worked on Duncan Fraser Black's farm, and one or two nights at a house in Bulawayo when he had gone up to take his examinations. He had been tempted several times by Kalahari women but always at the back of his mind was the word *disease*. He could recall the fearfulness and horror with which his mother had used it. It had been enough to make him draw back. Now, with money in his pocket and freedom to do as he pleased, he was aware of a change in himself. Disease was something one associated with poor people; the rich never suffered from it. Had Lily been more a fresh young native girl and less a weary product of Brock's imagination, he might have taken her just for the experience. Instead—well, instead there was always Rose, and the moment he had returned to the castle he had felt her sexuality spread out across the great withdrawing room to envelop him.

He had arrived back in the last stage of the Baron's evening. Like most other things, Baron von Steinberg's drinking was on a majestic scale. It was said that before he'd had his stroke he drank even more. But the sudden illness had frightened him into modifying his way of life slightly. He had eschewed the marriage bed, but not wholly the pleasures of his cellar. Traditionally, his drinking moved through four phases. The first was the sunset ceremony on the battlements during which he drank two litres of beer to clear his throat of dust and prepare himself for the serious business of the evening. The second stage was reached after he had been helped down the winding staircases to his own quarters where a large zinc bath stood waiting. By its side were cans of water, some hot, some cold, and it was Jonker's duty to mix an adequate amount at just the right temperature. In the meantime Kraai helped the Baron to undress. While he was in the bath he drank Cape brandy cut with water from one of the castle's two wells. The amount of brandy drunk depended on his mood. Occasionally he would ask the two Orlams if they were thirsty and tin mugs would appear from under their clothing as though by magic. They always drank the brandy neat, turning half away from the Baron as they did so, and coughing slightly after each sip.

At dinner he drank a Mosel or a Rhine wine, or one of each,

98

depending again on his mood. Over the years he had steadily increased his cellar. The wine was cellared deep in the subterranean passageways of the castle where, even in midsummer, it retained an earth chill. For the most part he drank Niersteiners and Oppenheimers from the Rheinhesse but on special occasions, when he had substantially increased the size of his cattle herds by shrewd trading with the Hereros, Kurt or Eva would be sent down to the cellar—he allowed none but white hands to touch his best bottles—to fetch two or three of the great Rheingau wines. Andrew had never heard of, much less tasted, a Johannisberger or a Steinberger before he came to Falkenberg. There were, it was true, a few burgundies and a dozen or so mixed Cape red wines in the cellar but since the Baron did not vary his diet he saw no reason to vary his wine. It was there for guests.

Years before, when he lived in Kaffraria, he had decided that mutton was the only meat worth eating in Southern Africa. It was fortunate, for his cook, who had come to him from the Little Karoo where sheep farming was beginning to burgeon, could only cook mutton, and in only one way—roasted. It suited the Baron perfectly. At noon every day he sat down to a roast leg of mutton—he could not be bothered with shoulders—accompanied by glazed carrots or baked pumpkin with cinnamon, or whatever vegetable was ready in the kitchen garden, saffron rice with raisins, and potatoes roasted to a dark brown colour and crisp to the centre. In the evening the same joint would be placed cold before him and he would sit hunched over it like a huge predator, slicing pieces from it with a sharp hunting knife and eating them from the blade. In the evenings he did not bother with vegetables. The remainder of his family, who had not developed his taste for mutton to the same degree, usually subsisted on a supper of scrambled eggs and ham. Occasionally Eva would revolt at the diet and prepare Swabian sausages, or *bratwurst*, or even, on one memorable evening, fish. It had come all the way from Walfisch Bay and was pickled in brine, but it was fish nevertheless. Sometimes she would bake *honigkuchen* or *Berliner kränze*, but except for Rose, the household was not given to sweetmeats, and once Eva had established that she was working mainly for the Baroness, she only baked when she herself felt the need for a less harsh diet.

From odd snatches of conversation Andrew knew that after her early attempts at Cape Malay curries had lain untasted on the table, Rose had never gone near the kitchen again. She was content to leave the Baron to his mutton.

After dinner the Baron entered the fourth stage of the evening's drinking, reverting once more to brandy—not Cape brandy this time, but genuine cognac and sometimes armagnac. The big cut-glass decanter was brought up and he would sit with it near his right hand, drinking from a tulip-shaped glass. He had been told by the Government Medical Officer who had visited him after his stroke that brandy was excellent for the heart; since then schnapps had not passed his lips.

It was during this fourth phase that Andrew returned to the castle. The first person he saw when he entered the huge withdrawing room was Eva. She was sitting at the piano, a large Bechstein grand which the Baron had taken in lieu of a debt twelve years before and which had nearly killed two spans of sixteen bullocks on its journey from Windhuk to Falkenberg. The chandelier had not been lit and the only light in the dark, shadowy room came from two oil lamps. The glow gave her an almost ethereal beauty. Her head was bowed over the keys and she was playing something soft and sad. For a moment he stood in the doorway watching her. There was a serenity about her that made the episode at the police camp seem even more unpleasant by comparison. She looked up and saw him, and stopped immediately. 'Have you had any supper?' she asked.

'Please don't stop. I'm not hungry.' He felt himself pronouncing the words with care.

It was typical of her that in spite of the gulf between them she should show concern for his welfare and he felt grateful. He moved into the room as she took up the melody. Kurt was sprawled out in one of the big leather armchairs watching his stepmother over the top of a month-old Cape newspaper. Rose was bent over her crewel-work, an occupation so foreign to her nature that it amused Andrew every time he saw her at it. Now she looked up and stared at him like a cat. Just for a moment he felt her cloying aura reach out and touch him. But he knew this was done only partially for his own benefit; it was also done to annoy Kurt. Andrew guessed that for the past hour or so she had been raising Kurt's hopes with hidden smiles and soft looks, raising him up as far as she could, waiting for the opportunity to

100

let him go crashing down. Andrew's arrival had supplied the opportunity. He had only to glance at Kurt to see the difference in him.

Since his coming to Falkenberg Andrew's opinion of Kurt had changed drastically. He no longer seemed the good companion of the Kalahari; instead he played the part of jackal to his father's lion. This in itself was understandable since it was unlikely that any family would produce two like the Baron. But in his relationship with Rose he became even less than a jackal and she was pitiless. She seemed to be amused by his patent adoration, one minute allowing him to indulge his hope, the next brutally exploding his ambition. There was nothing subtle about Rose. Once when Andrew knew that Kurt could hear them she had told him how much she disliked his pink eyes. She had described him as a white rabbit. Even Andrew had been embarrassed.

Later she had told him at least part of the reason for her antagonism. Two years before, Kurt had tried to force himself on her. As far as Andrew could make out it wasn't the attempted rape which had caused her irritation—she seemed to take that as a compliment—but the fact that Kurt had been unable to hold himself in and had stained, beyond restoration, a new silk evening dress which she had ordered from Berlin and for which she had been waiting six months—and all for nothing, before he had even achieved anything. In her uninhibited way Rose was able to give a ludicrous picture of Kurt, all passion spent, drooping before her like some disgusting schoolboy.

It amused Andrew to think of him like that and yet at the back of his mind he knew it was not possible to dismiss the 'white rabbit'. There was an unsettling quality at the back of his eyes which made Andrew wary. He tried to keep out of his way as much as he could.

The Baron came into the room. He walked slowly and heavily towards a great chair near the empty fireplace. It was made of wood and leather, studded with brass, and resembled pictures of medieval thrones which Andrew had seen in children's books. One of his arms was held by Kraai and the other by Jonker. The two Orlams, with their flattened yellow faces and scarred legs, looked totally out of place in the room. They helped the Baron into his chair. Sitting there hunched and slightly out of breath,

101

he reminded Andrew of a buffalo he had once wounded. He had put a shot into the spine and had paralysed the hindquarters of the animal, but it had remained enraged and battle-ready, raising itself on its forelegs. There was something of the old buffalo bull about the Baron, with his thick neck and his hunched shoulders and the small eyes set close together in the broad face. He sat there, hands stretched forward on the arms of the massive chair, wheezing slightly, until at last, getting his breath, he jerked his head at the servants. 'All right, get out.'

They muttered their good nights and disappeared into the shadows.

'Where's that damn kaffir?'

Watch entered the room with the brandy decanter and glasses on a tray. Andrew watched the scene with annoyance.

'Watch too old for running,' the Nyasa said severely.

'Don't talk back to me.'

Watch placed the tray on a table near the Baron's right hand. He nodded and Watch picked up one of the glasses. 'Not like that! Haven't I told you never to touch the rim with your fingers!' He leant forward, took the glass and threw it half way across the room. It struck Kurt on the leg and rolled, unbroken, across the carpet. Eva stopped playing. Then Watch calmly poured a second glass without touching it at all and moved the tray nearer the Baron. 'That's better.'

Watch ignored him and, turning so his back was to the Baron, he looked pointedly at Andrew and said : 'Is the Captain finished with me?'

Andrew nodded. 'Yes, all right, Watch. Go to bed.'

In the silence that followed Watch's departure he felt the Baron's eyes on him. He didn't care. For several weeks now the old man had simply co-opted Watch's services and he didn't like it. Not that he minded Watch working for the family—that was only reasonable since they were feeding him. But he didn't like the constant insults and the humiliations which the Baron dispensed for his own pleasure.

The Baron finished lighting a dark cheroot and blew the smoke up in a cloud. 'I'll have that boy flogged,' he said. 'He's too damned cheeky.'

Andrew opened his mouth to reply, then closed it again. There was no point in making an issue of it at this stage and starting a row; better to wait until it actually happened. He began to fuss with his pipe, aware that a look of disappointment had crossed Eva's face. Well, he was *her* father, let her deal with him. Andrew was getting sick of the whole bloody family. For days he had been thinking about the possibility of leaving. There were now about a hundred horses grazing the veld. When those were sold he'd pack it up. Kurt was already talking about another trip south to the north-western Cape to buy more, but even though the money was good it seemed hardly worth it if he had to go on living in this sort of atmosphere.

He was tired of the Baron's extravagances and tired of Eva's soulful, accusatory eyes and tired of Kurt's foxy cunning and . . . yes, he was even tired of Rose. There was no reason, now that he had a little capital, why he shouldn't go into business for himself, for the authorities were badly in need of horses. They tried to dispel fears of a native rising, at the same time purchasing re-mounts as fast as they could. It was ludicrous. And that was another damn good reason for getting out; he had no wish to be in the middle of Hereroland when the bullets started flying, though deep down inside himself he doubted very much whether it would come to anything—the blacks just didn't have it in them.

'Why always church music?' the Baron said abruptly. 'This isn't Kaufmann's mission. Why don't you play something lively for a change. We could all do with it.'

Eva came to the end of the piece and closed the lid of the piano. 'I don't know anything lively,' she said.

'A waste of good money, that's all.'

She looked up at him coolly. 'It was your idea, not mine. You said it was the only grand piano in the colony. Naturally you wanted it.'

'I didn't expect you to play church music.'

She didn't bother to reply. What the Baron called 'church' music was simple transcriptions of Bach, Handel, Mozart and Telemann which she had learnt in a postal tuition course coming all the way from Leipzig. It was impossible for him to realize the amount of effort she had to put into learning scales and finger exercises when so far from any source of advice and encouragement.

He turned to Rose. 'Come, *liebchen*, you show her.'

103

The Baroness allowed herself a small smile of triumph and went across to the piano. The room was suddenly filled with the strident, vamping chords of 'Suikerbossie', 'Sarie Marais' and 'Vat jou goed . . .' played as polkas. After the quiet, meditative playing of Eva they sounded out of place.

'That's better,' the Baron said, thumping the time loudly on the chair arm.

When Rose had finished he called her to him and she sat on a large cushion at his feet. He began to fondle her with the unembarrassed and casual intimacy of a father stroking the body of a baby daughter.

Immediately Andrew noticed a change in Kurt. He seemed somehow to come alive. There was lust and anger in the little pink eyes. Eva rose to her feet. 'I'm going to bed,' she said shortly.

'Sit down,' the Baron said. 'I've got something to say that concerns you all. I've heard there is going to be a rising. I don't believe it, but I hope it's true.' Eva opened her mouth to protest but her father waved her into silence. 'Yes, I hope so. If we have war, troops will come from the Fatherland and clear this place once and for all. It is the best thing that could happen. I haven't lived here all these years without hoping for something like this. We're prepared. We have the men and the arms. I tell you, when it's all over there won't be one Herero left! Not one!'

Andrew wondered how he was able to delude himself to this extent. As far as he knew, German troops in the Colony numbered only a couple of hundred. Windhuk was practically defenceless. At the last census the Hereros had been given at nearly 100,000.

'We may have to defend Falkenberg,' the Baron went on. 'That's why I tell you this. I want a report on all the servants. Cooks, maids, gardeners, everyone. Do you understand? Kurt, you will look to the doors and gates. Make sure the bolts are strong. I want sandboxes in each room in case of fire. When the time comes you will issue rifles to all those you think are trustworthy. Is that clear?'

He spoke about food supplies, water, firing positions, everything that might be necessary to withstand a siege, becoming more and more animated as he did so. Finally, he talked about the guns. Turning to Andrew, he said : 'You will see that every-

104

thing is oiled and cleaned. And that the right ammunition boxes are placed next to the correct calibres.'

Andrew nodded. The Baron had spoken as though he were one of the servants, but it was the way he spoke to most people.

'I am having a chair built,' he went on. 'Four of the servants will carry it, one at each corner. In this way I shall have mobility.'

'And a laurel crown?' Eva asked. 'Where will you get that?'

He ignored her, turning once more to Andrew. 'In the next few days I'm expecting officers from Okahandja for the horses. When you've sold the herd I want you to go south and find more. We need all the remounts we can get. Is that clear?'

Andrew was tempted to say right then what had been in his mind, but there was something about the Baron's excitement that affected him. 'Clear enough,' he said.

The Baron went on to describe how the attack, if there was one, would be organized. How the Hereros would be caught in a crossfire between the castle and the police post. How. . . .

But Andrew was remembering that the Baron had lost an entire cavalry regiment on ground of his own choosing and in warfare for which he had been specially trained. This was rather different. If he did go south, perhaps he'd simply keep going.

He was drowsily occupied with these thoughts when he felt Rose stir beside him. Her hand reached out for him automatically, touched his chest and travelled down his body. He turned towards her. She was very small, not above five foot, and her body was compact and hard as though she went in for athletic sports. Her hair was black against the white bolster and in the cold light of the moon he could see the outline of her breasts. They seemed to belong to an adolescent—small tight mounds like rounded pyramids but with unusually long nipples that had risen now into hard little towers. He noticed then that her eyes were still closed and thought how little difference it made. Waking or asleep she would be ready for him—or anyone else, he told himself cynically.

Still with her eyes closed she moved across the lumpy wool mattress and he felt her hair on his neck and lips. Her body was cool and sinewy, more, he imagined, like a young boy's than a woman's. Slowly she began to move against him and immediately the coolness of both their bodies gave way to sudden heat and he felt the sweat break out between their bellies. Their movements began to make a rhythmical sucking noise. She giggled and he looked into her eyes. They were watching his face with a terrible intensity. She quickened the tempo of her rhythm, increasing, at the same time, the frequency of the sucking noise. Both their skins were now slippery with sweat. Andrew was embarrassed, not only by her amusement, which was childish and, in the circumstances, offensive, but also by the rigidity of her stare. This, he had discovered, was an essential part of coition for her. She needed to see every change and movement of his face produced, unwittingly, by the sensitive nerve endings in other parts of his body. At the beginning it had been part of the unfamiliar excitement of her, but now, under her scrutiny, he would try to keep his face as immobile as possible. He pulled her head onto his shoulder and she giggled again as their wet skins broke wind against each other. He lay on his back, staring past her through the window, letting her grind herself on him, letting her use him.

It was then that he realized something important about their relationship : they never kissed; there was no tenderness between them. Even as she was reaching her climax he was wondering how this same act would be with Eva, whether in fact it would be any different with anyone, or if this was all there ever was between men and women. He was again conscious of a need, of a great unfulfilled longing.

They lay together, yet apart. Once again his skin cooled with the drying sweat.

'Rose,' he said.

'Mmmmm.'

'I was down at the police post last night.'

'With the kaffir girl?'

'She was there. I had a drink with Brock.'

'He smells. So does she.'

'Perhaps. While. . . .'

'I'm telling you. They both do.'

'All right. While I was there two Hereros brought a note from you.'

'From me?'

'Yes. It said they'd been cheeky.'

'Oh, yes, I remember now.'

'One was Februarie. I've seen him in the garden.'

'He was cheeky,' she said defensively.

'Who was the other one?'

'Why? What do you want with him?'

'Nothing. It's just that he looked familiar, yet I've never seen him about here.'

'I don't know,' she said. 'I can't remember every boy I send to the post.'

'He had a beard.'

'A lot of boys have beards.' She turned away. 'I told you I can't remember.'

'His face was pitted by smallpox.'

'Don't talk about it. Why do you talk about things like that here? What's the matter with you? Don't you love me any more? You said you loved me and now you talk about things like that when you're with me!'

God, had he ever said he loved her? He could hardly remember. 'Of course I do,' he said wearily. 'It's just that there was something about him.'

'Well, I don't know.' Her face and tone were petulant. 'He's new. Yes, he's new in the garden. That's all I know about him and I don't want to know any more.'

'What did he do?'

She turned back to him and began lightly stroking his stomach with the tips of her fingers. 'What does it matter?'

Deliberately he moved away. 'I want to know what he did.'

'He *looked* at me.'

'Looked at you?'

'Yes, looked, looked. The way you look at me. No kaffir can look at me that way.'

'I see.'

'All right, you see. Where are you going?'

He had swung his legs over the edge of the bed and was standing up. 'It's nearly dawn,' he said. 'I'm tired.'

She moved quickly across the bed on her knees and held him, rubbing her cheek up and down against his forearm. 'Don't go yet,' she whispered, but he was already pulling on his clothes. 'I'm tired,' he repeated.

He walked along the winding corridors, finding his way almost

107

by instinct now. Something white detached itself from the wall. He stopped abruptly, every sense alert, his heart hammering in his ears. If this was the Baron. . . . He struck a match and found himself looking down into Kurt's angry eyes.

'Where have you been?'

'Been?' Andrew repeated, trying to make his voice as normal as possible. 'I haven't been anywhere. I couldn't sleep so I went up on top to smoke a pipe.'

'Do you usually carry your boots?' There was something pent-up and savage about his manner as he indicated the boots in Andrew's hand.

Andrew let the match burn out and drop onto the floor. 'Only when other people are asleep,' he said, and pushed past.

After breakfast the following morning he wandered out into the garden. In some vague way he hoped he might find Eva there. Before the meal he had prepared the ramrods, the oil and the pull-throughs and at the back of his mind was the thought that she might help him with the guns. He had never stopped to consider such a thought, for the reaction from the night before had left his mind peculiarly vulnerable.

They breakfasted early at Schloss Falkenberg and by the time he found himself in the garden the day had not yet begun to show its ugliness. Instead of the dusty, scorched place it would become by midmorning, the patches of green, where water had been channelled to the vegetables, were fresh and soothing.

The Baron had built his castle as though it overlooked the Rhine and as though he expected it, one day, to withstand a siege. On two sides it was guarded by cliffs and on the other was bounded by a high bailey. Within the bailey, in the outer court, he had laid out the gardens. For the most part they consisted of rockeries planted with a profusion of desert succulents. Between them was a central walk flanked by stunted cypresses and an occasional stone seat. Nearer the bailey, where one of the two wells had been sunk, was the vegetable garden and now, in the growing season, it was head-high with maize and there were runner-beans and tomatoes, pumpkins, gem squashes and melons. Further down were two or three orange trees and a grove of fig trees that twined in and out of each other like a hedge.

Usually by January, if the rains had been good, parts of the garden were leafy and green, with shady trees and soft grass beneath them, but the season had not been kind. There had been little rain since October and well water was not to be wasted on flowers.

Now in the comparative coolness of the early morning, with the smell of the irrigated water on the damp earth and the trees giving long black shadows, the garden was not unpleasant. As Andrew walked along the central aisle he heard the swither of frightened lizards and the drowsy droning of the bumble-bees. Eva was not in the garden.

He walked on towards the vegetables where he could see two natives hoeing weeds between the beans. As he drew nearer he recognized them as the two Hereros who had been flogged at the police post the previous night. His pace faltered but then, as though drawn on, he moved towards them. He reached the fringe of the vegetable area and stopped. The two men had not seen him and went on with their hoeing. Each raising and lowering of the implement was slow and painful and he wondered how anyone could stand up, let alone work, after the beating they had taken.

Februarie stopped as though sensing an alien presence and looked around. He saw who it was and his eyes widened with fright. Andrew nodded.

'Morning, Master.'

'Morning, Master.'

Was it his imagination or had the Herero with the smallpox scars accented the last word just enough to give it a trace of irony?

Andrew wanted to say something to them, if only to dissociate himself from Brock and Lily, but he could think of nothing; nor indeed could he account for the way he felt. He was embarrassed standing there like a tongue-tied youth, and embarrassment led to irritation. 'What are you doing?' he asked sharply.

Februarie stood in the sun staring at him. He was an old man with grey peppercorns of hair and a patch of weeping eczema on the left side of his nose. His legs and arms were painfully thin and his hands were like the claws of a bird. At the corners of his mouth Andrew could see bubbles of froth. The old man seemed to sway slightly as though in a high wind—but there was none.

109

'What's wrong with him?'

Andrew had taken a step forward to inspect him more closely and now Februarie gave a slight cry of fear and held the hoe between them, not as a weapon but as a shield.

'He's hurt, Master.' The scarred Herero came forward and held Februarie's arm.

Andrew looked hard at him. 'What's your name?'

The Herero paused fractionally and said, 'Joseph, Master.'

'Don't I know you?'

'Last night, Master. At the police.'

'I mean before that.'

'I don't come from here, Master.'

'I thought . . . well, it doesn't matter. Where does he hurt?'

'His back, Master.'

Andrew reached out to lift Februarie's tattered shirt. 'All right, all right. I won't hurt you.' He felt vaguely affronted at the reception he was getting. After the first instinct to jerk away Februarie stood trembling while Andrew raised the shirt. He had steeled himself for an unpleasant sight but nothing could have prepared him for what he saw. In some places the shirt was stuck fast to Februarie's back by a hard crust of dried pus, in others, where it was still wet with suppuration, it came away and he was able to see the weals on the emaciated rib-cage. They were more than weals, gouges, rather, where the flesh had come off in patches as though Februarie's back was the surface of a sofa at which a thousand moths had been at work. Some of the wounds had been bound with filthy bandages, others were open to the flies.

'Christ,' Andrew said, swallowing a mouthful of saliva. 'Joseph, come here.' Joseph's back was not nearly as bad. He had more flesh and muscle on his bones, was generally more robust, and the wounds seemed less damaging. What puzzled Andrew was that the damage did not seem to have been caused by a whip or even a lash—and then he remembered the rope's end of which Brock had been so proud : '. . . first it is dipped in pitch and then in sand and then the end is bound with wire. . . .'

Andrew turned to Februarie. 'I'm trying to help you. Can't you understand that?' But the Herero was too far gone. 'Take him back to the huts,' he said. 'I'll see what I can do.'

He watched them go through the gate in the wall towards

110

the collection of huts that had been built to house labourers and their families; then he turned to the castle. He was angry and yet he was not sure what he was angry about. It wasn't enough to say he was angry at Brock's brutality. He had never pretended that life was anything but brutal, although in this case it seemed needlessly so and, to Andrew's police-trained mind, needless actions were often criminal.

No, it was more an anger directed against himself. He didn't like being in a position where he had to make moral judgements, in fact it was unfamiliar territory and the very unfamiliarity of it disturbed him. He had never been disturbed before; why now? He had felt it when the Reverend Kaufmann came to the castle; he had felt it the previous night; now he was feeling it again. What, he wondered, was happening to him? Was he becoming soft? Perhaps it was this place and its people. He couldn't remember being disturbed by doubts when he was alone in the desert. There, everything was clear-cut and straightforward.

The first person he saw on entering the castle was Eva. She made as if to pass him but he stopped her. 'Did you know that Rose had two garden boys flogged last night?'

'Oh God, not again!'

'They're not fit for work,' he said, gaining some satisfaction from the distress on her face. 'One of them may not live. I've sent them to the huts.'

'That was kind of you,' she said acidly.

'Kind or not, I can't doctor them in the middle of the garden.'

'I'm sorry.' She looked up suddenly and he was aware of a new expression in her eyes. 'I've got bandages. I'll go with you.'

'It's no sight for a woman.'

'Do you think I've not seen sights like this before?'

He was about to argue further but the bitterness in her voice touched an unexpected chord in him. She shrugged. 'We'll go together.'

Andrew had never been to the village before and he was surprised at its size. There were two parts to it, by far the larger consisting of rows of neat thatched dwellings which housed the Herero labourers. The smaller and less attractive section was some distance away; in it lived a settlement of Hottentots, the traditional enemies of the Hereros. The Baron had been shrewd in choosing his labour force for he was aware of the old antipathies between the two races and had reasoned that in any crisis the Hottentots would remain loyal to him if he had trouble with the Hereros, and vice versa, each preferring the white man to the other. And so it had turned out. Apart from Jonker and Kraai, the Baron had what could be described as a bodyguard of Hottentots. He knew that in this particular sphere he could trust them. The house servants, however, were Hereros because no Hottentot could be trusted not to pilfer liquor, food, money, clothes—anything he could lay his hands on. This the Baron considered to be characteristic of them as a race, for they had originally come up from South Africa as freebooters, dispossessed there of their lands and possessions, while the Hereros had always been pastoralists and farmers. 'Divide and rule,' the Baron never tired of repeating. 'Divide and rule.' He said it as though he had personally invented both the phrase and the philosophy.

Eva had brought a bottle of warm water, bandages, lint and a large pot of zinc ointment which she used in treating the veld sores and skin ulcers which were practically endemic to South-West. Andrew carried an enamel basin and a sponge. The moment they entered the village he became aware of the tension. Normally anyone from the castle would have been greeted feudally. Children would have followed in procession, women would have come out of their huts and even the old people would have pushed themselves painfully to their feet and given respectful greetings.

At first Eva seemed unaware of the atmosphere for she went forward and squatted down by a baby girl playing in the dust. 'Hello,' she said, putting out her finger and touching the child lightly on the point of the nose. She looked over her shoulder at Andrew. 'This is my namesake. She gave us a great deal of trouble, didn't you, *liebchen*?'

'Trouble?'

'Here, hold these.' Eva handed Andrew the medical equipment and scooped the child up in her arms. 'Yes, a great deal of trouble. You just wouldn't be born right, would you?' Again she turned to Andrew. 'We nearly lost her. She was a month early.'

'You mean you come down here and. . . .'

'What else do you expect? We haven't a doctor in the village.'

A woman came scurrying out of a nearby hut.

112

'There's her mother. Good morning, Hannah.'

The Herero woman paused and Andrew sensed the struggle inside her. She opened her mouth to say something, decided against it and held out her arms for the child. Her eyes were filled with pain and indecision. Gravely, Eva handed the baby to her. 'All right, Hannah, I know how you must feel. Which is the hut?' Still without speaking, the Herero woman nodded her head at the far side of the village.

They went on through silent, hostile alleys. Children stopped their games and moved closer to the doorways of the huts; the few adults visible were sullen and silent.

'I'm very fond of Hannah,' Eva said. 'She used to work in the castle once. We played together as children.'

'She didn't seem very pleased to see you.'

'No, old Februarie's her grandfather.'

They did not have to seek further directions for a small crowd was gathered at the doorway of one of the larger huts. Andrew went ahead and tried to push his way through, leaving a pathway for Eva. The crowd gave way but immediately closed in around him, forming a solid wall of black bodies between him and Eva. Andrew was suddenly aware of the smell of sweat. They all seemed to be men, and big ones at that. 'Move!' he shouted. But they did not move. 'What the hell do you think you're at!' He started pushing at them but it was like pushing a rubber wall. He was aware of a blur of faces, all sullen and grim.

'Not like that!' he heard Eva saying. 'They're probably all relatives of his.' She spoke rapidly in Herero and, reluctantly, some of the men gave ground. But others pressed more firmly against Andrew. Suddenly he was afraid. Christ, he thought, a knife or a spear now and I'm finished. I wouldn't even know who pushed it. He gripped the bowl of warm water more tightly; it was the only weapon he had.

And then, as abruptly as they had menaced him, he felt the pressure give way. The men turned from him. He was aware of Joseph talking softly and rapidly. It sounded as though he was rebuking them, but Andrew couldn't be sure. The Hereros listened with what seemed an unwilling respect. Andrew's immediate reaction was one of anger. Why should they listen to Joseph when they wouldn't pay any attention to him?

'What the hell's happening?' he shouted.

113

'Nothing is happening now, Master. They are afraid, that is all.'

'Afraid! Why should. . . .'

'You're Joseph,' Eva broke in, and when the Herero nodded, she went on : 'You were beaten too.'

'Yes, Miss Eva.'

'When I've finished old Februarie I'll dress your cuts.'

'Thank you, Miss Eva.'

Andrew glowered at him. What *was* it about the man? Dignity? Or was he mixing it up with plain impudence? He couldn't tell. He followed Eva into the hut.

The interior was dark and filled with the acrid smell of dead dung fires. At one side of the doorway he could make out a bundle of rags lying on a skin pallet. Beside it an old woman rocked back and forth on her heels, mumbling and muttering. As he bent over, Andrew was able to see that the bundle of rags was Februarie. He lay on his stomach and his breathing was so weak that at first it seemed he was dead.

'Shouting only makes things more unpleasant,' Eva murmured, going down on her knees on the hard dung floor.

He frowned at the rebuke but suddenly he noticed her smile. It seemed to light up her whole face, changing it from a natural and somewhat cold serenity to a face filled with life and humour, and automatically he found himself smiling back at her. Her smile was like an award and he couldn't think what he had done to win it.

'Come,' she said. 'Don't be so awkward. Hold the basin.'

He went down on his haunches beside her and held the basin as she poured warm water into it. Then she added salt and stirred until it had dissolved. With great care she began to sponge Februarie's ruined back. Watching her deft and practised movements, Andrew wondered how many times she had had to perform this office during her years at Falkenberg. She soaked off the strips of shirt and then the rags and slowly cleaned the whole suppurating area. Then she spread the ointment over the wounds and finally bound chest and back with clean white bandages.

When she'd finished she turned to the old crone and said, 'I'll send over special food and I'll come back tomorrow. Keep him quiet and don't touch the bandages.' The old woman stared uncomprehendingly. 'She's his wife,' Eva said. 'Deaf as a post I'll tell

Hannah on the way down. First we'll see to Joseph.' But when they asked about Joseph no one seemed to know where he was.

As they made their way out of the village Andrew said: 'Do you think he'll live?' He spoke more to break the silence than anything else.

'I'm going down to the mission. Herr Kaufmann and I will pray for him. Why don't you join us?' She was looking at him again with that searching gaze which seemed to weigh him and find him wanting.

He felt a stab of irritation. Why couldn't they simply go on walking and talking together? Why did she want to involve him with missionaries and prayers? 'I've got the guns to see to,' he said abruptly.

'Oh yes, the guns. I'd forgotten about the guns. When we're tired of flogging them we can always shoot them.'

The irritation stayed with Andrew all the way to the gun-room but there, with the smell of oil in his nostrils and the feel of steel and wood in his hands, it gradually fell away, leaving him absorbed in his task.

The Baron was right: the gun-room was a miniature arsenal. Opening off from his apartments, it was a large, gloomy place with one high slit-window. In it were the normal sporting guns one might have expected to find, but there was also rack after rack of military rifles which had once belonged to the armies of half a dozen different nations: Mannlichers, Mausers, one or two Winchesters, .461 Gibbs-Metfords, a double-barrelled Rigby and even some Martini-Henrys. The boxes of cartridges stood on shelves and though each box had been labelled the writing was so faint on some as to be almost illegible. They had been thrown down in untidy heaps and it took Andrew a couple of hours to clean the guns, relabel the boxes and pack them neatly in sections.

He stood for a moment looking along the lines of guns and began to light his pipe. Down here the silence was complete. He was standing with his back to the door when he heard a slight noise. It was the sound of heavy breathing. He turned, but no one was in the doorway. He held his breath, listening for a moment, and thought he heard the softest *thud, thud, thud* of running bare feet. He sprang to the door and looked down the corridor. In the gloom he could just see a figure at the far end.

'Hey!' he called, but the figure went on, whisked around a corner and was gone. For a moment he wondered whether he had imagined it, wondered if it was a castle ghost. He shrugged, locked the gun-room door behind him, and made his way through the Baron's apartments to the living quarters. As he neared the withdrawing room he heard voices, and laughter. He paused for a moment wondering who it was, decided it could only be Brock, and turned away.

'Captain!' It was Watch. 'The soldiers have come.'

He went to the main door and saw half a dozen horses. A group of Hottentot troopers squatted in the shade of the pepper trees. As he crossed the hall and entered the room he heard the Baron's voice: 'Ah, here *is* Herr Black. We have been searching for you. Come, take a glass.'

The Baron was seated in his great studded chair but the rest were standing, grouped, it seemed, round Rose. Andrew noticed that Eva was missing. 'Herr Black, what shall it be, wine, beer, cognac?' The Baron was in an animated mood; it was a pleasure for him to see new faces in Falkenberg and he always revised his behaviour towards Andrew in the presence of possible buyers.

Two German cavalrymen stood in the centre of the room, dwarfing Rose and Kurt. Both were big men and moved with the assurance of fighting soldiers. They were covered with dust and every movement brought a creak of leather or a jingling of spurs.

'Major von Langsdorff, this is Herr Black, the man you've come to see. And Lieutenant Seegert.' Kurt completed the introductions with a blandness that gave no reminder of his anger the night before. Once again Andrew was struck by the man's foxiness.

He shook hands with the major. At close quarters he seemed even bigger and his hand was as hard and dry as sandstone. He was dark complexioned, with a high-bridged nose and a luxuriant Kaiser moustache. His eyes were disturbing, amber flecked with gold, and reminded Andrew of a leopard's. By contrast Seegert was much younger and had the fair complexion, sandy hair and rosy cheeks of the North Baltic. He was almost as big as von Langsdorff but when they stood together he seemed to shrink against the major's springy toughness.

116

'We have ridden far,' von Langsdorff said. 'We hope it is not for nothing.'

Andrew poured himself a stein of beer and held it up. 'I hope not,' he said. '*Prosit!*'

For another second von Langsdorff's eyes held him and then the German turned back to Rose. Her face was shining with pleasure.

'No talk of business now, please,' Kurt said, circling the group like an albino jackal. 'Let us drink together and have a meal. Then you can have Herr Black to yourselves. You must not deprive us of your company. It is not often we have distinguished visitors.'

Later that afternoon, when the sun had relented slightly, Andrew and the two German officers rode down to the kraal into which the horses had been driven.

'I've heard of you, Herr Black,' von Langsdorff said.

Andrew nodded. 'They know me in Windhuk.'

'Tell me, what is an Englishman doing mixed up in something like this?'

'I'm not English, I'm South African, and the reason is profit.'

'That's an honest answer, anyway,' von Langsdorff said, smiling a thin, chilly smile.

Baron von Steinberg was never sure exactly how much land he owned, although he knew it was somewhere between 40,000 and 60,000 hectares. When he had first come to German South-West he had acquired it at the equivalent rate of threepence a hectare and had secured over 125,000 acres for something under £700. Since then he had added bits and pieces so the total might have gone above 150,000 acres. He had never seen it all, never would, but since the Swakopmund-Windhuk railway had been built over his land he had taken the opportunity of travelling by train over some of the more remote parts of Falkenberg. He had done this once or twice for reasons of curiosity but it had quickly developed into a habit. Now, once or twice a month, he would travel the twenty kilometres to the nearest point of the line, board the train, have dinner in the saloon, sit drinking with whichever passengers he was interested in, and finally leave the train at a halt called Brakwater, where a second wagon would be waiting

117

to take him back to the castle. In the beginning the expedition had taken some thought and organization but it now worked like clockwork and on the whole had been very profitable. He had met cattle traders and government officials and mining engineers who were willing to pay him prospecting rights; he had played poker with a windmill salesman from Dresden and won so much from him that the man had agreed both to bore for water and set up windmills at half price—a fact which contributed to the Baron's ability to increase his cattle herds; but best of all the train supplied him with the latest news and gossip from the two major urban areas in the territory.

Now, two days after the completion of the horse sales, the Baron, Kurt, Andrew and the two German officers were proposing to make a night of it in the dining saloon. They had arrived at the side of the track just as dusk was falling, and the light was still strong enough to show the twin lines of steel stretching away on either side of them and narrowing until they became a single silver streak. The presence of the track and the telegraph line that ran beside it seemed to give an added dimension of loneliness to the place. They waited, talking quietly until, as full darkness arrived, they saw the far-off light of the train, dipping and reappearing as the engine rose and fell on the swell of the land.

'Wave the light,' the Baron ordered, and Andrew lit the red lantern and moved out onto the track. Standing with one foot on the rail, he could feel in his body the throbbing of the oncoming train even before he heard the engine. He began to wave the lantern from side to side and was answered almost immediately by a hoot from the driver. The train, all four coaches of it, came slowly to a halt, steaming and hissing and smelling of hot oil.

A voice said: 'It's the Baron.' A door opened and the *schaffner* dropped down onto the track. 'Good evening, Excellency. Good evening gentlemen.' Heads craned out of windows, doors slammed. Andrew found himself gazing up at the big lighted windows of the saloon thinking how civilized, how welcoming it looked. They helped the Baron aboard and were met at the top of the steps by the *oberkellner*.

'Welcome, Excellency.'

'Good evening, Hoppe. I hope you can look after us.'

'Of course, Excellency.' The *oberkellner*, bowing and walk-

118

ing backwards down the middle aisle of the saloon, showed the party to two tables at the far end.

'Is there ice?'

'Specially for you, Excellency.'

'Good, good.' It was always doubtful whether the ice taken aboard at Windhuk or Swakopmund would last half-way through the journey and after one or two occasions when the Baron had had to drink his wine warm and Hoppe's tip had decreased in consequence, the latter had made sure that a supply was kept in a vacuum flask until the train had passed Falkenberg.

'The Piesporter?'

'If you please.' The Baron raised his eyebrows to his guests and they all nodded their agreement. The bottles came in ice buckets, already sweating. Within five minutes the remnant of the ice would be floating in its own water but it would have chilled the wine sufficiently. It was like a furnace in the saloon.

'I hope you have something special,' the Baron said, when he'd despatched the first glass of wine.

'Extra special, Excellency. *Sauerbraten.*' Hoppe waited for the inevitable question.

'Any mutton?'

'Of course, Excellency. Cold leg.'

'I'll have that.'

They made a heavy meal of *jägersuppe, sauerbraten* (except for the Baron) and *mandelkuchen,* opening their tunics as the meal progressed and feeling the sweat trickling down the front of their chests. While he ate Andrew looked around. Since it was pitch dark outside the windows reflected back the scene within the saloon so that the dining area seemed much bigger than it was. The saloon was decorated in plush and gilt and three fans hanging from the ceiling stirred the hot air sluggishly. On each table was a small bowl of Namaqualand everlastings, put there in a defiant effort to make the carriage as festive as possible. In the corners of the windows and even on the flowers themselves Andrew could see the fine red dust of the desert.

The saloon was almost empty and he had a strange feeling of being rushed through time and space at great velocity, for the train was lurching and swaying, causing glassware and cutlery to chink softly together. Only when he placed his face against the window glass and shaded his eyes from the light could he

119

see the limitless, moon-bathed veld. It was apparent then that the train was travelling with almost painful slowness.

'Looking for Hereros?'

Unlike the others, who were already looking damp and dishevelled with the food, wine and heat, von Langsdorff appeared dry and composed.

'All we hear is talk,' the Baron broke in. 'Talk of this and talk of that. It will come to nothing, unfortunately. I wish you fellows could have your chance. But the Hereros . . . they're good enough at fighting Hottentots, but when it comes to German steel. . . .'

'Has the Baron not heard?' The *oberkellner* had paused at their table.

'Heard what?'

'There have been attacks, Excellency.'

'By Hereros?'

'Yes. On farmers. They say some have been killed south of here.'

'Who is *they*?'

'In Windhuk, Excellency, everyone is talking. They say that women and children have been murdered. The police reserves are being called up.'

'Is that true?' von Langsdorff said sharply.

'Yes, Major. I thought you would have known, being in the military.'

A stony expression crossed von Langsdorff's face. 'We've been riding for weeks.'

'We must get back,' Seegert said.

'A train was attacked,' the *oberkellner* said, his body quivering with the excitement of being able to impart information to so select a group.

'A train! My God, that should do it,' the Baron said delightedly.

'Just a few shots. But they broke some windows.'

'Excellent!'

'Do you know what you're talking about?' von Langsdorff said. 'Do you think it's going to be as easy as stopping a few hundred Bondelswart Hottentots?'

The Baron checked an angry reply and said in a voice uncharacteristically humble: 'You fellows will see to them. I've no doubt of that. And we'll give all the help we can.'

'By selling us beef and horses, I suppose.'

120

'And by using our guns.'

'Thank you,' von Langsdorff said dryly. 'That will make a big difference. Do you realize how many there are of us? A handful! That's all, a handful! And as for guns, let me tell you that wherever I've gone in this country I've seen guns. You people have been trading guns for cattle for years. There are thousands of guns among the Hereros and now you say, "You fellows will take care of it!"'

'Guns, yes,' Kurt said, 'but very little ammunition.'

'Perhaps enough!'

'I can assure you, Major, that we will fight as hard as anyone,' the Baron said stiffly. 'We will clear them from the land, you'll see!'

'Yes,' von Langsdorff said. 'We'll see. If they really rise I'm sorry for us.'

They sat in a brooding silence. The chief steward left the table quietly and ordered cards to be placed before them. Over their brandy and coffee they played a few hands but no one was in a mood for gambling and it was with a sense of relief that Andrew felt the train begin to slow down. The door at the far end of the saloon opened and the *schaffner* came towards them. 'Brakwater, Excellency.'

Brakwater was a tiny pool of light in the immensity of the semi-desert. As the name implies, a well of poor water was Brakwater's sole reason for existence. During the building of the railway it had been of some minor importance as a base camp for labourers who had lived in cabooses. Now the siding buildings housed two linesmen, a dozen Herero gangers and a signalman and his wife. Near the well was a water-tower, drinking-troughs and stock-pens. As the train jerked to a halt Andrew saw the door of the signal cabin open and a figure run towards the coaches waving a piece of paper. The Baron's party began to clamber down the steps onto the dark, clinker-strewn verge. The signalman paused as if to greet the Baron, then plunged on.

'What's the matter with that fellow?' the Baron asked. He was looking around and his face quickly took on an expression of petulant anger. 'By God, I told them to be here with the wagon!'

There was no one at the side of the train to meet them. 'Kotze!' he shouted, but the signalman had found the conductor and they were staring at the piece of paper. 'Kotze!'

'Excellency?'

'Where the hell is my wagon? Have you seen it?'

'No, Excellency, it has not been here this evening.'

Von Langsdorff had been standing slightly to one side and now, with a slight explosion of annoyance, he turned away and began to pace up and down, his boots crunching harshly on the clinkers. The Baron glowered at him but said nothing. They stood in a small group next to the train, looking slightly lost. The conductor came hurrying towards them. He waved the paper. 'It has started, Excellency. Really begun. We must get on! We must hurry!' He leapt onto the steps of the coach, blew his whistle and waved his arms at the driver. Slowly the train began to gather speed.

'What do you mean, started? What's going on here?' the Baron shouted, unused to being ignored, unused to having his arrangements go awry.

'Excuse me, Excellency.' It was the signalman.

The Baron turned. 'Well?'

'He meant the rising. The news came on the telegraph not an hour ago. It started two days ago. That is *official*.'

Von Langsdorff pushed his way roughly to the front of the group. 'Where? What happened?'

'I only know what the message said. It gave no details. Just that there had been attacks by the Hereros and that the *schaffner* was to darken the train.'

'Damn,' von Langsdorff said, and then, turning to the Baron, added pointedly, 'Now, if we are to fight your glorious war for you I'd be obliged if you'd get us to our horses.'

The Baron was nonplussed. 'The wagon should have been here,' he muttered, looking at Kurt and Andrew as though trying to find someone to blame.

'They may have been attacked,' Kotze said. 'You never know.'

For the first time Andrew felt the faintest touch of apprehension. So far he had managed to ignore all thoughts of a rising. It was only a theoretical, if fortunate, way of making money, but now, standing on the deserted track, the only light coming from the oil lamp in Kotze's house, he had that feeling of vulnerability which all white men have felt in the lonely places of Africa.

'Have you no transport?' Kurt asked. 'No horses, even?'

122

The signalman shook his head. 'We only use the train. But wait, there was someone. Watering bullocks over by the stock-pen. He was here this afternoon with a wagon. He won't have gone far.'

'I'll go and see,' Andrew said.

Von Langsdorff said : 'I'll go with you.'

Together they crossed the tracks and walked under the dripping water-tower; they skirted the stock-pens and came to the long drinking-troughs. About fifty yards further on they could make out the black humps of the bullocks and beyond them, under a clump of acacia trees, was the wagon. It was a big Cape wagon and as Andrew came up to it he found it vaguely familiar.

'Hello! Good evening! Is anyone there?' von Langsdorff called.

A light flickered and glowed inside the dirty-white canvas tent and the wagon rocked as someone moved to the front. The flaps opened and Andrew found himself looking up at Matthew South-gate.

'Well, it's been coming for a long time, and now it's come,' said Fricke to Andrew about a week after the uprising had been officially declared. He was sitting in his usual place on the high stool behind the counter. His own precautions had consisted of slamming and bolting his shutters and now the interior of the store, always dim, had become stygian. 'And everyone is sur-prised. Surprised! Last thing they would have thought of, if you listen to them. And injured, too. What has happened to our dear children, the Hereros? Rubbish! Anyone could have foreseen it.'

Andrew had heard some of the more honest German settlers admit that the Hereros had good enough reasons for insurrection. Some remembered that only a few months before a farmer called Dietrich had murdered the wife of a Herero under-chief, Bar-menias Zerua, after trying to rape her. Evidence was given at his trial that he had been drunk and had simply shot wildly, fear-ing he himself was being attacked. He was acquitted because, as the judges said, they accepted as a fact that he had acted in good faith. Andrew had heard that the prosecution was appeal-ing against the acquittal. As far as he could make out, liberal opinion held that while no one expected a man to be gaoled for long simply for killing a black woman, an acquittal did seem a little on the easy side, especially as Zerua was an under-chief.

Several had admitted to Andrew over drinks in the canteen that there was injustice there. And they mentioned the business about flogging. It seemed that Governor Leutwein himself had said that if a Herero died under the lash it could not be construed as murder. What the Governor didn't seem to understand was that while the distinction was well taken by a sophisticated mind, the Hereros weren't sophisticated.

'There is an English phrase, "the writing on the wall",' old Fricke went on. 'Well, Herr Black, the writing has been on the wall here for many years.' Andrew was never certain whose side Fricke was on at any given moment and had to content himself with the thought that the old man's dislikes were so widespread that he could fairly be said not to be on any side at all.

'Take this business of death compensation. If a native is beaten to death the farmer compensates the family with a couple of dozen head of small stock. I'm not saying his life is as valuable as ours, what I'm saying is that you can't throw up your hands in surprise at an insurrection when you do things like that. And the whole question of evidence in court: you know, Herr Black, we Germans are bureaucrats at heart. Everything has to be set down, cut and dried. So the Kolonialamt decrees that the word of a white man is equal to that of seven coloured people. Why seven? I tell you, it's unrealistic not to have expected trouble!'

The reasons for the war were debated endlessly in Falkenberg and two factors had emerged which Andrew knew in his heart were its real causes. In May 1903 Governor Leutwein had issued a circular limiting the number of native reserves and making it impossible for the Hereros ever to get back the land adjoining their territory which was owned by Germans. The second, and more important, struck a close personal note. It was the Credit Ordinance of July 1903, which gave traders and farmers a year to collect all their debts. Andrew remembered how Kurt had gone out to 'collect' his from the Hereros. No, there wasn't much point in being surprised.

In those first weeks, the course of the war was not easy to follow in so remote a place as Falkenberg, but the Baron was determined to try and keep up with it and had had a large-scale map mounted on wood and placed above the fireplace. Here he fought the battles of Okahandja and Omaruru and half a dozen other hamlets which were besieged by the Hereros early on. The moment news came through that German flying columns had beaten back the attackers and raised the sieges the small black flags of the enemy were replaced by yellow flags denoting Germans. In the beginning the black flags were spread widely across the map.

Falkenberg existed on news brought to it by the odd officer or sergeant who came through in the early days, and by contact with the trains which still ran through Brakwater in spite of attacks on the line.

But most of all it existed on rumours. The canteen was the place for them and Andrew was spending much of his time there now. Had he believed them all he would have leapt on Duke's back and fled the country, for it was said that 100,000 warriors were pouring down to wipe out Windhuk, that 500 German farmers with their wives and children had been murdered in their beds, that gun-runners were supplying the Hereros with the latest machine-guns and rifles. Only later was he able to sift fact from fiction. Occasionally a soldier who had seen the fighting in several parts of the colony would come through Falkenberg and Andrew would buy him drink after drink in an effort to see the whole situation. In this way, he learnt that the figure of 500 civilian deaths was in fact more like 120, that only about 4,000 Hereros had arms and that ammunition was very scarce; that the Hereros were encumbered by vast herds of cattle and sheep which greatly reduced their mobility. And, more important, he learnt there had been a proclamation by Samuel Maherero to the effect that no Englishmen, Boers, Bastards, Bergdamas, Namas, missionaries or German women and children were to be touched. The war was to be directed solely at the German male, in or out of uniform. Andrew kept all this information to himself for, during those first weeks of open conflict, no one would have wanted to hear it. The Germans felt bereft; even the Baron believed they had been forgotten by the Fatherland and that they might, indeed, be pushed into the sea by the Herero hordes. Nothing they heard from Windhuk made the picture any brighter, for the town itself was under a partial siege and every available man—with the exception of three elderly grandfathers—had been called to arms.

The fighting blazed like a forest fire, leaving burnt patches throughout the central portions of the colony, and like a forest fire it leapt in various directions, leaving other areas untouched; sometimes they remained so, sometimes the fire would return.

In Falkenberg the defence had been organized by the Baron. Like some grand seigneur of the Dark Ages, he was looking after his people. He had had the bush cut down between the castle and the police post to open up the field of fire; he had instituted a signalling system by means of flags; and he had bullied Fricke into setting up a heliograph on his roof. He had instructed Eva and Rose to prepare dressings and bandages—in consequence the castle was now short of linen; he had organized water barrels at strategic points in case of fire; he had consulted for hours at a time with Brock, had brought the herds as close to the village as possible—sheep were grazing even in the garden—so the day was filled with their lowing and bleating, and in general had done what he could to preserve and hold what he had.

At any time of the day his chair, a rickety, hastily-built affair on a platform of planks, manned at each corner by a servant, would come bobbing into view and a whole string of orders would explode from his throat. It could be seen that he was in his element. Forgotten was the cavalry regiment that had foundered under his command, forgotten the years of exile in East Prussia, the stigma, the disgrace, his wife's suicide, forgotten even the years of struggle in South Africa and German South-West itself. One thing alone had burnt itself into his mind : they were at war and he was in command.

It was a trying time for everyone, for the plain fact was that nothing happened. After the first few weeks when all their attentions were foscused on the possibility of attack, interest flagged and boredom set in. They were like castaways on an island; around them were the hostile plains; there was nowhere to go, they were marooned. The fact that this had always been so, that they had remained in Falkenberg by their own choice, seemed to be forgotten. Now they were *forced* to remain—and there was the difference.

It had always been Andrew's unconscious resolve to become as little involved in other people's lives as possible. His character

126

had been forged by loneliness as a child, by an alone-ness when he worked on his uncle's farm—heightened by the knowledge that although he was a Black he was not a Fraser Black—and by the remoteness of his desert life. He had turned in on himself, had become preoccupied with his own psyche to the exclusion of almost everything and everyone else.

That had remained substantially true even when he had come to live at Falkenberg. He had assumed a position on the periphery of the family. But now, with the coming of Matthew Southgate, he felt he was standing on the edge of a whirlpool and that his feet were already wet. It was too late to draw back; it would, be impossible to remain at Falkenberg in a state of isolation. All he could do was to try and maintain the position he held.

It had taken him days to get over the shock of seeing South-gate's face in the lantern light. He had not thought of him more than a dozen times since coming to German South-West; had, if he were honest with himself, written Southgate off as a casualty of the desert—which was the fate he deserved. So when his face had emerged from the tent flap, it was like seeing a corpse which had been decently recumbent for a long time suddenly sit up and give tongue. In the days that followed their journey back to Falkenberg Andrew had been the prey of casual images which flashed through his mind at unexpected times: the trunk in the desert with the copy of *Through the Looking-glass*, the death of Chik, the Herero refugees, starving and listless in the sun, Seit-sang handcuffed to the acacia tree, the letter from Headquarter House, the dumping of the body in the water-pit. He tried to force this particular memory to the back of his mind, but it failed to remain there and he cursed at himself for allowing his feelings —those same feelings which had begun to plague him of late by their persistence—to make him uncomfortable. There was one image which dominated all others, and that was working on Southgate's nearly dead body at Kela Pan, and the triumph he had felt in saving him.

But his immediate reaction to Matthew's sudden re-entry into his life was more characteristic: with his knowledge of what had happened in the reed-bed he could do infinitely more harm to Southgate than Southgate could do to him, for desert philosophy was adamant on one point: there could be no more heinous crime than letting a companion down, no matter what the colour

127

of his skin, for desert people were ultimately the same and were interdependent. Andrew wasn't sure where the destruction of a well came in the pantheon of crimes—high, indeed, but not as high as the death of Chik.

Curiously enough, the thought did not do much to reassure him, for almost as soon as he had mumbled something to von Langsdorff about having known Southgate when they were children in South Africa—a near-fiction which had been accepted readily at Falkenberg—he had registered that Matthew was more than willing to assume the role of old acquaintance. Yet even as he did so there was a faint smile on his lips that seemed to say, 'You know, and I know. . . .' and this irritated Andrew.

Southgate was greatly changed in the three months since Andrew had seen him last. He was thin as a leather strap and burnt to a reddish teak by the sun. His hair was bleached in parts and hung down past his ears in unkempt rat-tails. But it was his eyes that Andrew noticed in particular. They were sunk deep into violet sockets; sad, bewildered—neither of those words quite described them, for there was also a quiet strength that seemed to lie deep. It was as though he had seen something that other men hadn't and had gained from it both pity and understanding. He seemed much older.

He was also more withdrawn and when Andrew had put to him a self-consciously casual question about the intervening months, he had answered shortly that he had been trading in Hereroland. There was not a word about the last time they had parted, nor about the Sand Veld, to the mercy of whose waterless desolation he had been condemned, nor even a hint at the hardships he must have endured. In a way he seemed to have forgotten, or seemed to *wish* to forget, the whole affair in Bechuanaland. Well, that was fine with Andrew. He had done his duty—of that he was certain.

But there was something else bothering him; the way in which Southgate had made himself at home at Falkenberg. It was as though he, and not Andrew, was the established guest. Not that he made it obvious; quite the contrary. He did not assume a favoured position; in his withdrawn way he assumed no position at all, and yet it appeared that within a few days he was being treated with a courtesy and respect which Andrew himself had failed to attract. This was especially true of the Baron, because

128

Matthew had been in the right place at the right time to save his face in front of von Langsdorff, and because he was the son of Sir George Southgate, whom the Baron had met on a visit to the Cape. This immediately gave Southgate a certain rank and he was treated accordingly. Even Watch had seemed pleased to see him again, which annoyed Andrew.

It was also a factor in Matthew's favour that he had arrived with his wagon and bullocks, for Falkenberg, with its excellent fortifications, was fast becoming one of several important supply depots in that part of the Colony. It was already a market-place for cattle, sheep and horses, but as the months passed it also became a staging-post for war materials and Matthew was kept busy with his wagon between the village and the railway. It was dangerous work, for there were no men to spare to ride with him as a security patrol, but this did not seem to bother him. And that was the point: as far as Andrew could discover, *nothing* seemed to bother him.

Yet this was the man who had railed against German brutality, who had first talked of the sufferings of the Hereros—and here he was working for the Germans.

One day when they had found themselves alone in the withdrawing room Andrew had put it to Matthew that this was indeed a strange reversal and he had replied: 'It's a matter of survival.' The words themselves were noncommittal to the point of blandness, but the way in which they were spoken and the look in his eyes gave them an intensity which lingered long after he had left the room. *Survival*. Yet his whole attitude bespoke an indifference to his own survival and, if not to his own, then whose? These thoughts, at first no more than disquieting pressures, troubled Andrew more and more as the days became weeks and the weeks months and the war showed no signs of ending.

Andrew stood in the shadow cast by an embrasure on the highest point of the battlements. Beside him, mounted on its stand, was the Baron's huge brass telescope and, resting against one of the sandstone blocks, the Jeffries. In a basket near his feet was a large German Imperial flag that was to be run up the new flagpole the moment he noticed any sign of suspicious movement. Brock, at the police post, was supposed to have the flagpole in view every waking minute but since he was constantly about his own business the watching had been delegated to Lily in his absence. Andrew had little faith in the Baron's overcomplicated arrangements.

Still, if that was what the Baron wanted it was all right with him, so long as he was up here with the Jeffries where he had room to manœuvre and time to add his own refinement to the system. From the battlements he could see into the courtyard of the post and he had already decided to put a bullet through the corrugated-iron well-cover the moment anything went wrong. That would bring them out fast enough. One bullet through the tin and . . . yes, why not? One at the big bell that hung outside the mission, if his aim was good enough. There was no reason why Kaufmann shouldn't have time to get into the post.

Andrew's opinion of the Hereros had changed substantially. The day after they had heard the news at Brakwater he had mentally dismissed the whole affair as a minor outbreak of violence which had been exaggerated out of all proportion. He had met Samuel Maherero and he knew he was incapable of leading anyone anywhere.

'Met' was not really the word to describe what had happened. Andrew had been at the Alte Feste in Windhuk—the big, low-built fort that dominated the town—on business one afternoon when there was a commotion at the main gate. Two officers had been helping a native down to his horse, which was tied near the guard-house steps, when one of them seemed to trip and the three fell in a sprawling heap against the barred gate. Andrew, who was passing through the gate at the time, stopped and looked down at them curiously, for the officers were of high rank and appeared to be giggling. He bent down to help one of them and the stench of rum hit him in the face. Between them they managed to get the native onto his horse and with arms and coat flapping he set off at a perilous canter down the hill.

The odd circumstances had caused Andrew to take particular notice of the native. He had worn a white shirt without a collar which was fastened at the neck with a cheap brass stud, and a dark jacket with the German colours worn as an armband above his left elbow. The lower part of his body was encased in formal grey morning trousers and dusty black shoes and on his head he wore the wide-brimmed hat with the right brim buttoned to the crown which was the uniform hat of the *schutztruppe* and was called the '*sudwester*'. He had a *sjambok* hanging from his right wrist and he wore a small moustache. Andrew would have put his age at about fifty. In his youth he might have been good-looking; now his wide-spaced eyes were bloodshot and watery and his weak, self-indulgent mouth was open in a vacuous smile.

What caused the incident to remain vivid was the fact that moments after his cantering horse had borne the native down the hill, the two officers staggered back through the gate and Andrew heard one say, 'They tell me Samuel's father was a real man. How he could have spawned that thing I'll never understand.'

So that was the great Herero chief—nothing but a common drunk. In a way Andrew had felt cheated for, ever since he had arrived in German territory, the Hereros had dominated people's thoughts. It had not been difficult to find out more about Samuel; in fact the officers at the Alte Feste had been on more than one drinking bout with him. He was a direct descendant of the great chiefs Tjamuaha, who had died in 1859, and Maherero, who had died in 1890, still claiming Windhuk for himself and devising ways of clearing the Germans from his soil. At first the settlers had wondered whether Samuel was going to prove as intransigent, but the nature of his weakness was soon apparent and it became German policy to see that his supplies of rum never dwindled. It was not difficult, in the circumstances, to obtain his support.

Now he was leading his people in open insurrection and Andrew found the idea of his sudden determination difficult to accommodate; yet the accommodation had to be made, especially after the letter Samuel had written to the Governor. Andrew had heard about it from an officer passing through Falkenberg to Okahandja and he had said it was not the sort of letter he would have associated with Samuel. It was tough and to the point. It accused the Germans of starting the war and the implication was that the Hereros would finish it. Andrew heard that Governor Leutwein had been most upset.

But there it was; something inside Samuel, some residue of greatness passed down from Tjamuaha and Maherero, must have slowly come to the surface. It was one thing to turn one's back on a steady supply of rum, quite another to lead a nation. Still, facts were facts and since he could not formulate a reason for Samuel's change of character Andrew simply put it down to the eccentricity of the war. And it *was* an odd war. He was told that a regiment of marines were fighting near Karibib—who had ever heard of marines in a desert? The gunboat *Habicht* was at anchor off Swakopmund and some of her sailors had gone to war on horseback. He would dearly have loved to have seen them. And what of his own case? Here he was, a stranger in a strange war, his rifle still unfired, his person still unthreatened, getting richer all the time. For it had taken the arrival of reinforcements from Germany, with their sea-sick horses which were totally unfitted to the terrain, to prod Supply into action. Now they were buying everything they could lay their hands on. Farmers in remote areas who had speculated in horses had little means of knowing this and in fact little inclination to drive their herds hundreds of miles through territory that might be under Herero control. But the farmers did know that a man called Andrew Black at Falkenberg had always been ready to pay a fair price. Within a few weeks Falkenberg became the only source of supply for an area of a few thousand square miles.

What gave a slight edge to Andrew's situation was the knowledge that he was not German and that the Hereros had specifically exempted people like himself from retribution—although he didn't know exactly how he was going to make this clear to a couple of thousand warriors when the castle came under attack. So, like Kurt, he was happy to do his watch duty of four hours on, four hours off, especially since it gave him time to himself to work things out. There were many thing to work out, and they all seemed to centre on Southgate.

The effect of Matthew on Rose had been automatic and predictable, as hers had been on him. For Rose he was another man in what had become a Utopia of masculine arrivals and departures. Now that he was assuming the role of a *Reichsmarschall*, the Baron had even less time for his wife and family and Rose made it plain that she found Matthew handsome and desirable. He ignored her—not pointedly, because it was not in his nature to hurt people; but as though he simply did not recognize the

132

display she presented for his benefit. At any other time this sort of reaction in a closed community might have been the start of ugly tensions; however, with the coming and going of officers on their way to and from the various battle areas, Rose was in the position of having at her disposal an endless supply of men. With the natural discretion of the professional whore she gave the impression of flirting with them all while taking none to her bed. At least, this is what Andrew thought, for he had had no first-hand knowledge of her since he had helped Eva to doctor Februarie. That first joint visit had been followed by several others, and when the old man's back had healed Andrew had, in a sense, been disappointed. He no longer saw Eva, who now spent more and more time at the Mission. The Reverend Kaufmann had had a heart attack and she was looking after him.

One night, after an evening spent playing *skat* with four *Seebataillon* officers in their tent in the village square and sampling rather too much of a fiery peach brandy which one of them had bought from a farmer in the south, he went back to the castle and decided on the spur of the moment to visit Rose. Before, they had made their arrangements with some care but now, with officers staying in Falkenberg itself and strangers wandering up and down the corridors at all hours calling for coffee or beds, the place was more like a barracks than a private home. Andrew wanted her; he wanted her at that moment.

Her bedroom door was locked. He pushed at it tentatively until he realized that the big bolt on the inside had been thrown across.

'Rose,' he called softly, putting his mouth to the door-jamb. He heard a movement inside the room. 'Rose, it's me. Open the door.' There was the creak of a bed and he heard her breathing on the far side of the door panel. A faint draught must have been coming through the open window for he suddenly caught the smell of her: heated, sweaty, the smell of rumpled bedclothes. 'Let me in!' he whispered more urgently.

He thought he heard a low rumble of speech and then a smothered giggle. Then she spoke, her voice seemingly choked with ... sleep? Laughter?

'I'm tired,' she said. 'It's late.'

'For Christ's sake open this bloody door! D'you hear me?'

'I told you I'm tired.'

'Rose. . . .'

'Not tonight.'

He felt the anger rise inside him. He drew in a breath, checked himself and, with a sick feeling in his stomach, heard his voice say: 'Rose, darling, *please*. . . .'

Then came the third voice, a man's, deep and somewhat amused: 'You heard what she said. She's tired and she's going to be a lot more tired.' Rose giggled again. 'Now run along, cousin, your turn will come.'

He turned away from the door as though it had been sealed against plague. The feeling of sickness remained, but it was of a different kind, not so much at the shame of listening to his own importunate voice, but more at the thought that this could not be the first time. Like pigs, they all had their feet in the same trough. And where had these been feeding before? In the brothels of Hamburg and Berlin and Windhuk. He hurried to his room; he had an urgent need to wash himself.

Kurt was sitting on his bed. The shock of seeing him momentarily drove all other thoughts from his head. In the darkness the German's pink-rimmed eyes were not visible and he would have looked almost human if it had not been for the expression on his face. Even though it was blurred by the lack of light Andrew had never seen such a depth of hatred. It had actually brought out the sweat on his cheeks and in that instant Andrew was reminded of the Baron: they're insane, he thought; something has gone wrong with them. His mind flicked back to the Kalahari. He had seen a different Kurt then. He had had no idea, of course, that his father was a baron or that he lived in a fake medieval castle, and yet he *had* been different. Or—and for the first time he wondered if his own judgement was in question— was there something so different about deserts that one's terms of reference changed?

'You've been with her!' The accusation stung at him like a scorpion.

He stood just inside the doorway. It was a second or two before he saw the heavy military revolver in Kurt's hand and he knew then that if he denied it he'd probably be shot. There was no time for explanations and no time to turn for the door. He nodded and came forward half a pace. 'It's true,' he said in a voice as contrite and ashamed as he could make it.

'You pig!'

Andrew was watching the fractional movement of the gun barrel. 'Call me what you like, I couldn't help it.' He allowed his shoulders to slump in dejection.

'What!'

'*You* must know what it's like! You've suffered, anyone can see that. Can't you understand?'

Kurt was momentarily confused. He had not been prepared for the sudden switch. Andrew took another pace forward. 'It's the same for both of us,' he went on softly. 'We can't help it. We love her.' As he said it he struck. He used the cutting edge of his right palm, bringing it down like a striking snake on Kurt's forearm. The revolver jerked out of his hand as though on a spring and Andrew scooped it up from the bed. He caught Kurt with his free hand and pulled him up until their faces were only inches apart. 'You bloody white rabbit!' he shouted, shaking him with all his strength as the shame and rage of the past half-hour boiled up inside him. 'What do you mean by coming here with your threats? If you must know where I've been, ask them down in the village. I've been playing cards. Ask them!' He stopped shaking Kurt and for the first time realized the wetness on his cheeks was not caused by sweat but by tears. 'Oh, Christ,' he said wearily, letting the German drop back onto the bed. 'She's not worth it, man. She'd go to bed with a regiment if she could.'

'It was you who started it!'

'No, not me. It started a long time ago. Probably before she even met your father. You should be grateful to me. Look what I've saved you from.'

After that he and Kurt avoided each other as much as they could and even though Andrew felt fairly certain the German would not try to attack him again, especially now that he never went near Rose's room, he sometimes had a prickling sensation in the back of his neck as he walked along the tortuous and ill-lit corridors of the castle.

In a way he was pleased his affair with Rose was over. He would not have caused the break himself, perhaps, allowing things to drift on as they could, but the decision had been forced on him. He would not take his place in a queue. And in any event, he had been drawn more and more towards Eva. Things would be different now, he told himself. He was cleansed.

135

It did not take him long to discover that something had occurred, however, which would make any advances to Eva unwelcome and embarrassing. This was the situation which had arisen between her and Matthew.

He was not clear how long a 'situation' had existed, even though he had been preoccupied with the surveillance of Southgate. The relationship between Matthew and Eva finally emerged as an ironic by-product.

The process of spying on Matthew had begun almost unconsciously, springing as it did from several small incidents which, by themselves, seemed of little moment but which, when fitted together in the context of the war and Falkenberg's isolated position caused him to become suspicious. The first had occurred soon after Matthew had arrived. After a night of alarms and false reports, when the dogs had never ceased barking, when every shadow seen from the top of the battlements appeared to be a fully armed Herero warrior, a night in which the inhabitants of the castle had wakefully patrolled every vantage point, Andrew had gone into the garden at first light and stretched out under the fig-tree hedge to escape the noisy recapitulation of a series of non-happenings. He had slept for an hour or two and been wakened by voices which came from the kitchen garden on the other side of the fig-trees. Matthew and Joseph were talking rapidly in Herero and his first reaction was one of surprise at how well Matthew had mastered the language in the short time at his disposal. Although Andrew himself had picked up a smattering of Herero to use on his trading journeys, the dialogue between the two men was much too rapid and idiomatic for him to follow. He would have thought little more about it if it hadn't been for the *way* in which they were talking. Both were intense, bent towards each other and seemingly talking on equal terms. It was unlikely that Matthew was discussing the state of the beans and tomatoes. Andrew pushed himself up on his elbow to get a clearer view but just then the conversation reached its climax, with Matthew shaking his head vigorously. Andrew thought he could hear him saying: 'No, no . . .' in English, but he could not be sure. Matthew had then put out his hand and touched Joseph on the arm. It was a gesture at once friendly and familiar; then he had turned on his heel and walked away.

The second occasion was a week or so later when Andrew

136

was once again alone in the garden. He was walking slowly up and down the central pathway between the dusty cypresses when old Februarie approached him from the other end. Deep in thought about the war, which was going badly for the Germans, he was aware of the old Herero in that peripheral way in which white men are often aware of the presence of blacks without it really impinging on their consciousness. He was irritated and somewhat surprised when he found Februarie barring his way.

'Yes?'

The old man seemed not to recognize him—in fact, he hardly recognized anyone now. It was generally accepted that his thrashing had pushed an already feeble mind over the limits of reason into senility. He had been allowed to continue working in the garden only because Eva had insisted that he would starve to death if he was sacked. The eczema on the left side of his nose had grown much worse and was an angry red; his old eyes, purple and depthless, were weeping at the corners. Andrew watched him with distaste. 'Yes?' he asked again.

Slowly the man began to speak; Andrew could almost hear the creak of his jaws as he opened his mouth. The words spilled out as though he was disgorging a mouthful of pebbles. Andrew could only understand one in three of the Herero-German mixture. The word 'kill' was repeated frequently, and 'guns . . . Hereros . . . white men . . . Germans . . . ancestors. . . .' He could make neither head nor tail of what it was all about, but that it was the result of a manic anger he was in no doubt for the old man was trembling and chattering like an ancient machine that has been set in motion. It was his extreme hostility which got through, as though a pet canary had suddenly mounted a violent attack on its owner.

'Hold your tongue!' he said sharply and pushed past, but the old man turned and he was followed by a frothing stream of words. He called Joseph over from where he was leading water into the kitchen garden. 'See to Februarie,' he said. 'If he goes on like this I'll have him sacked.'

'He is an old man, Master.'

'I know that,' Andrew said shortly. There was something about the quiet dignity of Joseph's hideous pock-marked face that always affected him in spite of himself. Confused again by his presence, he added: 'I can't understand all he's saying, but he seems to be threatening everyone. If the Baron hears about it he'll be sent to Sergeant Brock again.'

'It was the whipping that caused it, Master.'

'Yes, well, see what you can do. . . .' He turned on his heel and walked up through the dead rose bushes and under the pepper trees, to the great main door of the castle.

The third incident had occurred recently. He had been in the withdrawing room after dinner, watching the festivities which had become almost a nightly ritual. Rose was thumping the piano at the centre of a group of half-drunk officers all singing the old songs, mainly out of tune; the Baron was seated like an emperor on his leather throne nodding in pleasure at the enjoyment of the officers, whom he had come to call, in his role of War Chief, 'my boys'; and Kurt was there, watchful and jealous as ever. Suddenly Andrew had become bored with it all and had wandered down to the village.

The economics of the war had made a difference to the canteen. A new room had been built on one side of it which had been taken over by officers as an unofficial mess. The non-commissioned ranks drank in the original bar.

He hardly ever went near the place these days, with its crude wall drawings, its smell of schnapps, the gobbets of phlegm on the unwashed floor and the rank smell of cheap tobacco. It had been weeks since anyone had found the time or the energy to clean it. The first person he saw through the haze of cigar smoke was Brock. He was standing with his back to the bar, his tunic black with sweat. Andrew paused in the doorway and would have turned away but it was too late for Brock had seen him and was waving him over.

'Ah, Herr Black, what will you drink?'

'Brandy.' Sometimes Andrew found himself worrying at the easy and imperceptible way in which he had succumbed to the drinking in German South-West. In the Kalahari he had hardly given liquor a thought from one month's end to the next; now almost every morning he awoke with a slight ache at the back of his head. It was the war, he told himself; things were different in a war.

The noise in the room was prodigious—shouting, laughing, cursing—and kept up a steady assault on his ears. He drank his brandy in silence and bought another round, fastidiously keeping his hands off the bar top which was swimming in spilt beer and schnapps.

'I've been meaning to ask you about Herr Southgate,' Brock said. 'You knew him before?'

Andrew nodded. 'At the Cape.'

'What sort of man is he?'

'Ordinary. Why?'

'They tell me he's doing good work between here and the railway.'

'Supply is pleased with him.'

'So I hear. And by himself, too. It must be thirty kilometres and yet he's never lost a load. You know that a Transvaler called Venter was attacked three nights ago riding transport north of the line. They killed him, took his bullocks and his load and burnt his wagon.'

'I heard. Southgate takes a longer route. It's slower, but he says it's safer.'

'Yes, well, some people are lucky.'

They carried on a desultory conversation for two more drinks and then Andrew excused himself on the ground that he had to keep watch. He wandered out into the square and looked up at the great lighted windows of the castle. He did not feel like returning, nor did he wish to go to bed, nor did he want to go on drinking with Brock. It was a still hot night and he made his way slowly up the Falkenberg, sat on an outcrop of rock and lit his pipe. His position was about forty yards from the outer bailey and somewhat above it. The castle was away to his right, the huts to his left. He had not been there for many minutes when he heard the crunch of leather-soled boots on the brittle schist. The sound stopped immediately, as though the owner of the boots was fearful of the noise they made. He shifted his position to try to get a better view but the sound had come from one of the densest areas of the garden, about twenty yards north of the gate which was guarded at all times by one of the Orlam Hottentots. In the starlight he could see the Orlam leaning against the wall, smoking. He seemed to have heard nothing. Just then there was a slight thud and a shadow detached itself from the outside of the wall and dodged quickly away into the broken, boulder-strewn ground. It made no sound and Andrew assumed it was one of the natives from the huts. There was no point in trying to follow him in the darkness for, by the time Andrew reached the lower ground, whoever it was would have already reached the huts and disposed of the load he'd been carrying. That was something Andrew *had* seen. Some sort of sack. It had given the figure a hunch-backed appearance. He had no doubt about what was happening : the servants were smuggling food out of the castle.

He ran lightly down to the gate, nodding to the Orlam as he passed through into the garden. The important thing was to find the culprit *inside* the castle.

He reached the point along the bailey at which he reckoned the sack must have been thrown but there was no sign of anyone. He circled around the kitchen garden and along the fig-tree hedge. He was moving with the stealth of a hunting leopard and his very technique almost brought him onto Southgate before he saw him. Matthew was standing quite still in the shadow of the hedge and Andrew froze. He could not have been more than ten feet away, yet Matthew seemed unaware of his presence. He stood with head slightly bowed as though lost in thought. A moment or so later he began walking slowly back towards the castle. Instinctively Andrew followed, keeping to the shadows. Matthew was half-way along the central pathway when a figure moved out from behind one of the cypress trees.

'Matthew?' The name was called softly, half-query, half-statement.

'Yes.'

'I waited. I thought you weren't coming.'

He watched, stupefied, as Matthew took the figure in his arms, for he was quite certain the voice had been Eva's. Standing there, listening to the low murmur of their voices, seeing the movement of their heads, the touching and the tenderness, he felt a growing sense of outrage. Southgate ! Southgate and Eva !

When he was alone in his room later that night, one question hammered at his mind : How had it happened? How had they suddenly become lovers? And yet all the signs had been there from the beginning and not only Andrew had remained unaware of them. Everyone must have been too concerned with themselves to notice the relationship bud and ripen.

Had Andrew given the possibility any thought he would have realized the inevitability of it, for if they were all marooned at

Falkenberg like castaways on an island, Eva was isolated within the environment itself. For her, the arrival of Matthew must have been like the fulfilment of a dream. For the first time she had someone to talk to about books and music, about the world outside, about great cities, about what people were thinking and doing—subjects which would have met with blank disinterest from her family. Until Matthew arrived there had only been the Reverend Kaufmann and much as she loved him he was little substitute for the enthusiasm of youth.

So, within the roiling, roistering life that the war had brought to Falkenberg her relationship with Matthew had gradually, almost imperceptibly, grown from the excitement of exploring ideas to a deeper understanding of him—not that she understood him completely, for as she penetrated the layers which surrounded the core of his being there always seemed to be another layer guarding—what? She didn't know. Instinctively she realized that whatever it was, it was fragile. She felt protective towards him.

Andrew would have been able to comprehend little of this even had it been explained to him for, lying on his bed, his brain a mass of confused thoughts, the one thing that stood out in sharp relief was that here was a personal problem. Lost now were the memories of Rose, the fact that only after that relationship had waned had he turned with greater attention to Eva. For a long time he had almost ignored her; now that he wanted her she belonged to someone else—no, not just someone else, Southgate. This is what hurt. Had she chosen von Langsdorff or Seegert or one of a dozen officers who had been in and out of the castle it might not have been so bad, but she had made her attitude to them quite plain: for her they simply didn't exist. And now Southgate, someone less than a man!

In any other circumstances Andrew might have seen the irrationality of his thoughts but for a long time the foundations on which he had built his life had been cracking and crumbling. Things were happening to him which had never happened before.

It was almost dawn before he dropped into an uneasy sleep.

For most of the following day he kept to himself. Instead of seeing things in a clearer light when he awoke, he found them, if

141

anything, more confused. He took his turn at watch duty on the battlements and up there alone in the hot shadows he came to a decision : it was not too late. It was *never* too late to go after something one wanted. He would see her privately, just the two of them in the garden, perhaps at dusk when it was at its best. He would tell her what was in his mind, what had been in his mind for a long time. He remembered the expression on her face when he had told her of the floggings, the new respect, the interest. Above all, he remembered her smile. Well, he'd reawaken that interest. It was not too late. Now that he thought about it the bewilderment and jealousy of the night before melted away and seemed like the angry passions of a schoolboy. The question that had to be answered was why she had chosen Matthew, and the answer was plain : because he, Andrew, had kept himself aloof. Not that he'd put it like that. She would have to be treated with circumspection. He wouldn't spring anything on her. Gently . . . tenderly . . . that was the way to go about things.

But what if she wouldn't listen? What if Southgate's influence on her was greater than he had thought? He felt a queer sensation in the pit of his stomach. The idea that she might be in love with Southgate was anathema to him. He remembered her voice in the garden, soft, low. Had her tone been full of meaning, a meaning which he had refused to register? No, it couldn't be. It wasn't possible. Yet when he'd first seen Southgate he had mentally written him off as someone who might only appeal to women. In that case, he'd tell her everything. He could visualize the scene in the garden : the pearly dusk, her pale, serious face, the steady brown eyes. He'd tell her everything, from the moment he had first seen Southgate when they were children. He'd tell her about saving him at Kela, about the buffalo hunt and Chik's death, about the Herero refugees . . . well, perhaps there was no need to go into that. He'd tell her the facts without exaggerating his own part in them. He'd tell her because she was precious to him and because he wished to spare her the inevitable unhappiness that would follow. But he'd tell her gently . . . tenderly . . . not to shock. And he would see understanding in her eyes and new respect.

Matthew had left for the railway at dawn and was due to be away for two days; Andrew waited for his chance. For most of the day when he wasn't on watch he kept to his room but a few

142

minutes after six o'clock he felt a sudden coolness in the air and realized that the breeze from the sea had finally reached Falkenberg. It was time. The first person he saw was Rose. She was standing at one of the withdrawing room windows looking out over the village and for once she was not surrounded by a group of ruttish officers. It was several weeks since they had been alone together and Andrew felt embarrassed. But her smile was the same as it had always been, the automatic, slightly charged smile which overtook her features the moment a male human-being crossed her line of vision. He flinched at the naked invitation.

'Have you seen Eva?'

'What would you want with her?' she asked archly.

'To talk.'

'Oh?'

'Have you seen her?'

'She's lucky. He's very good-looking.'

'Who?'

'Matthew.'

'I don't know what you're talking about.'

'She's not for you, Andrew, take my word for it.' He felt himself flushing. 'I can tell.'

'You can tell nothing!'

She shrugged. 'Find out for yourself.'

'I will.' He turned on his heel and made for the door.

'You'll find her down at the mission.'

He walked down the hill, seething with anger. How the hell could someone like Rose know anything about a situation like this? It was foreign territory to her. He went on past the shuttered store of Sauermann & Fricke, past the canteen and across the square. He was tempted to stop for a quick brandy and then realized he would smell of liquor and he didn't want that. He planned to meet Eva accidentally at the mission so they could walk back to the castle together. In that way he could naturally take the path through the garden.

The village was much changed since the outbreak of war. The square was covered in tents, horses were picketed behind the canteen, and the roads, such as they were, had been badly cut up by heavy vehicles. He picked his way over the scarred ground and through a jungle of guy-ropes and was almost opposite the

143

police post when he heard the screaming. It was a high-pitched, brittle, animal scream and it put every tooth in his head on edge. It ended as abruptly as it had begun, with a strangled gurgle. There was dead silence for a second and then he seemed to hear a cheer, faint and ironic perhaps, but it was a cheer nevertheless. He turned and ran towards the post. Through the archway he could see a crowd of soldiers. Some were laughing and it was apparent they were the ones who had sent up the cheer. There were others who did not seem amused but stared to the front of the crowd with expressions of shame and shock. Andrew forced his way between them until he came to the centre of the hollow square. The first thing he saw was the gallows. It was a miniature gallows, about eight feet high, but in all other respects it was a replica of the real thing.

A new hemp rope stretched down from the crosspiece and at the end of the rope hung a grey shape, still kicking. He stopped, feeling nausea reach up into his throat. The grey shape was Bismarck the baboon. Its paws were bound behind its back and a filthy rag had been tied around its eyes. The execution had been carried out to the letter. It hung there, twitching and jerking; its great dog-face was pulled up in a horrible grimace and froth dripped down the long incisor teeth. Andrew could not remember ever seeing so ghastly a sight.

'Justice has been done, Herr Black.'

He turned to see Brock at his side. 'He bit Lily, you see. And so we held a court. Oh, yes, a proper court. Ask these gentlemen.' He flung out his arm to embrace the twenty or thirty soldiers standing in the square. Some of them looked away in disgust. It was clear that Brock was drunk. 'Judge, jury, prosecution, defence. Justice. Absolutely! Without fear or favour, Herr Black. Guilty. Biting the hand that fed it.' Andrew saw Lily standing in front of the baboon watching its death agonies. Her right arm was bandaged but otherwise she seemed in no way impaired. 'Gratitude, Herr Black. I told you that before. Never expect gratitude from a baboon or a native! Now, what about a drink to send Bismarck on his way?'

He felt Brock's sweaty hand on his arm and threw it off. 'I don't drink with monsters,' he said angrily and began pushing his way back through the onlookers.

Eva was standing in the archway of the post. She looked past

144

him and then at him. A look of horror was spread across her face.

'Wait,' he called, shoving a path through the back ranks. 'Eva!' But she had left the doorway and was hurrying across the square. 'Eva, wait!' He felt a hand on his arm and threw it off. It gripped him again. 'Herr Black!' He turned and saw Seegert. 'Let me go!'

'A moment, please.' The voice was cold and authoritative.

'What is it? What now?'

'The Major wishes to see you.'

'Later. Tell him later.' He tried to run forward again but this time Seegert jerked him back.

'I told you the Major wishes to see you. Now! It will be better if you do as I say.'

There was a menace in Seegert's tone that penetrated. No one had spoken to Andrew like that for a long time. The breeze from the sea seemed suddenly chill.

Andrew had not seen von Langsdorff since the outbreak of hostilities, had been unaware of the Major's return to Falkenberg. Now, standing in the shadowy interior of the tent, he looked down at him, noticing again the dry, sandstone quality of the big man. His uniform was covered in red dust and the stubble on his cheeks was flecked with grey. He sat like a rock, glancing at the papers in front of him. His greeting was perfunctory and cold.

'We've been expecting you, Major,' Andrew began. 'The horses are exceptional.' The Major remained silent. After a pause Andrew said, 'I was told you wanted to see me.'

'That is correct. A moment, please.' He opened a folder and studied several sheets of paper. Minutes passed and Andrew began to feel irritated. At this moment Eva would be arriving at the castle, walking through the garden. . . .

'Your name is Andrew Black?' The voice was remote.

'Of course it is. Now, look here Major. . . .'

Von Langsdorff's head came slowly up and Andrew found himself looking into the leopard's eyes. 'You are Andrew Black. Yes or no?'

'I am Andrew Black. Yes.' He had meant to sound sarcastic but the Major simply nodded and bent his eyes to the dossier.

'Age?'

'What's this all about?'

'Age?'

'Twenty-four. Would you mind telling me what you want this information for?'

'Place of birth?'

'Look Major, I don't know what you think you're. . . .'

'Place of birth?'

'Cape Town.'

'Marital status?'

'Oh, for Christ's sake!'

'Marital status?'

'Single.'

'Father's name?'

'If you'd only tell me what this is all about perhaps we could dispense with the formalities.'

Von Langsdorff raised his eyes from the dossier and tapped his teeth with the end of a pencil. 'Just answer the questions and you'll be doing all that's required. Now, father's name?'

'Arthur.'

'What nationality are you?'

'South African.'

'Place of domicile?'

Andrew paused.

'Falkenberg.'

Once again von Langsdorff looked up. 'I see, Falkenberg.' He made a note in the margin.

So it went on, one question after another, school, occupation, reason for leaving last employment. Every facet of Andrew's life was noted. At the end of fifteen minutes von Langsdorff knew more about him than his own mother.

'Good,' von Langsdorff said, leaning back in the canvas chair and tapping again with a pencil. 'Now, according to my information you entered German territory from the British Protectorate of Bechuanaland between, let me see. . . .' He glanced at the folder and gave two dates a week apart. 'May I see your papers, please?'

'What papers?' The irritation at being questioned as though

he was some native who'd left his employment without reason drained away and Andrew felt the tip of a cold finger touch his heart.

'My dear Herr Black, it is necessary to have permission to enter German territory. The permission is granted by means of a document. May I see the document?'

'I'm sorry, I don't have it.'

'You've lost it?'

'No. I never had one. I didn't know it was necessary, I'm sorry. But I came in through the desert and there was no police post anywhere near.'

'But there's one here.'

'I suppose so.'

'You could have gone to Sergeant Brock for temporary permission.'

'I told you. I didn't know about it.'

'You didn't know about it. Tell me, when you were a member of the Bechuanaland Police did people have to obtain permission in writing before they entered the territory?'

'Yes.'

'Do you think this is a very rare law? By that I mean, do you think it only applies to British territory? Could I walk into South Africa, for instance, without permission?'

'No.'

'No, Herr Black, I couldn't.'

'Look, I can explain all this. You see. . . .'

'You don't have to explain. It is all here.'

Why was he being questioned? This wasn't simply routine, there was a purpose behind it. But he couldn't imagine what.

'For God's sake,' he burst out. 'I might have entered the territory illegally but I came here to help you people. So at least my reason was good enough.'

'Just so. I was about to get to that. You came here as a horse trader.'

'That's correct.'

'We certainly needed the horses, but we paid you for them, if I remember.'

'Yes.'

'So you also came to help yourself.'

'Well . . . I wouldn't put it like that.'

147

'How would you put it?'

'I—well——'

'Come, Herr Black, let's not pretend. You haven't even heard a shot fired. Is that correct?'

'Yes.'

Von Langsdorff leant back and fixed him with a contemptuous stare. 'You came to make a profit out of the war.' He lit a small shag pipe and blew the smoke across the wooden table. 'And now, Herr Black, we come to the point. You are what is known as an illegal immigrant. I was going to say undesirable alien, but I'll spare your feelings. As far as I am informed you have committed no criminal act while on German soil so there can be no charges other than entering the territory without permission. Normally we would give you the choice of which border you would like to be escorted to but we are in the middle of a war and we cannot spare the time or the men. However, we have a column moving east towards Bechuanaland and I will make arrangements for you to travel with them until you can be handed to the British authorities there. Will that suit you? I think you will agree that it is a most lenient arrangement.'

How much did he know? The thought kept hammering at Andrew. And who had told him? Kurt. Of course. It had to be Kurt. But Kurt didn't know everything, nor did von Langsdorff. There was still room for manœuvre.

'Can I sell my horses first? I've got a herd of nearly a hundred.'

'Yes, I know about them. No, Herr Black, I'm afraid that will not be possible. The horses will be forfeit. The spoils of war, I'm afraid.'

'But I paid good money for them.'

'And you made good money.'

Christ, it meant he was wiped out. Every mark he had was tied up in the herd. He'd be stripped clean and bounced back into British territory with a court martial hanging over his head.

'Now, Herr Black, this need not worry you too much. There is a way out.'

'What?'

'I'm told you are an expert in deserts. We are not. We have no experience of them. But the war is taking us further and further into the north-east towards the Omaheke Desert. We need men with experience, scouts and guides. If you could see your way clear to help us in this, we could find a means of helping you. The horses would remain your property—until we bought them, of course. And we would pay you for your trouble.'

'I'd like to think it over.'

'Certainly.' Von Langsdorff took out a watch and laid it on the table. 'Let's say two minutes.'

Andrew's mouth was as dry as limestone dust. 'When would I have to leave?'

'We ride in an hour for Windhuk.'

BOOK THREE

To The Red Wall

I achieved an equal understanding of the importance of physical terror towards the individual and the masses. . . . For while in the ranks of their supporters the victory achieved seems a triumph to the justice of their own cause, the defeated adversary in most case. despairs of the success of any further resistance.

Adolf Hitler, *Mein Kampf*

Extracts from the War Diary *of A. Black, Esq. (Herero Uprising 1904-05, Archive Mss. Catalogue No. 66 -2303.)*

WE LEFT WINDHUK at 0630 on a bitterly cold morning, riding north toward Okahandja. The front line is said to be somewhere between Okahandja and Otjiwarongo but no one seems to know exactly where, which is typical of this war. At Okahandja we are to strike north-east until we meet the eastern encircling column. As far as I can tell the eastern and western columns are moving in a pincer formation to a point south-east of Otjiwarongo. When the pincers close they hope to squeeze the Hereros between the two arms. From what I know of the country up there it will be a miracle if the columns sight each other, let alone the enemy.

Windhuk was a depressing place. After the initial success of the German forces in relieving beleaguered outposts they simply ran out of men and guns and the enemy took advantage of the situation by raiding down to Windhuk itself—the town lost some of its cattle in one attack—and burning and pillaging all along the railway line. But now things have changed, or at least that's what the rumours said and Windhuk exists on rumours. It was said that 4,000 hussars had embarked at Wilhelmshaven, others said the figure was nearer 10,000. I heard that a transport was lying off Swakopmund waiting to unload the latest quick-firers from Krupp's; that Argentine horses were beginning to arrive and camels from the Canary Islands and Somaliland. One simply did not know what to believe. And food was scarce in the capital. It was in the queues for the soup kitchens that the rumours collected.

They put me in the Home Guard. It isn't a real regiment but a composite made up of German farmers who have been in the Colony for years, a host of South African Dutch who have come north for the pickings and an occasional Englishman with experience of the country. No one is quite sure where we fit in. We're supposed to do a little of everything : scouting, guiding, transport riding, surveying, and in general seeing that the German troops reach the enemy without heavy losses, and then stand shoulder to shoulder with them when the bullets begin to fly.

Our uniform is brown corduroy with a soft grey hat and long boots. Now that winter has come it's serviceable and warm. I feel sorry for the Germans; in their thin khaki they'll suffer both from the cold and from the thorn bush.

It was good to be leaving the rumours and intrigues behind. This is really not my war at all and I must make the point that I am an impressed man. I was trading horses in the small village of Falkenberg, north-west of Windhuk, when the Germans took me. They said they were taking all able-bodied men and that I could either join or leave the territory. Since my money was tied up in horses which I hoped to sell as remounts the latter was impossible.

I rode to Windhuk with a Major von Langsdorff with whom I have done business before for the Army. He seems to occupy an indefinable position. At first he was in Supply but now appears to combine that with Intelligence work. This is not as surprising as it seems since regular German officers are so scarce that they frequently overlap in their duties.

He is a hard man and the journey to Windhuk was made unpleasant for me by his manner. He seems to believe that I am lucky to be allowed to fight in his army. We did not talk much and each looked to his own food and cooking.

I did not see him again in Windhuk but heard that after a few days he had returned to Falkenberg for the horses. I hope he left my money there but I have no great confidence.

I have tried to analyse my feelings about this war and I find it difficult. For a policeman, it is plain that what the Germans are doing is a criminal act : they want, therefore they take. And yet they say they are going to civilize the people once they conquer them. There was much talk in Windhuk about the *kultur*-position of the natives. This is a fashionable phrase and is frequently used. The Germans appear to be very proud of their *kultur*. If they do civilize the races, I suppose there is some merit in what they say. But I am still confused about my own attitude. It seems I will have to fight, but there will be no relish in it. At the Alte Feste in Windhuk every German soldier professes to be aching to reach the front line and throw himself at the enemy. I wonder what the true position is up there in the north.

As the sky lightened soon after we left Windhuk I could see layers of grey cloud. It was a dark brooding morning with a cold wind from the east. The weeks of waiting have softened me and my buttocks are still sore in the saddle, but Duke is prime from rest and good feeding. I looked across at my companion. We had met only an hour before. He is a young lad called Walter—I have not learnt his other name—a heliographer in the *Seebataillon*, and it is my business to get him to the front where signallers are scarce. He is riding an East Prussian grey, a big gelding, heavy in the haunches, more like a cart horse than a cavalry mount, and I feel sorry for him. He is a fresh-faced boy who looks about sixteen perched up there on the big horse. I know he is feeling the saddle even more than I am, but it isn't that so much that worries me, it is the colour of his horse. When the warm weather comes the flies will drive it mad; they do that to greys.

We had not come a dozen kilometres from Windhuk before we saw the fires, away in the distance on either side of us, flickering on the tops of hills like St Elmo's Fire.

'What's happening?' Walter asked. 'Why are they burning? Are they ours?'

I shook my head. 'No, not ours. It's the enemy. They're burning the grazing.'

He looked frightened. 'It's what happened to Napoleon,' he said after a moment. 'I learnt it at school. Scorched earth, that's all they left him.'

'They?'

'The Russians.'

'There aren't any Russians here. They're only burning it to keep us from moving north. They've got their own herds up there. Don't worry, they won't burn everything.' He did not seem to take much comfort from my words.

All that dark morning we rode through a wasteland. The grass is gone, the camelthorn trees are blackened stumps. The wind blew the feathery ash in our faces until we became streaked with soot. Everywhere there are signs of war. We are on the great road to the front and it is marked all the way by death and destruction. Mules, horses and bullocks lie where they have fallen, some only skeletons after the jackals and vultures have picked them clean, some blown up like dark brown balloons, some half-eaten. Everywhere lie the broken wheels of splintered wagons, torn flapping canvas, yokes and leather thongs. For hours we picked our way through this desolation.

I talked to Walter, trying to keep his spirits up, but he became more and more depressed and I could see my task was not going to be easy.

'Tell me about yourself. Where are you from? What made you come out here?'

'I wish I hadn't,' he said.

Bit by bit he told me his story. He came from a village outside Kiel where his father was the local baker. He and a friend had joined the Army more out of boredom than anything else. He had left school the year before and had been helping in his father's bakery but hadn't cared either for the hard work or for getting up at two and three in the morning. So, in the autumn of 1903, when he heard that the 85th were looking for recruits on three-year commissions, he and his friend had signed on.

'We thought, why not see the world? We'd go to all our Colonies and the Government would pay the fares.'

He said it so naïvely it was difficult not to laugh. And yet I could see his reasons clearly enough for I had experienced something similar myself.

'You didn't expect this.'

'None of us did. Even when they said we were coming out here we thought it would be like a desert island with palm trees and beautiful brown women. My father asked me to bring him back a coconut. We all thought the war would be over by the time we got here.'

'Where is your friend now?'

He waved his hand ahead of us. 'Up there somewhere.'

It is difficult not to feel sorry for him. He looks so young and innocent and new. Everything about him is new, his knapsack and his white sleeping blanket, his cartridge belt and his rifle with its barrel cover, his bread bag and his army flask. He is still wearing the yellow boots he was issued with in Germany.

At noon we stopped at a ruined farmhouse. The roof beams had been burnt and what remained of the roof had fallen into the rooms. The furniture had been taken outside and most of it

156

lay in splinters. In one of the rooms a wooden motto still hung crazily from its nail. It said in German : 'Love your enemies'.

Outside we found three graves. Someone had made a cross out of boxwood and had burnt on it the name 'Scheel', and then 'Wilhelm, Anna, Maria'. Underneath that was the sentence : 'Fallen by the hand of the murderer'. I wanted to have our food in the shelter of one of the walls but the scene had affected Walter so much that we went on. We had no lunch, for our road took us once again through the blown and stinking corpses of mules and bullocks, and the wind blew the ash and dust in our faces. It was not a place for picnicking. Left and right in the far distance the black hills were haloed by flames.

It is pitch dark and bitterly cold. I write this by the light of a small fire of camelthorn. We should not really light a fire at all but I am afraid for Walter. I have given him one of my spare shirts but even so he feels the cold badly. The enemy could be anywhere in the bush around us. I keep my rifle close at hand.

Yesterday we left Okahandja. We saw the fort where the besieged white settlers had been relieved by Captain Franke and the small field hospital under the shadow of Mount Kaiser Wilhelm. There is almost nothing left of the sacred cemetery where the Herero chiefs were buried.

More rumours. They say that the Hereros are running short of ammunition and are falling back to the north with their women, children and huge herds of domestic stock.

They say we are preparing for a great advance. A new general has arrived who is going to finish everything off in a matter of days. But it is wishful thinking. Unless we get reinforcements nothing will be finished off. I know the country, and it suits the enemy.

But the arrival of the new general has produced a wave of optimism. His name is said to be von Trotha. I have never heard of him but he is known to every German soldier. They say he was in the Chinese Boxer rebellion and that he put down the rebellion in German East Africa with a severity unknown even to the Arabs. Perhaps we need a strong man.

We should join the column tomorrow or the day after, all going well.

*

We have been with the column for a week and nothing I have seen yet gives me confidence. We found headquarters by the huge elliptical balloon that flies over it and can be seen shimmering in the sunlight for many kilometres. If we can see it, so can the enemy. As we drew closer we noticed the signalling posts built on platforms high up in the tallest trees. Walter seemed to brighten up a bit at this. The men working the heliographs shouted greetings and Walter said he thought he might enjoy his job if it meant sitting up in a tree all day.

But we were quite unprepared for the reality of the column. The men were depressed and morale was low. The first thing we saw was a sort of gigantic mattress. It had been made by folding a tent in two and stuffing it with grass. Between thirty and forty men lay on it and I found out later that half were suffering from dysentery and the rest from wounds received in an encounter with the enemy two days before.

The months of campaigning have wreaked havoc with their dress. Boots have fallen apart, trousers are nothing but shreds and rags, thorns have penetrated jackets, leaving great rents in them. Everyone seems to be suffering from veld sores and skin ulcers. Food is scarce and disgusting. The first meal I ate was a mess of pancakes made of dirty water and flour. The drinking water tastes horribly of *glaubersalz*. It looks like yellow pea soup and smells of sulphur.

What makes matters worse is the fact that the soldiers feel they have been forgotten. Windhuk seems like another country to them and Germany itself, according to the few letters and newspapers reaching the front line, is more interested in the Russo-Japanese War than in anything happening in South-West Africa.

I haven't seen Walter since we arrived. I hope he has found his friend. I have been ordered to join the mess of a group of Home Guards. The difference between these grizzled, sunburnt men, some in their sixties, and the fair-skinned youths of the regular army, is very great. I feel safer with the Guards. If it comes to a fight at least I know I'll be in capable company.

Day after day it is the same : breakfast, if that is what it can be called, in the cold dawn; then we see to the inspanning of the bullocks that pull the heavy guns and supplies. The drivers are

Hottentots and Bergdamas. Then we, the Home Guards, move out into the bush looking for the easiest route to the water-pits located the previous day. Sometimes we only manage five kilometres. Then comes the search for more water until the final order at dusk : 'Stack arms and take blankets.' One is always conscious of the long, winding column and the responsibility. What if we lead them into an ambush? What if we don't find water? They look at us, these young German boys, with a childlike confidence and trust : we will look after them, we will lead them to water, we will see that they come through unharmed, we will send them back whole to their mothers in the Fatherland. I wonder.

A week ago I saw action for the first time. One of our scouting parties brought in news that the enemy was breaking out to the east and was threatening to cut our supply line. Orders were given to check our northward advance and to return south to water-pits where we had camped three days previously. We were to fortify our camp and wait until news came. We started the return journey at dawn. The men seemed very depressed. They were weary and dull and the thought of going back on their tracks aggravated the lowness of their morale.

In camp that night we saw signals to the south-west. Red and white rockets burst into the black night sky. There was much excitement and the rumour was that elements of the main western column had come across to engage the enemy. Only later we found out that a flying column had been ambushed by the enemy and the Hereros had taken the rockets from the dead bodies and were firing them off in celebration.

Walter came to see me that night. He was thin and wretched-looking. He took me aside from the mess fires and gave me a large silver watch which he said his father had presented to him on his embarkation. He asked me to look after it for him and I said I would. There is no sense in pretending about these matters.

The next morning was Sunday. Some of the men lit a big fire of camelthorn and held an impromptu service around it. I went more out of curiosity than anything else. No one seemed to be in charge and there were many denominations present. They sang '*Stille Nacht, Heilige Nacht*,' because it was known to everyone, I suppose. It was strange to look at the worn, grey company and hear a Christmas carol in such a place.

About six o'clock we broke camp and continued southward in the following order: first the small group of cavalry, a third of what had originally sallied forth, now riding their emaciated horses with long stirrups and bent backs; then a company of infantry; then the cannon; then about fifty wagons—some carrying wounded—each with a team of twenty-four bullocks; then a second company of infantry. About 300 yards to the rear marched half a platoon. The whole column was about two and a half miles long as it wound in and out of the thick bush and through the dry beds of *omurambas*. I rode on the left flank and sometimes it was impossible to see anything of the column other than a long thin snake of rising dust. Occasionally one heard the long-drawn cry of the drivers as they urged the bullocks on.

Out of nowhere came the crack of guns. I wheeled Duke and raced for the column. It was in confusion. 'It's all right,' someone was shouting. 'They saw a buck! Took a couple of shots!' Slowly the column got started again but then a corporal came running through the dust. 'The rear! The rear is under fire!'

The officers immediately ordered us to press forward into the bushes. I could not see anything to fire at. The whole point about being mounted was that it was supposed to give one manœuvrability but here in the thick bush, with dust obscuring everything, and the bullocks bellowing and frightened, and wagons suddenly lurching out of the dust threatening to unhorse one and trample one in the sand, it seemed better to dismount, take cover and watch for an opportunity. I sprang down from the saddle and pulled Duke into a dense thicket, unaware of the long white slashing thorns.

The soldiers had dropped to one knee and were firing blind. Bullets were cutting through the bush, making clattering noises as they ricocheted from branches to leaves. I wondered how many men would fall to their comrades' rifles.

Near me I could see an under-officer whose left arm was bleeding badly. He had propped his rifle on a dead branch and was firing at regular intervals. Away to my right the bush had been set alight and the smoke was drifting down on us making visibility even more difficult.

Through the swirling smoke and rising dust I saw the enemy

160

for the first time, nightmare figures dressed in ragged civilian suits looted from farms, cord uniforms which they had stripped from dead Home Guards, and some even in khaki. They flashed through the smoke like black ghosts, spraying the bush with their heavy Martini-Henrys. I fired snap shots whenever I saw even a shadow, and the barrel of the Jeffries grew hot in my hands.

'Keep low and fall back!'

I pulled the under-officer, a Thuringian, to his feet and helped him across Duke's saddle. In this way we made our passage to the centre of the column. The Germans had formed a square with infantry and wagons, and the 3.7s and Maxims had opened fire. As others came to join us they were ordered to lie down in front of the square while the cannons fired over their heads.

The Hereros were all around us but we now had the comparative cover of the wagons. When the cannons began using shrapnel the enemy fell back. The roar of the flying steel through the bush was terrifying; it sounded like an avalanche. After two hours we broke from the square and followed the enemy but they had melted away into the bush and one was left wondering if they had been there at all.

But the dead were real enough. We had lost eleven killed and nearly thirty had been wounded. Towards evening, as the sun was setting, the dead were laid in a communal grave and twenty infantrymen fired over the bodies. An old major talked of the Fatherland and God and of Death and the fact that it was Sunday.

I sat leaning against the side of a wagon, feeling stiff and sore. Around me others were lying in exhausted stupors. The Thuringian under-officer, whose arm had been tied in a sling, brought me a cook-pan of water. I suppose it was his way of saying thank you. I would happily have drunk a gallon, for my mouth was thick with scum, but there was no water near us. It was terrible for the beasts. Some of the cavalrymen were trying to feed their horses on weaver-bird nests, for equally there was no grazing. I thought of the melons in the Kalahari and the desert seemed suddenly to be a most inviting place.

The following morning we had a little rice and zwieback and a mouthful or two of water, then the sick and wounded were loaded into the wagons. The column ground slowly forward. I was leading Duke and as we passed the communal grave I found

161

Walter at my side. His eyes had sunk far back into his head and his dusty face was flushed. 'Here you are,' I said, taking out the watch. 'You won't be wanting me to keep this any longer.' But he seemed not to hear. His eyes were on the grave. Then he took the watch and crept back to his place in the column.

At about midnight I awoke from an uneasy sleep. A Rhinelander was sitting on an ammunition box near me. He complained of weakness in his feet and knees. His eyes reminded me of Walter's. Great drops of sweat were bursting from his forehead. One of the surgeons, a young one-year volunteer, came up and felt his pulse. Then he turned to me and said : 'This is the twelfth in seven days,' and went away again. I found out later that he meant typhoid.

Time passes in an endless cycle of hot noons, cold nights, thirst and dust. It is evening and supper is over. We sit around the cooking-hole talking in soft voices. These cooking-holes are made as carefully as possible with a knee-deep gutter cut in a circle around them so we can put our feet in it and sit comfortably. I mess with five other Home Guards. Away to our right are the cooking fires of the regular soldiers. Someone is singing a melancholy song. I listen to the words.

> *Doch mein Schicksal will es nimmer,*
> *Durch die Welt ich wandern muss.*
> *Trautes Heim, dein denk'ich immer,*
> *Trautes Heim, dir gilt mein Gruss.*
> *Sei gegrüsst in weiter Ferne,*
> *Teure Heimat, sei gegrüsst. . . .*

The voice trembles and fades. We go back to our talk.

One of the older men who has been farming in the Colony for ten or more years says suddenly, and for no apparent reason except that it must have been on his mind, 'What the hell can you expect? They're acting just like the North Germans in 1813. This is *their* struggle for independence.' No one has to ask him who he means. Almost all our conversation now is about the Hereros. Until their last attack no one realized how courageous they are. We have a certain admiration for them.

'But what about the cruelty?' someone else says.

'Do you think there wouldn't be cruelty if the Germans rose against a foreign oppressor?' the old man answers. 'And aren't we cruel to them? Granted they don't take prisoners; do we? Look around, where are they all?'

No one answered and the old man went on: 'You've got two sorts of Germans out here. You've got the missionaries who arrived and said, "You are our dear brothers in the Lord and we want to bring you Faith, Love and Hope, for these are our benefits." And then you've got the soldiers and the farmers and the traders and what they're saying is, "We want your cattle and your land and we want to make you slaves without legal rights." But the two things don't go side by side. Either it's right to colonize and take away their rights and make slaves of them, or it's right to Christianize them and proclaim brotherly love. The trouble is the missionaries said, "Ye are our brothers" and that turned their heads. They're not our brothers. It'll take a century or more before they reach that state. First they must learn to irrigate the land, to make wells, to plant corn and build houses and weave clothing. Then perhaps they'll become our brothers. . . .'

Another old man, a transport rider from South Africa, broke in sourly: 'The Germans want this, the Germans want that! They don't understand the first thing about governing colonies. There'll be a thousand or two German graves in this country before you get what you want and you might not get it even then.'

All this talk of missionaries reminds me of the Reverend Kaufmann who is in charge of the mission at Falkenberg. (I was about to write 'home' for that is now how I think of it.) I remember him saying to Baron von Steinberg: 'I cannot allow you and others like you to stand for examples of us all. I would not want the Hereros to reject our entire civilization just because of you.' I was not certain what he meant then, but I am clearer now.

Three things have happened in the past ten days which have changed the pattern of the war for us. The first was the arrival of a supply train from Okahandja with food, clothing, blankets and medicines. We were able to load all our sick and wounded into the wagons and send them back to hospital. Morale rose immediately, especially since the news is good. The enemy has retreated to the water-holes near the Waterberg Mountains and is said to be preparing for a final stand. Reinforcements are on the way to us and we are in a much better position to fulfil our part in the pincer movement. The plan is now to encircle the Hereros at the Waterberg and try to drive them southwards into the teeth of our advancing guns.

The second occurrence was more melancholy.

I had been out with a mounted patrol when someone saw a strange animal or bird in the fork of a tree. When we got closer we realized it was no animal. It was the body of Walter. We could only conjecture as to what had happened. He must have been shot while on his signalling platform and his body had fallen almost to the ground. He had been stripped of his clothing by the enemy, and mutilated. His genitalia had been removed and his throat had been cut. By the amount of blood on his upper legs it seemed to us that he must have been mutilated while he was still alive. We took his body back to camp and foolishly allowed several of the men to see it. It caused much distress and throughout the following day I was pestered by soldiers coming up to me and asking me to describe what we had seen.

I mention this for it seems to have had a great influence on the men, as witnessed by the third occurrence. This was the arrival in camp of General von Trotha and his staff. They rode in without any warning. I had returned from a patrol and was rubbing Duke down near our headquarters tent and so had a good view of all that happened. When it became known that the general was in camp the men began to group around headquarters and each time they saw him they gave a small cheer. He came among us asking about food and conditions and saying that the war was almost over and that only one final push was needed. He was a fierce-looking man of about fifty with piercing eyes and a heavy bristling moustache. His hair was white at the temples and he wore a white pointed beard, but his moustache was dark brown.

Just then a Herero woman was led into camp. Occasionally we did come across old women or children who had been left behind while the others made for the Waterberg, but most of them had been sick or close to death. This woman, although weak, was able to walk. I suppose she was about thirty.

His Excellency saw her being led into camp and ordered her to be brought to him. We all stood around as he asked her questions. She said her people had gone north but that she had been too weak to keep up. This was apparent for she was painfully

164

thin and wasted. After she had answered as well as she could through an interpreter his Excellency ordered that she should be taken away and bayoneted. The interpreter, who looked like a Rehoboth Bastard, took her to one side. He seemed to be trembling with fright at what he had to do. Then a soldier went over to him and offered him a bayonet. The interpreter started to shake his head. I heard him saying, 'No, Master, I can't do it.' Then the soldier said, 'All right, I'll show you what a German soldier can do!' With that he took the woman aside a few paces and drove the bayonet through her body. He then withdrew it and held it up so the blood dripped down onto his hand and arm. 'You see,' he said, 'I have done it.' I'm not sure whether he was observed by His Excellency but certainly several other officers saw him and made no move to stop him.

When His Excellency and his staff left us an hour or so later the cheering was tremendous.

The woman's body was thrown beyond the perimeter of the camp to be eaten by jackals and hyenas.

We approach the Waterberg. I have seen its great red wall from the tops of hills. The enemy is said to be massing beneath it. We are in constant communication now with the western column. Water is scarce again. It is said the enemy have taken up positions around the water-pits. If we lose the battle we lose the water and so we shall either die by bullets or by thirst. It is now August and we cannot expect rain for two months at the least. It is odd how small things come to haunt one at a time like this. I am obsessed by the thought of Walter's watch. I should have looked for it beneath the tree. It might have fallen from his pocket and been missed by the Hereros. I could have sent it to his father in Germany. I seem to see it lying there, forgotten in the dusty bush, like so many other things in this war.

We started the final advance about 2330. It was said that our division would reach the enemy at dawn. There were all kinds of rumours. I had been told that nearly 50,000 Hereros were waiting for us but I knew that most of them would be women and children and that only a proportion of the men would have any ammunition. A group of Witbooi Hottentots rode ahead of us to spy out the land, then came our company. One part had been detached to ride at the side of the track, the other kept to the main path. Behind us came the artillery. We tried to move as silently as possible but the night was filled with the sounds of jolting wheels, snorting horses, jingling harnesses, shouts and whip cracks. It was very cold and I allowed the reins to fall on Duke's back while I warmed my hands in my pockets. I did not want to have stiff fingers when the shooting started.

We marched all night and were almost under the Waterberg when the sun rose. Here, beneath the great overhanging slopes of the mountain everything was bathed in red.

I was riding near a young German from Hamburg who had shared his coffee with me before we started. He seemed much affected by the dawn and turning, said to me : 'Everyone has to experience something if he wants to become a serious person. That's why I came out here.'

According to rumours we should have sighted the enemy at dawn and sitting there in the bitter cold I gradually began to feel depressed. I had not been looking forward to the action but since it was inevitable I wanted it started and finished one way or the other. Just then, away to our right, we heard the opening barrage of the mountain battery. We moved forward but the bush was so dense it was impossible to keep any formation. By ten o'clock the sun was fierce and the horses were becoming exhausted. A lieutenant rode past and said, 'We aren't two kilometres from the water-holes.' Almost as he said it we heard the first smack of a heavy rifle and then the zipping noise of the bullet in the undergrowth. We dismounted hurriedly and handed the reins of our horses to a detail. For the purpose of this battle I had been drafted into a mixed company of mounted infantry. There were marines, one or two sailors, part of an infantry regiment and a parcel of scouts and cavalrymen. We were about ninety strong. As we pushed ahead into the thick bush we could hear the wild battle cries of the enemy but we were not able to see them. They seemed all around us and the firing grew warm. Someone near me, I think the serious young man from Hamburg, gave a slight cry and fell forward. There was no time to look more carefully. I dropped to my belly and took a snap shot at a naked brown arm. I didn't hit it. Someone was shouting, 'I hit one !

I hit one!' I saw a marine crawl past me with a bullet in his shoulder.

The firing grew heavier on our left flank and there seemed to be a dozen or more of our company lying on the ground with wounds. The noise of screaming and shouting grew and I thought they would rush us. I saw an officer to the rear and shouted, 'We have wounded!'

'Hold your position! I'm sending help.'

We fired blind into the bush hoping that the rapid volleys from our 98s would discourage the Hereros.

I heard groaning and cursing; then, right next to me, I saw the barrel of a revolving cannon. 'Out of the way!' a voice shouted. I rolled over and the cannon was pulled into place. It began to spit out shrapnel at the enclosing bush at a very rapid rate. Each explosion sounded beautiful.

The attack on our left was beaten off and we lay there in silence for a while. Then the mountain battery opened up again. 'Forward! Forward! Double quick!' We sprang to our feet and plunged forward. We were met by a volley of flying lead. The attack faltered and stopped. That one volley had knocked down about half the group near me. We dropped to our bellies again.

All of us were dripping with sweat. My mouth and throat were parched but as I had only a little scummy water left in the water-bottle I decided to do what I had done in the Kalahari. I told myself I would have a mouthful after the next engagement.

The wounded were being dragged back. On the other side of a clearing I saw a medical orderly dealing with a man who had taken a piece of shrapnel on the inner side of his thigh. He was bleeding badly. The orderly, in his panic, had tied the tourniquet *below* the wound. I shouted to him but the noise of firing was too great. By the time I'd got to my elbows to wriggle over to them he'd dragged the man out of my vision. I never saw him again.

If the enemy had attacked then they could have wiped us out, but inexplicably their firing seemed to become weaker instead of stronger and I remembered about the ammunition. A staff lieutenant dropped down beside me. His tunic was torn and he'd lost his *sudwester*. 'The captain is dead. So is the first lieutenant and most of the under-officers. Go to the General and tell him we are about five hundred metres from the water-holes.'

167

I ran back, ducking behind trees and ant-hills for cover until I saw the balloon shimmering in the sky. The headquarters tent was in a clearing. In front of it were long rows of bullocks, their tongues lolling out of their mouths. Many were bellowing mournfully. They had smelt the water. As I ran past the men holding our horses one of them shouted: 'For God's sake push on to the water! What's holding you?' I delivered my message. I heard someone say to the General, 'The animals can't hold out any longer, sir, and the men are dying of thirst.' I crossed over and rested in the shade of a hospital wagon. Just then we were attacked from all sides. A doctor shouted to his staff, 'Get your white coats off!' They dropped their coats and picked up rifles and began to pour a heavy fire into the bush. But they were firing wildly. 'Shoot more calmly!' I shouted. I was lying underneath the wagon firing through the wheel spokes. My words must have had some effect for the doctors and orderlies began to shoot more deliberately. After a few minutes the firing died down. I returned to my position at the front.

I have little idea how much time was passing but I think it was early afternoon when our guns opened up with a fearsome barrage, every available cannon and machine-gun was firing. Then word came up the ranks, 'We are going to charge.' The barrage suddenly died away and I found myself on my feet and running forward. The noise had been so tremendous that now in the silence I could not hear my own feet thudding across the hard ground. There were shrieks and cries and bloodthirsty yells but they all sounded far away and remote. I saw tattered black figures rising up from the bush almost at my feet. I fired as well as I could but they sped away like duikers. All at once the water-holes were before us. We flung ourselves down in a defensive perimeter. The whole camp had followed us with a rush and now the area around the holes was teeming with bullocks and horses, wagons and wounded. Everyone was thirsty to the point of death.

Behind us our men were filling buckets and kettles, basins, water-bags—anything that would hold water. First they helped themselves, then the wounded, and then, after they had brought us full cook-pans, they began to water the stock.

The sun went down. Some of us went out and cut thorn-bush with our bayonets and built a stockade around the water-holes. Then the mountain battery set up its cannon and machine-guns.

As darkness fell we heard the bellowing of animals still waiting for water.

We knew that the enemy was all around us. Occasionally we heard the crack of a rifle and the bush would light up for a fraction of a second. About midnight the firing faded away. We passed a little zwieback from hand to hand.

What, I wondered, was in store for us? Around us was a huge tribe of men, women and children. If only a fraction was armed it still meant they could crush us by their very weight of numbers.

We lay there in the dark silence waiting. And then someone said, 'Listen!' In the distance I seemed to hear a soft groaning noise. I listened more carefully and realized that what I was hearing was the combined bellowing of a vast herd perhaps two or three miles away. It was an organic sound, seeming to come from the very earth itself; it was the sound of thirsty cattle.

At dawn we expected another attack. We did what we could to prepare for it. The sun rose. Nothing happened. We suspected a trick. The light strengthened. Still we lay waiting. A party of Witbooi Hottentots were sent out to reconnoitre. In an hour they were back. They told us an amazing thing. The Hereros were gone; men, women, children, cattle, sheep and goats. A whole nation had taken flight to the east.

How am I to describe what we have done—what we are doing? Someone whose business is words might well find difficulty in choosing the right ones; for me it is almost impossible. It is now nearly a month since the battle at the Waterberg and ever since then we have been riding, riding, riding.

As long as I live I shall remember these past weeks. Until the Waterberg we were fighting a war against an enemy and my mind is often a blur when I try to separate days and weeks from each other. I can remember hardship as well as comradeship. But since the battle everything has changed. Men and young boys, who seemed out of place in such a war and in such a country because of their gentleness, have become hard and ruthless. The reasons for the change are obvious. They saw their comrades mowed down in battle and they have seen other sights, like Walter's body, which turned the stomachs of the bravest. But perhaps the real reason is that we have been ordered to kill by

169

the highest authority—not as one is ordered to kill in battle, but rather as a pest-control officer will set about wiping out vermin. We are the exterminators.

General von Trotha issued the decree. We are to kill the Hereros, men, women and children, wherever they may be found. We are to wipe them off the face of the earth. It is not enough that they have been defeated in a war; they are to be erased from the human census so that never again will the Germans be troubled by them. It was this *vernichtungsbefehl* of the general's that seemed to turn the men's heads. Our plan is simple. We keep driving the Hereros east into the desert known to me as the Sand Veld, and which the Germans call the Omaheke. Those we do not kill with bullets we sentence to death in its waterless wastes.

Sun, heat, distance, sand, dust . . . and always riding, riding. . . . Everything has become a nightmare.

Dawn—that first dawn after the Waterberg when we awaited the attack that did not come—I remember it clearly. About two hundred of us, those whose horses were not on the point of extinction, were ordered to follow the enemy. It was like following the path of a tornado. The ground was trodden down into a roadway about 300 metres wide, like a dusty river winding into the parched hillocks. It had been made by thousands of naked feet and thousands of hooves as the Hereros, with their flocks, had stormed away from us in fright. Scattered all along its length were blankets, skins, wooden implements, ostrich feathers, pots and pans, beads, bangles, dead and dying cattle, dead and dying men. In the hot windless morning the smell of death and decay hung over everything like a pall.

Each time we reached the crest of a rise we would stop and scour the countryside ahead and each time we would see the gigantic cloud of dust on the far horizon that marked the passage of the enemy. Although we rode hard it seemed always to keep the same distance ahead of us.

I say rode hard and I mean only in those circumstances. It was impossible to ride at more than a fast walk for the horses were already beginning to drop.

And everywhere were dead cattle, goats and dogs, and old men and children lying apathetic in the sun, unable to keep up with the frenzied rush of their people. I saw babies lying next to the corpses of their mothers trying to reach the nipples of dead breasts; I saw old women with spears in their chests where they had been helped into the next world by relatives too kind to leave them to die of thirst. I saw a dog which had bitten into the neck of a dying cow and was lapping at the blood. I found a baby girl about two years old lying completely forsaken in the sun. I dismounted, picked her up and took her to the shade of a bush near an old fire-place. She saw an old bone and began to gnaw at it. She neither cried nor showed any fear and I had an uncanny feeling that she had simply materialized one day and had grown up there on the hard yellow ground without any human help.

When we returned to camp in the evening we sent out the native drivers to finish off the wounded and dying. It seemed the most reasonable thing to do.

In camp at Ombakaha north of Gobabis. Some days ago our commanding officer sent an envoy to a party of Hereros camped about thirty kilometres away, offering peace terms if their leaders came into camp and discussed the matter. A Herero sub-chief called Traugott, who had been a school teacher, came to confirm this. He was told that if they came in and made peace their lives would be spared and they would be allowed to keep their cattle and small stock. The following day a party of Hereros entered camp. I understand that they were the chiefs Saul and Joel, the under-chiefs Traugott, Elephas, Albanus, Johannes Munqunda, Elephas Mumpurua and two others whose names I never discovered. They brought with them seventy Herero soldiers. The women and children were left behind. The Hereros were halted on the perimeter of the camp under a clump of camel-thorn trees. The Germans wanted to know where the Herero leader Samuel Maherero could be found. One of the chiefs said he had fled with a group of Hereros towards Bechuanaland. The German commander then gave an order and the Hereros were wiped out by machine-gun fire.

Near the Waterberg, Saturday. We came upon an old Herero woman of about fifty or sixty digging in the hard ground for wild

171

onions. General von Trotha and his staff were present. A soldier named Konig jumped from his horse and shot the woman through the forehead at a range of about two feet. Before he shot her he said, 'I am going to kill you.' She simply looked up and said, 'I thank you.'

I have found a copy of the Extermination Order issued by General von Trotha. It belongs to a Holsteiner who had it from a member of the General's staff. He carries it about with him as though it came from the Gospels. I have prevailed upon him to let me copy it. He was unwilling but I pretended a sincere admiration for the General. Now he thinks of me as a friend.

Here is part of the document which I took down by the light of a camelthorn fire near Hamakari on the edge of the Omaheke Desert in October 1904 :

'I, the great General of the German soldiers, send this letter to the Herero nation. The Hereros are no longer German subjects. They have murdered and robbed, they have cut off the ears and the noses and privy parts of wounded soldiers and they are now too cowardly to fight. . . . The Herero nation must now leave the country. If the people do it not I will compel them with the big tube. Within the German frontier every Herero, with or without a rifle, with or without cattle, will be shot. I will not take over any more women and children, but I will either drive them back to your people or have them fired upon. These are my words to the nation of the Hereros.

(Signed) The great General of the Mighty
Emperor, von Trotha.'

Midnight, near Eiseb. We had been following a party of Hereros about four hundred strong—this is happening more often now as the nation splits up into its sub-chieftainships and spreads out across the edge of the Omaheke Desert. We had news that this party was trying to break west through our cordon to reach water-holes. We followed them for two and a half days but never came up with them. In all that time we found no water.

At midnight we started our return journey. Horses were dropping every mile of the way. At first, when a horse fell, the rider would take the saddle on his back and trudge through the sand in his heavy boots, but soon saddles were simply dumped and marked our trail all along its length. We dismounted and began to lead our horses. It was a hot oppressive night in spring. One man in front of me began to talk wildly. He shouted that he wanted to kill every Herero in the world and drink all the blood. We put him on a horse and two men held him. I felt a deep feeling of revulsion for what he had said and yet I knew that I would drink blood if I had to. Often when we passed dying beasts I had felt the urge to tap the jugular vein.

Our problem is that we have all become less than human, even if some of us have not given way entirely to barbarism. It is the land and the conditions. Although it is spring no rain has fallen. It is easy to feel sorry for ourselves. Whenever I do I remember how much worse it must be for the enemy.

Beyond Hamakari. We were in camp near a water-hole. One of our men found a small baby boy about nine months old lying in the bush. The child was crying and he brought it into camp. The soldiers formed a ring and began throwing it from one to another as though it were a black ball. The child was terrified and began to shriek. After a while the men grew bored with their game and one of the soldiers fixed his bayonet on his rifle and shouted for them to throw the baby into the air. He missed the child twice but the third time it landed on the tip of the bayonet and he held it up to show the others. There was a great deal of laughter and I felt physically ill. When the child died some minutes later I took the small body and buried it.

Dusk, somewhere near Okaua on the edge of the Omaheke. The Holsteiner who carries General von Trotha's message next to his heart asked the lieutenant for water.

The lieutenant shook his head and then said encouragingly, 'Cheer up, the war must be nearly over. We'll soon be home.'

'They say the tribe was ninety thousand strong. There can't be more than fifteen or twenty thousand left by now. But what

173

good does that do me? I'll die here without water. Haven't you got a drop?'

The lieutenant held up his water-bottle. It was dry. 'Rest,' he said. 'The night will refresh you.'

The guardsman lay down for a while then pushed himself to his feet and walked down the slope of a hill to a bushed area.

'What's he up to?' the lieutenant said.

'Probably going to see if he can dig for water.'

We heard a sudden cry, then a shout and sounds of a scuffle. The Holsteiner came out of the bushes holding a tall thin Herero by the neck. The man was dressed in European clothing and carried a rifle. The Holsteiner tore the gun from his hand and dragged him up the slope, swearing at him in German all the time. 'Look at this!' he shouted as he came up to us. 'This bastard's got a German rifle.' The Holsteiner seemed to have forgotten his thirst and his depression. He kept on abusing the Herero and started to kick him on the knees. Between curses he asked him where he got the rifle. He accused him of murdering a good German soldier to steal it. He said he must have killed a German farmer to get the clothing. The Herero kept on saying the same thing over and over. One of the men near me who could speak the language quite well said, 'He says he has not taken part in the war.'

'Not taken part! How the hell does he get this rifle then?' the Holsteiner said. 'He's just stuffing me with lies.' He seemed on the very brink of insanity. Suddenly he flung the Herero down on the ground. The black crouched there like a terrified animal.

The Holsteiner said in a more normal voice, 'The missionary said to me, "Beloved, don't forget that the blacks are our brothers." Now I will give my brother his reward.' He pushed the Herero again. 'Run! Run away!' The man sprang up and raced across the clearing, zigzagging and leaping. He had not taken more than five jumps when the Holsteiner shot him through the head.

I couldn't help myself. I walked over and threw a blanket across the body. The lieutenant looked at me severely. 'It is safer,' he said. 'He can't fire a rifle at us any more and he can't breed children to fight us. It's the best way.'

The Holsteiner sat with his head on his arms. Every now and then he looked at the corpse. In spite of the heat he was shivering. He began complaining of a severe pain in his chest. Then he said, 'When we were sitting around our fires at the beginning of the war our Captain said that two million Germans would live here. But I'll not see anything of it. I am sick; sick. Are you sure you haven't a drop of water left?'

Later the lieutenant came to sit by my side. 'The missionary was right, you know. All men *are* brothers.'

'Then we've killed our brother,' I replied.

In a hoarse, painful voice, he said, 'For a long time we'll have to be hard; we'll have to go on killing. But at the same time we as individuals will have to strive towards high thoughts and noble deeds so we may contribute our part to our future brothers.' He looked thoughtfully at the dead body. 'You see, Black,' he said finally, 'the great difference between the Hereros and us is our *kultur*-position. When they have attained that there will be no need to kill them any longer.'

I turned away from him and felt overcome by shame.

BOOK FOUR

The Great Thirst

All human culture, all the results of art, science and technology that we see before us today are almost exclusively the creative product of the Aryan. This very fact admits of the not unfounded inference that he alone was the founder of all higher humanity, therefore representing the prototype of all that we understand by the word 'man'.

Adolf Hitler, *Mein Kampf*

A BATELEUR EAGLE planing on outstretched pinions below the cliffs of the Falkenberg would have seen the horse with its rider come slowly up out of the plain, at first as a dark speck against the yellow *t'wa* grass, then as an unfamiliar mass ascending a slight rise. At the crest of the hillock the shape stopped and remained motionless, an irregularity amid the grass and camelthorn trees.

Andrew Black leant forward in the saddle, allowing the blood to flow to his buttocks and ease the numbness. He raised his eyes against the brutal glare and saw the rippling peak of the Falkenberg in the distance. The heatwaves obscured the castle outlines but he could make out the colour of the ramparts. He touched Duke with the heel of one broken boot.

Wearily, the horse picked up his stumbling walk. Andrew let the reins drop on his neck and put both hands on the pommel for support. 'Hang on,' he told himself. 'You're nearly there.' He rode with long stirrups, his body bent forward, and swayed to the rhythm of the horse's gait as though riding in his sleep. Over and over in his mind ran a line of verse he had picked up somewhere: 'Home is the sailor, home from the sea, And the hunter home from the hill.' Home, he thought.

He rode past the peeling mission, seeing but hardly registering the sagging roof, and on past the police post without memory of the last time he had been there, and past his tree in the middle of the square, empty now of tents or human life, but strewn with a mass of broken bottles and rusting food tins, and past. . . . Something stirred in his mind. He pulled on Duke's head and the horse stopped. He turned in the saddle and stared once more at the camelthorn tree under which he had so often drunk a litre of Dortmund beer. Three black shapes, like large pods, hung from its branches. He wiped his hand across his eyes and looked again. It was a sight with which he was all too familiar. Three naked Hereros hung by their necks. To one side were the ammunition boxes which had acted as rude platforms before being kicked out from under them. The leather thongs which had been tied under one ear had bitten so deeply into the black skin that in parts they had disappeared. Each head was cocked at a slight angle as though the dead man was listening to an epigram. Dirty rags covered the callouses on their ankles where chains had rubbed. Here too, Andrew thought, urging Duke forward again. They moved past the canteen, now an empty, burnt-out shell, and past Sauermann & Fricke, bolted and barred, and up the rocky path to the castle and past the Hottentot guard sitting sleepily by the gate until, reaching the shade of the pepper trees, he slid to the ground and stood shakily, trying to keep his balance. He looked vaguely around for a Hottentot groom and, seeing none, threw Duke's reins over a bush. 'I'll be back,' he said, in the way he had now of talking to the stallion.

He walked unsteadily to the steps leading up to the huge Gothic door. As he reached the top it opened and he saw Eva standing in the dim interior of the hall. 'What do you want?' she said, her voice shrill. 'You'll get nothing to drink here! Don't you know the war's over?' She was about to say something more, then she took a pace towards him. 'Oh, God,' she said, examining his face. 'Can it. . . ? Andrew. . . ? Andrew! It's you!'

He nodded. 'Yes. It's me.'

'Forgive me. Come in, please come in.'

She took him through to the withdrawing room. In spite of his weariness he noticed the torn cushions and the ripped leather, the scarred panelling, the lop-sided piano, and the carpets mottled by a hundred carelessly thrown cigar butts. She followed his eyes. 'Soldiers at play,' she said.

He sank down into one of the chairs and in the light falling on him from a window she was able to see the thin, bony face, the torn and dusty garments, the cracks and ulcers on his hands, the flapping soles of his boots, and she felt a quick surge of sympathy.

'The horse,' he muttered, trying to push himself to his feet. 'I must see to the horse.'

She held him back. 'Don't be silly. I'll have him seen to.' She went into the hall to call a servant, then remembered that only the cook and one or two others remained. She stopped, wonder-

180

ing whose need was the greatest, and turned back into the room. Andrew was asleep in the chair.

The next few weeks remained in his mind like a series of photographs that had been taken out of focus; in parts there was some definition and these parts he could recall clearly, but mostly the images lay on the periphery of his memory, irritatingly there yet not substantial enough to see. He and Eva were thrown almost completely into each other's company, for great changes had taken place not only in the village but also in the castle since he had left nearly nine months before.

The war, in the sense of set-piece battles with the Hereros, was over and Falkenberg had been abandoned by the Army and left to set itself to rights as best it could. From what Eva told him he was able to piece the months together into some sort of coherent picture. There had been no attack on Falkenberg, unless the rape of the village by the Army could be described as an attack. He had seen the results of roistering German officers on the castle furniture, and now learnt that the canteen had been burnt down one night in a display of exuberance that had caused Herr Fricke to make up his mind once and for all. He had fixed a huge padlock to the door of his store and vanished.

Of the people Andrew had known, most were gone. Rose had left the Baron on a flood-tide of men and was said to be living with von Langsdorff in Windhuk. Kurt had followed her with the excuse that the capital was now the place to be to take advantage of the speculation in land that would result from a German victory. Eva did not tell him of the rumours that Kurt was to be seen at almost any time of the day or night, drinking by himself in one of the bars. In fact, she did not give any details of the incident which had precipitated Rose's departure. He heard them later from Watch.

The evening had, apparently, started like many other evenings in the latter stages of the war. Since the fighting was now nearing the Waterberg the Baron had considered conditions safe enough to leave only the Orlams on guard during the night and he had rejoined 'his boys'. He had been half drunk when he was helped into the withdrawing room by Jonker and Kraai and so, it appeared, were most of the officers. Rose was thumping out her polka selection on the piano that was already looking and sounding the worse for wear, four or five men were singing

181

accompaniment in loud throaty voices, and others were arguing, shouting and laughing. Seeing the Baron at the doorway, three lieutenants greeted him with a loud whoop and, lifting him to their shoulders, rushed him around the room in two full circuits, yelling and shouting, before depositing him in his chair. Then one raised his glass and cried: 'To the Emperor of South-West!' There was a roar of acclaim and a dozen or more brandy goblets were drained and smashed in the fireplace. Laughing with pleasure, the Baron threw back his own cognac and hurled his glass after the rest.

Someone began to dance and soon the others joined in, their heavy boots stamping out the polka. They swung each other round and round, crashing onto chairs and sofas, mincing backwards to a waltz, laughing all the while at their own male antics —for Rose was the only woman in the room and she was at the piano. But as the dancers went on and on and showed no sign of stopping, her arms began to tire and she was glad to give up her place to a major with an even heavier touch than her own.

The Baron called her over and she sat at his feet. His face red and sweating, he hovered above her, laughing and thumping his hand on the arm of his chair in time to the music. Unconsciously, his other hand had begun to stroke her neck and it was not long before one of the dancers in the midst of executing a grotesque pirouette suddenly stopped as though he'd been shot. He stared for a moment at a sight he had not seen for many months and with a shout gathered Rose up and swung her away in a fast waltz, laughing and pointing with one hand to one small naked breast which jigged in time to the step. Quickly the other officers formed a circle and Rose was whirled from one to the next. She seemed oblivious of the fact that she was now stripped to the waist. So indeed was the Baron, who was still thundering out the time but had slipped sideways in his studded chair. His eyes were almost closed.

It was likely that within another five minutes Rose would have been stripped entirely had not von Langsdorff chosen that moment to enter the room with Kurt at his side. Kurt was the first to see what was happening and with a cry he grabbed for a holstered revolver lying on a table just inside the door. Rose was now in the arms of Seegert and it was apparent that any shot from the gun might kill them both. But no one had seen what was happening except von Langsdorff, and as Kurt brought the barrel round the major knocked his arm up and the bullet crashed into the ceiling.

The roar of the shot in the confined space stopped everything abruptly and the silence was almost as loud as the preceding din. Rose stood in the centre of the officers, half-naked, flushed and excited. Then she saw von Langsdorff and her eyes became frightened.

Everyone stood quite still and then, as von Langsdorff moved, a path seemed to open for him and he walked slowly forward and stood in front of her. He hit her twice with his open right hand, once with the palm, the second with the back of his fingers, and each time the noise of the slaps came with almost the same violence as the revolver shot. 'If you wish to behave like an animal,' he said, smiling thinly at her, 'I will give you the opportunity.' He removed his tunic, wrapped it around her and carried her from the room under one arm as though she were a rolled-up rug.

Watch told Andrew that she made no effort to resist him. Even Kurt had appeared too stunned to intervene. By the time anyone glanced at the Baron he had slid half-way down the chair and was totally unconscious. No one saw Rose again.

On the other hand, Brock was much in evidence. He had turned into a man-hunter on a prodigious scale and spent all his time scouring the countryside for Hereros. Those he caught he brought back to the police post and to a final resting place in the lower branches of the camelthorn tree. Lily was no more. In a night of drunken debauch he had raffled her favours among a group of hardbitten cavalrymen. By the light of a full moon they had tried to teach her tent-pegging. She had fallen from the horse and broken her back.

At the mention of her name Andrew recalled the ghastly scene in the police post the last time he had seen Eva and he tried to explain what had really happened. She stopped him. 'You don't have to explain,' she said. 'I know what happened.'

During those slow, healing weeks in the mid-summer of 1905, the past, the time 'before the war', as it was now being called, seemed to recede into the mists of memory. He could hardly remember a time when he had sweated with jealousy over Eva. They now took their evening walks in the garden with the passionless ease of old friends. There was little emotion in either of them; it had all been spent.

By turns they filled in the gaps. Andrew told her what he could remember of his war and about the diary he had kept which was now buried in his saddlebags. He felt no desire to dig it out and she never asked if she could read it. She listened to his account of the Waterberg battle and the hunting down of starving Hereros and the final weeks of typhoid fever in the hospital at Okahandja with sympathy but without comment.

When he asked her, she told him about Matthew. Again her voice was expressionless, the result, it seemed, of iron self-discipline. About a week after the news of General von Trotha's Extermination Order had reached Falkenberg Matthew had left. He had told her there was something he had to do and had packed his wagon and gone in the night. She had not heard from him again.

'We were to have been married when the war was over,' she said.

'He'll be back,' Andrew said.

'Perhaps.'

It was plain that she did not care to discuss him any further and they let the matter drop.

The castle itself was in a state of decay. The moment every Herero became a target for a German rifle, the Baron's servants had fled into the hills, and some weeks later, when news reached Falkenberg that the Witbooi Hottentots in the south had risen against the Germans, most of the Hottentot servants, with the exception of the Baron's Orlam bodyguard, had looted what food they could and ridden away.

Andrew had heard about the Hottentot rising just before he had gone down with fever. At first he thought he might be sent to fight another campaign, but troops were now pouring into the Colony at a greater rate than at any time during the rising proper and there were more than enough to hunt the Hereros into the northern desert as well as to take on the Witboois in the south.

In the absence of the regular servants it had been Eva, with the aid of Watch, who had kept the castle going. Watch. . . . Andrew could remember the worried black face hovering over him when he awoke in the withdrawing room on that first day of his return. It had been Watch who had helped him along the corridors and put him to bed; Watch who had sponged his body and thrown away his clothes and fed him meat soup; and Watch who had muttered unceasingly about 'the Germans', using the word as another might use a particularly unpleasant expletive. Watch and Eva . . . between them they had seen the bones in Andrew's face slowly disappear under a new layer of flesh and the strength return to his muscles, but they had yet to see him smile and it would take more than a plate of soup to remove the look of hopelessness that lay behind his eyes.

In spite of the castle's decrepitude the one dominating presence in it remained: the Baron. Andrew had seen him on only two or three occasions since his return and those had been enough to convince him that von Steinberg's own private war was still in full swing. The Baron had moved away from the main rooms of the castle and no longer ate in the dining-room or held court in the withdrawing room. Instead he lived like some brooding Minotaur in his lair in the bowels of the building. The first time Andrew saw him was a day or two after his return. He was nearly knocked down as the four Orlam carriers padded down a corridor with the huge chair on their shoulders.

'*Achtung! Achtung!*' they shouted as they bobbed round a corner. Andrew flattened himself against the wall as the party surged past. He had time to glimpse the Baron, a fantastical figure in an olive-green cavalry jacket that was much too small for him. Its black facings were almost as green with age as the rest of it and the braiding hung down in moth-eaten strips. Andrew remembered the derelict uniforms hanging in an upstairs cupboard and realized where this one had come from. Around the Baron's waist was a cavalry sabre and his feet had been crammed into black leather cavalry boots.

'Halt !' he cried, seeing Andrew.

The swaying chair came to an abrupt stop.

'Good day, Excellency,' Andrew greeted him.

'Stand to attention when you speak to an officer.' Andrew automatically drew himself up.

'That's better. What news from the front, Sergeant ?'

Andrew was about to stroll forward and hold out his hand when he noticed an expression of tolerant amusement on Jonker's face and the barest shake of his head. He looked up at the Baron again, noticing this time the brandy bottle he held in his hand

and the heavy flush on his face. His eyes still had the vengeful look of a wounded buffalo but his mouth was slack and foolish-looking. Andrew realized that he was very, very drunk at ten o'clock in the morning.

'Good, Excellency. The news is good.'

'I told them! Steel, I said! The French have never stood up to steel!' He brought his hand up in salute, the carriers sprang into motion and the strange palanquin disappeared down the corridor.

When Andrew mentioned the meeting to Eva later in the day the first thing she said was, 'Did he recognize you?'

'No. He thought I was a sergeant in the Prussian Army, I think. He talked about the French.'

Apparently the collapse had not been sudden. According to Eva it had started a long time before Andrew's arrival and the war had only hastened a process already moving inexorably towards its conclusion.

'His drinking makes it worse,' she said. 'When Rose left he was so drunk he didn't miss her for three days. He still thinks she's only gone to Windhuk for a short holiday. Some days he's all right and others he's like this.'

She said it matter-of-factly and Andrew wondered at the courage needed for her to remain at Falkenberg and look after her father when everyone else had deserted.

For himself, he stayed on because he could think of nothing else to do. His guess about the cash for the horse sales had been correct. Whether or not the Army had paid for them, or whether Kurt had simply kept the money for himself he never knew; but there was nothing in his money-belt other than the marks he had earned as a mercenary and these did not amount to more than about fifty English pounds. Anyway, where was he to go and what was he to do? The war had left his thoughts strangely muddy, and the fever's legacy was depression and listlessness. He wanted to make no decisions. He knew that life itself would force action from him in the end and he was content to wait for that moment. In the meantime he and Eva lived the strangely gentle lives of two people convalescing in a remote sanatorium. In the mornings he would help with chores around the house; in the afternoons he slept in his cell-like room near the top of the castle; and in the evenings, after walking in the garden, he and Eva would sit down to a simple supper, followed by a game or two of draughts. Once he asked her to play for him and she raised the lid of the piano and showed him where a sabre cut had slashed the strings. 'They also poured beer into it,' she said, quietly.

From time to time he remembered his plans for her and cringed. He realized now how unthinkable it would have been to go to her with a denigratory tale about Southgate and expect anything from her but contempt, and he mentally thanked Brock for his excesses on that day which had prevented him. Looking back, he could hardly recognize himself as the same person; it was like peering into the past through the wrong end of the Baron's telescope.

How long he could have continued to exist like a pumpkin slowly ripening in the summer sun is speculative but in the event it was life, as he had expected, which forced itself upon him; life in the shape of nightmares.

In hospital at Okahandja he had suffered two or three nightmares of prodigious terror but they had not returned either in the hospital or when he first came back to Falkenberg. Now they attacked him again. They came in different forms, sometimes as phantasmagoric images without connection which burst into his subconscious like exploding lyddite, and sometimes as coherent narratives which contained a terrifying logical development. But whether incoherent or understandable many of the images were the same. He saw again the baby on the tip of the bayonet, the buck-springing Herero soldier shot through the head, the child gnawing at the decaying bone. In one dream he bent to pick her up and she changed into the snarling, spitting form of Bismarck, in others she simply dissolved into powder that blew away on the hot wind. But one image more than any other recurred : a figure standing alone at the lip of a water-pit, looking down at something formless lying half in and half out of the water. Slowly the thing in the water would begin to change until it became recognizable as himself. He would turn slowly, like some giant salamander, and stare up at the figure on the bank and see the death's head under the dusty *sudwester*, the skeleton fingers poking out from the ends of the torn sleeves, the bones of the feet in the broken boots, and he knew that this figure, too, was himself.

187

One night he woke up screaming to find Éva hunched over him. His naked body was slippery with sweat and her hands slid on his shoulders as she tried to hold him down. Seeing her face in the darkness, he felt an overwhelming sense of relief.

'What is it, Andrew? What's wrong?'

'Bad dream,' he said, after a moment.

'You sounded terrified. Here.' She brought him his towel from the back of a chair and he rubbed his face and chest. He could feel his heart hammering under the rib-cage. 'Better?' He nodded. 'It was about the war, wasn't it?'

'Yes.'

She did not tell him that this was not the first time she had heard the screams, nor that she had stood in the doorway three or four nights running and watched the terror take him, too frightened herself to wake him lest the sudden shock might harm him more than the dream. She lit the lamp and turned the wick down low.

'Do you want to talk about it?'

'I can't remember it now,' he said. 'It's gone.'

'You talked about your brother. You've never mentioned him before.'

He lay back on the bolster, drained and shaken. He thought of telling her what it meant. But he said, 'I have no brother.'

'Talking about things often helps. Why don't you go down and see the Reverend Kaufmann?'

He leant out of bed and lit a small cheroot from the lamp's flame, letting the heat at the top of the funnel singe the tobacco before he pulled on it.

'He's a good man, Andrew. I'm sure it would help.'

'Perhaps.'

They talked quietly for about an hour until his heart was beating normally again and the physical world had reasserted itself and blotted out the turmoil in his subconscious. She had been sitting on his bed and when she rose to go he found he had been holding her hand as a small boy would. There had been something unconscious and natural about the gesture.

The regularity and horror of the dreams began to affect him and he found that as the summer dusk crept into the castle corridors he would experience a growing unease, a vague apprehension that grew stronger as night fell, and he realized that he was

188

becoming frightened to go to sleep. So he changed his habits. He cat-napped during the day and lay reading on his bed at night. Sometimes he dozed and would wake with a start, grateful that the lamp was still lit and the corners of his small room were not in darkness. He drew further into himself, creating his own vacuum within the wider one in which the castle now existed.

But the castle was not the world and things were happening outside. The Hereros had been blown across the face of the desert like tumbleweed, scattering before the growing German forces. Except for a few groups of guerrilla fighters they had, in their search for water and food, split up into units of twos and threes. Brock seldom went out now without bringing back a pathetic starving group to the cells at the police post. Some of the men he hanged from the tree in the square, some he sent in long manacled lines, their women and children staggering alongside them, to the railway to be shipped Andrew knew not where.

One guerrilla band lived in the wild Tjirue Mountains, a tangled chain of hills that lay about forty kilometres from Falkenberg. And it was on these that Brock had fixed his ambitions. The destruction of a whole band would be an achievement of some significance, the result of which might mean promotion. But he needed more men. He wanted Andrew to bring the Baron's Orlams but Andrew had expressed an utter lack of interest and Brock knew that to approach the Baron himself would be hopeless.

It was said that this particular band had, in their desperate search for food, raided almost as far as Omaruru and Okahandja and Brock awaited the possibility of their arrival in Falkenberg with mounting impatience, for he had received a Maxim from the Army and it was now mounted on the tower of the police post. The next best thing to going out after them would be for them to come to him.

What gave him a special interest in this band was not only its nearness but also the fact that it was said largely to consist of the Baron's former servants. What plagued him was the thought that the terror in which they had held the Baron while working for him might even now keep them away, and if this was so it was possible that a military column might mop them up before Brock could get a chance.

Andrew did not believe this. It was easy for people who had

189

never fought the Hereros to denigrate them now they were refugees. Andrew knew differently.

But knowing did not overcome his lethargy. He never bothered to keep watch on the battlements now, leaving it to the Baron and his servants. He never even bothered to keep his rifle clean and ready. If they came, they came, and that would be that; he supposed he would have to fight; he was content to leave a decision until the time came.

Brock found his attitude inexplicable. 'My dear Herr Black, we must rid ourselves of these vermin. Berlin has said so.'

'Are you sure it was Berlin? As I understood it, the edict was von Trotha's.'

'It is an order and we must obey.'

Brock's conscientiousness had thinned him down somewhat, or perhaps it was the lack of Lily's company, but he still stank of body sweat and Andrew turned away from him. 'They may be your orders,' he said. 'Not mine.'

One night as he lay trying to fight off sleep he heard a dull crash somewhere below in the innards of the castle and his first thought was that Brock's wish had come true and the Hereros were attacking. His second was that he could not recall, at that moment, when he had last seen his rifle. There would be little point in looking for it now and instead he ran lightly down the twisting staircase towards the gun-room. He did not get far for he heard a second crash, this time much nearer, and realized it had come from the Baron's private apartments. He saw a slit of light under the Baron's door and knocked, but there was no response. He pushed and the door swung open. Whatever he had expected was nothing compared with reality. The room looked as though it had been savaged by a maddened rhino. The Baron was lying on his side, a pathetic figure in his ancient uniform, his head resting near the edge of a pool of vomit. His stertorous breathing thudded on the air. Before he had collapsed he had attacked the room physically as though each piece of furniture was an individual enemy. He had taken down the lances from the wall and used them with fearful energy on the splintered chairs and scarred sideboard. The portraits of his ancestors hung in ribbons, the carpet was gouged and ripped, the liquor decanters smashed against the dripping walls, the curtains torn and shredded. What particular battle this one represented in the old man's molten brain Andrew could not know, only that here again the Baron had lost.

Eva was bending over him and she looked up as Andrew opened the door. Two patches of anger burnt on her cheeks, giving dramatic colouring to her pale skin; her hair was plaited and hung down across her breast. He was momentarily breathtaken by a beauty he had never seen before.

'What do you want?' she said, and her voice was harsh with bitterness and shame. 'Why don't you leave us alone?'

Normally he would have approached such a situation with extreme distaste; it was untidy and dirty. But of the many changes the war had brought about in Andrew one of the most important was a relaxation of some of his most rigid conventions. He went forward and took the rag from her hand, dipped it in the basin of water which stood near the Baron's head and began to clean him up. He noticed that the skin colouring around the lips was less red than bright purple and he said, 'I don't like the look of him. He may have overdone it this time.'

'Oh God, I hope he has! No, I don't mean that. It's just that sometimes. . . .' The harshness had been replaced by a note of exhaustion.

'Help me to get him to bed,' Andrew said. 'We'll know in the morning.'

In the morning the Baron was much improved and two days later his palanquin could be seen once again on the battlements where he awaited an enemy that might never come.

For Andrew the results of that night were twofold. First, he could not get out of his mind the sight of Eva. Never before had he felt sexually drawn to her; his fantasy relationship had always been based on childlike innocence. But now his imagination saw her once more in her nightgown, bending over her father's recumbent form, and painted into the picture the swell of her breasts, the marks of the nipples on the flimsy material, the glittering, angry eyes. It was still fantasy, but this time the fantasy of an adult.

Secondly, as the days passed, each one drawing to its inevitable conclusion in fearful darkness where sleep and nightmares lay in wait, he grew more and more troubled and in the moments of depression he saw again the ruined room and began to wonder at the madness that had caused it. He began to see himself lying there in his own vomit, his energies spent in a futile attack on half-formed things that lurked far beyond vision. He began to worry about his own deterioration.

A week after the Baron's extravagance he found himself outside the mission. He had not made any positive decision to seek the Reverend Kaufmann's help. It had started when he had dug out of his saddlebags the diary he had kept. He had decided to read it carefully in case he came upon something hidden to him which could be causing the dreams. If he could discover it and, in a sense, show it to himself, familiarity might draw its poison, might give him back a sense of safety in which the nightmares would fade. But when he had brought out the school exercise book, now stained with dust and travel, he could not open it. He sat staring at it for a long time, then stuffed it into his pocket and left the castle, pretending to himself that a long walk in the veld would help. Instead he circled the village in the direction of the mission.

The building was in a state of massive decay. Part of the roof had fallen in and thatch was strewn down the centre aisle of the small church section. The wooden benches were thick with red dust and one of the windows was smashed. The little harmonium leant drunkenly against the wall and the music which had been piled next to it on a table now lay in scattered heaps. He bent to pick up one of the sheets and blew the dust off the title page. It was the chorale prelude '*Es ist ein' Ros' entsprungen*'. He dropped it onto the table and went forward.

The Reverend Kaufmann's rooms lay at the rear of the church, connected to the hall by a small door. Andrew knocked and a voice told him to enter.

The missionary was sitting in a cheap rocking-chair with his back to a window. In spite of the heat his shoulders were draped in a shawl. A big clasped Bible was on his knees and his hands and fingers trembled as they rested on the pages. His hair was almost completely white now and his face was grey; he appeared to be twenty years older than the last time Andrew had seen him.

The immediate warmth and welcome in his eyes faded

abruptly and Andrew realized that he must have been expecting Eva.

'Ah, Herr Black, back from the wars at last.'

'I've brought something for you to read,' Andrew said abruptly.

'I do very little reading these days except for this.' His fingers tapped the Bible.

'It's a diary of the war.'

'You mean a series of daily lists? "Killed so many Hereros today". Or "Found so many starving children today". Like that?'

'Not quite like that.' Andrew leant forward and put the exercise book on the Bible, but the priest made no move to pick it up.

'I've been expecting you,' he said. 'Eva has told me something of your troubles. Now you're searching for your panacea. The forgiveness of Christ on Calvary. It's just so much rubbish, isn't it, until you *need* it?'

'Will you read it?'

'Yes, for Eva's sake. Not for yours. That doesn't sound very pleasant, does it, coming from a priest. And it isn't. But I don't fool myself any longer. Self-deception is also a sin, Herr Black. If I am not what I might be or should be, you have the Baron to thank. If it hadn't been for him, or men like him, this war would never have begun. If it hadn't been for him my church would have been full of worshippers. If it hadn't been for him we would have lived here in peace. Why did he have to come here and corrupt an old priest so? Now fetch me my spectacles.'

There was hatred in his voice. In a sense the Baron had won his long campaign of attrition, for instead of emerging from his martyrdom into sainthood, the Reverend Kaufmann had become soured and bitter, his health gone, his congregation gone, all his work in tatters.

He opened the exercise book and began to read slowly, holding it close to his spectacles so the light from the window fell on it. Occasionally he would raise his eyes, but he said nothing. Half-way through, he suggested Andrew should make them a glass of black tea.

Watching him, Andrew was struck by another thought: the similarity, at least in one sense, between Kaufmann and the Baron. They were both trapped by their own creations, both living on

193

like animals in their lairs, neither willing to leave the battlefield to the other.

It was an hour before the priest closed the book. 'Well,' he said, 'what do you want me to say?' He held it out and took off his spectacles.

'I don't know,' Andrew said dully.

'I am not a Roman. I can't tell you to go away and say so many Hail Marys and tell you you're absolved and don't do it again. I'm glad I can't. You fought a brutal war and now you're sorry, is that it?'

'The war's over. Anyway, it wasn't my war.'

'It's over, is it? The battles might be over, but the bodies you see hanging in the square are not ghosts of the mind—they're real enough. No. Herr Black, your war, the sort of war you people understand, may be over, but our whole lives are only part of a war, a war against cruelty and oppression, a war against disease and ignorance. That's the war you should be fighting. You say to yourself, It was horrible for the Hereros while it lasted but it's over now, let's forget and forgive. But it's not we who have to do the forgiving. In a thousand years we shall not be forgiven for what we've done here . . . and what we are doing. Have you heard of Shark Island?'

He talked of concentration camps at Shark Island off Lüderitz and another on the beach at Swakopmund where dozens of starving Herero prisoners died each day, unable to withstand, in their weakened condition, the cold, moist climate. He described letters he had received from colleagues in missions throughout the country, letters filled with horror about what was happening to an already broken people, how women in spans of eight were yoked like animals to the shafts of Scotch-carts and made to pull heavy loads for anything up to ten kilometres. Some of those who collapsed from exhaustion were simply bayoneted where they lay.

As he spoke his voice grew stronger. He had collected the letters for a purpose. He was going to send them all to a Herr Erzberger in Germany, who was making a reputation by exposing Colonial scandals in the Reichstag.

'I won't be the only one,' he said. 'They write to him from every Colony. Now there is a sad fact, Herr Black! Not only from here, but from every Colony; the same stories of brutality.

194

What has happened to us? Where did we go wrong? There is an old Herero proverb which says, "Where my cattle have grazed is Hereroland." What right had we to come and change it? What right had we to come with our custom of parental chastisement? What right had the German to regard himself as master, *in loco parentis* to the native, to thrash him whenever he wished and for any reason whatsoever, without fear of punishment? Who gave us such rights? God? Bismarck? Even Bismarck knew our limitations. Once he wrote, "No success could be hoped for from transplanting the Prussian Government official and his bureaucratic system to Africa." And he was right, Herr Black, he was right. But it wasn't only the system. We wanted to build up on African soil a New Germany and create daughter states. We tried it here in South-West and the only things we've produced are one native rising after another. We tried to assume the functions of Providence and we're trying to exterminate a native race whom our own lack of wisdom has goaded into rebellion. Certainly we've succeeded in breaking up the native tribes, but we haven't succeeded in creating a New Germany, Herr Black, and we never shall.'

He paused and looked down at his trembling hands and suddenly the fire that had illuminated his words seemed to flicker and fade. After a while he said, without looking up. 'Now take your little book and go. I cannot help you. I no longer have the strength to shoulder another's guilt as well as my own.'

Andrew kept silent for a few moments, unwilling to accept the terrible finality of the answer.

'Won't you send it to Berlin?' he asked. 'You spoke of a man. . . .'

'No. What you've written is subjective. If we're to have any hope of a hearing, our evidence must be objective and everything must be corroborated.' He saw the misery in Andrew's eyes, began to speak again, then checked himself. 'I'm sorry,' he said, and it was obvious that the conversation was at an end.

Andrew wandered out into the crushing sunlight. He felt an overwhelming sense of grief and for the first time for many years was aware that tears were close behind his eyes. He had wanted the solace of confession, needed the excoriation of penitence, hoped for the peace of catharsis and all he had received was an implacable wall of hard fact. The grief that had risen so

195

quickly was caused by knowledge of what had happened during and before the war, things which he himself had caused and done, and the hopelessness that accompanied it was the perception that he would have to live with it, that there was no easy solace, no second time around.

He walked up through the square, hardly noticing the five new bodies that dangled from their ropes; his eyes misted over with self-pity.

Instead of going down to supper that evening he lay on his bed smoking. On his chest, unopened, rested the copy of *Through the Looking-glass* which his fingers had touched when he reburied his diary in the saddlebag. Now he picked it up, turned once more to the title page and its childlike handwriting, and re-read Matthew Edward Southgate's address: ' "Morgenster", Ronde-bosch, Cape Town, Cape of Good Hope, Cape Colony, South Africa, Southern Hemisphere, the Earth, the Universe'. It was all so innocent and redolent of the nursery and yet it was the find-ing of this book and the others in that strangely bereft cabin-trunk in the middle of the Kalahari that had started the chain of events which had placed him here on this bed in this castle at this time.

He began to think about Southgate, wondering if he had mis-judged him, if he had mistaken weakness for strength; wondering whether weakness and strength were really things that could be isolated in themselves and judged separately or whether they shaded into a more complex set of qualities too subtle for simple assessment. What would the Andrew of a year ago have said about the Andrew who now lay wakeful on his bed, too frightened to sleep, too full of self-pity, too lacking in dynamic to face the future? Was this not weakness far in excess of any he had en-countered before?

What, in fact, *was* he going to do? Could he simply drift on in a twilight, leaning on Eva's shoulder when he needed to? Abruptly he swung his legs off the bed, picked up the book and went in search of her.

He found her in a little sewing-room off the main corridor. She was darning a pair of his socks and he was struck by the in-timacy of the domestic scene. It was as though they had been married for years and years. Springing as it did from instantaneous nostalgia, there was a bitter-sweetness about such a thought which momentarily confused him with hope. He held out the book. 'I've got something for you,' he said. 'I've had it all this time without recalling it. I found it today and I think you should have it.'

She took it and looked at it with raised eyebrows. 'Don't you think I'm a little young for this?' she said, smiling at him and hoping for a smile in return.

'Look inside the cover.'

She turned the page and he noticed the blood leave her cheeks. She read the inscription and her eyes filled with tears and spilled down over her lower lashes onto her face. In that second he knew that he loved her, not idealistically, not as a figure to place on a pedestal, not as a mother-figure on which to lean, but with a painful simplicity that seemed to wrench his heart from his body. It was not like any feeling he had experienced before and he realized that this time he did not want her simply *because* Southgate had her. The weeks together had developed precisely the kind of feeling for which he had always longed.

'Do you miss him very much?'

'It's as though I'd lost an arm or a leg,' she said, more to herself than to him.

'I could cherish you,' he said, hope still fighting with reality.

She seemed not to hear. 'And it's lying out there somewhere—anywhere—but the ache remains. Do you think you can understand?'

'Aches pass. You'll see. We could. . . .'

At that moment they heard the first shot. Automatically they stopped talking and held their breaths, listening. It had been some distance away and might simply have meant Brock was taking a pot shot at a hyena. There came a second and a third, this time closer. Then the tearing sound of a Maxim. 'Christ!' Andrew said. 'They've come.' He stood as though unwilling to allow anything to intrude on the earlier moment. Then he took hold of himself. 'Find your father,' he said. 'See if you can keep him somewhere safe.'

Even as he spoke they heard the Baron's voice, '*Achtung! Achtung!*' There was a drumming of feet in the passageways as the Orlams ran for the chair. 'Stay here,' Andrew shouted. 'Keep

197

away from the windows.' He ran into the corridor. He saw a milling group of Hottentots at the far end, all clutching rifles; then the chair appeared from the deep stair-well, and the Baron swayed into view like some triumphant Roman emperor on his way to the Forum. He was holding his sabre in one hand and a rifle in the other. He saw Andrew and recognized him. 'Black! See to the ammunition!' Andrew remembered, a long time ago, that in the Baron's plans for the defence of the castle he had been placed in charge of the gun-room. Now, without questioning the order, he shouted for Watch and they plunged down the narrow winding stair. As he did so he could hear the deep thud, thud, thud of Martini-Henrys close by the ramparts.

He flung open the the gun-room door, letting Watch go first, with the lamp. Everything was as he'd left it, the neatly labelled boxes of ammunition on their shelves, the rifles in their racks along the wall. He stopped and looked at them more closely. He didn't remember these guns. He crossed to the racks and pulled out an old muzzle-loader. The barrel was split and the stock had been bound with copper wire. He flung it down and pulled out an army weapon; the bolt was missing. Hastily he examined all the rifles. Not one of them was whole; not one had been there almost a year ago. These guns were totally useless. He ran to the ammunition boxes, picked one up and breathed a sigh of relief when he felt its weight. But when he opened it he found a row of cartridges on top and only loose stones beneath. Each box was the same. Momentarily bewildered, he stood holding one of the boxes. What in Christ's name was going on? He was certain they had been full. He tried to recall the scene as well as he could. Yes, he'd checked every box and there on the side was his hand-writing to prove it. How. . . ? And then he remembered the foot-steps in the corridor and the figure that had flitted round a corner and he knew what had happened. The place had been plundered under their noses. Old, useless weapons had replaced the first-class rifles he'd cleaned, and gravel and small stones had replaced the ammunition. And he remembered the figure in the garden passing something over the wall. He had assumed that it was stolen food; it had been a parcel of ammunition.

He flung the pebbles out of one box and told Watch to fill it with what cartridges were left and take it up to the battlements. Then he raced up the stairs to his own quarters, found the

Jeffries and his bandolier and jumped the winding stairs three at a time. He burst out into the starlit night and the first thing he saw was a fire. The flames were on the roof of Sauermann & Fricke and by their light he could make out flitting figures in the village. The firing had grown more intense and the hammering of the Maxim was a brittle counterpoint to the steady thud of heavy rifles. He flung himself down at a loophole and began to take stock of the situation. To his right he could see the forms of the Orlams as they lay in the embrasures. Every now and then, as one of them found a target, he would hear the sharp crack of a rifle. Further along he saw the massive outlines of the Baron's chair. Von Steinberg was resting the barrel of a heavy rifle on the top of his telescope stand. It enabled him to swing the barrel in an arc of about forty-five degrees and every now and then Andrew saw him jerk backwards with the recoil. The gun's boom was unmistakable and sounded as though it might be a .550 or a .600, perhaps even double-barrelled, an elephant gun.

Now he began to see the efficacy of the Baron's defensive planning. The bush which had been cut down had not grown back and the area was open to cross-fire from the castle and the police post. But the theory, as far as he could remember it, was that either the police post or the castle or both were to be targets for the Hereros, and this did not seem to be the present situation. As he watched the muzzle flashes of the attackers' rifles it became apparent that the real interest centred on the store, and the firing directed at the castle and at the fort was no more than an attempt to pin down the defenders. Andrew fired off one or two shots to show willing, then lay with his cheek to the stock trying to see some coherent plan of campaign. Occasionally a bullet whined overhead or struck sparks from the sandstone buttresses.

There seemed to be only one possible explanation. Since no one had heard of any other group of Hereros closer than the Tjirue Mountains it was safe to assume that these were they. Since most of them had once worked at Falkenberg they would be familiar with the target area. Assuming they had stripped the Baron's arsenal, it was likely that the castle would be relatively safe since there was nothing in it they required. What they wanted was food and the place to find it was the store.

It was clear that his presence on the ramparts was unnecessary and he went down to see how Eva was. The little sewing-room was empty. He went along the corridors to her room, but that was empty too. She was not in the Baron's apartments or in the great darkened kitchen where the few remaining servants crouched in corners, their frightened faces lit by wide saucer eyes. 'It's all right,' he said. 'You have nothing to fear.' He might have saved his breath for all the comfort they took. They had not seen Miss Eva either. He began to feel worried. He ran back along the corridor, thinking she might be watching the skirmish from the withdrawing room. 'Eva?' he called, standing with his hand on the Baron's throne-chair. But the huge shadowy room was empty. As he turned, his foot crunched on something brittle. Glass. He went over to the windows and found a pane had been smashed and glass was strewn across the rug. He assumed it had been caused by a spent bullet until his foot again touched something unfamiliar. This time it was a stone about half the size of a man's fist. He stood for a moment examining it but it was simply a stone like ten million others around the castle. He crossed to the window and pitched it into the night. A stone meant that someone had got into the garden. He slipped the safety on the Jeffries and crossed softly to the door. In doing so he had to pass the piano and he noticed something lying on the shiny top. It was the copy of *Through the Looking-glass*; by its side was a piece of torn brown paper. Badly frightened now, he crouched below the line of the windows, keeping the piano between himself and a possible rifle shot, and lit a match. The note was only three or four lines long. It was addressed to no one; nor was it signed. It read simply : 'Keep away from the windows. They have promised the castle will not be attacked. You have nothing to fear as long as you stay inside.'

At first he thought it might have come from Brock, but the sergeant was far too busy to detach one of his men to act as a runner and, anyway, how would he know what 'they' had promised? Could it be Kaufmann? But the same would apply. He shoved the note into his pocket and ran out into the main hall; the front door was ajar. He opened it wider. 'Eva!' he shouted. He stood uncertainly for a moment, waiting for a reply that did not come, and then he slipped out under the pepper trees and began to search the garden by the walls. His soft skin shoes made almost no sound on the loose gravel as he circled the outer bailey by the vegetable garden and then dropped down past the fig-trees to the central path. He kept clear of open spaces and flitted like a nightbird from the cover of one cypress tree to the next. Half-way along, he thought he heard a slight sound. He stopped and turned and a shadow detached itself from the deeper shadow of the tree. It came towards him. 'Matthew!' a voice whispered. 'Matthew, I'm here.' He saw the look on her face as she came towards him, excited, exultant, and he knew then precisely how matters stood with her. 'It's me—*Andrew*,' he said, gripping her above the elbows and watching, with a kind of bitter satisfaction, the light go out of her eyes and the excitement fade.

'He's here!' she cried, unwilling to believe that the figure which had come so stealthily to their former meeting place was not that of Matthew.

'How do you know?'

'He wrote a note. He threw it through the window.'

'I've read it. There's no signature.'

'Do you think I don't know his writing!'

'What the hell's he doing here then?' As he put the question the answer was beginning to form in his mind : he could see again the meeting with Joseph in this same garden, and there was the 'thing' Matthew had told Eva he had to do. Even speculating, the thought was fantastic. But what else was there?

'Come on,' he said. 'You're going back to the house.'

'No. We must find him!'

'It's not safe here!'

She struggled briefly, crying softly, and then she allowed Andrew to lead her back to the castle. He sat with her in the sewing-room for a long time, neither of them speaking. The firing was becoming more sporadic now and minutes went by without the sound of a shot. The roof of Sauermann & Fricke had fallen in and the shop was smouldering sullenly. It was possible that the Hereros had taken what they wanted and gone, that the shots he heard were defenders firing at shadows. After a while he made a pot of coffee and brought her a cup. Her face was gaunt and old and her eyes were red from crying. 'I've waited and waited,' she said. 'I've wanted him to come, to take me away from this. Any-where, it didn't matter.' There was a note of such utter despair in her voice that he realized her whole existence had been pinned on this one hope, that she hadn't stayed on at the castle to look after her father, she had stayed because this was the one place Southgate could find her. All her days had been spent in waiting.

By dawn the firing had ceased altogether. He went out into the cool morning air expecting to see great changes, but the garden was as it had been the day before. He opened the gate in the outer bailey and carefully made his way down to the village, moving from one piece of cover to the next, but no one fired at him; it wasn't so much the Hereros of whom he was afraid, for he was certain they had long since gone; what he feared was a bullet either from the castle or the fort.

Sauermann & Fricke was a ruin. It had been completely gutted and greasy smoke was still rising sluggishly from the collapsed roof. The bodies of the hanged Hereros were no longer suspended from the branches of the tree but lay in two separate heaps near the ammunition boxes. It seemed as though an attempt had been made to carry them away but that it had had to be given up in the face of the machine-gun. Except for the police post the village was now a complete wreck. He thought that as the years passed and the wind blew and the rain fell it would slowly decay even further until eventually grass would grow over it and it would cease to exist.

Away to his right he heard the rumble of thunder and he looked up to see great purple thunderheads. A summer storm was on its way. As he turned to go back to the castle he felt the first huge drops of rain on his head.

'Herr Black! A moment!' Brock came hurrying out of the fort, his baby-waddle more pronounced with the speed of movement. 'Are you all right at the castle? Are there any casualties?'

Andrew allowed him to catch up. 'Not that I know of.'

'Good. Good. We have none either. What a night! I tell you, Herr Black, there must have been a hundred of them, perhaps more!' There was no mistaking the post-battle euphoria.

'A hundred?' Andrew asked dryly.

'At least! And only four of us. Myself and three troopers. I tell you, for a moment it was touch and go.'

'Why? Did they attack the fort?'

'Of course! Didn't you see?'

'I thought it was the store.'

'Secondary target,' Brock said, tossing the phrase off with an attempt at a Staff Officer's aplomb.

202

'Ah.'

'We must have killed a dozen or twenty. Look, there's one!'
The corpse lay on the far side of the square and they walked
over to it. Brock turned it over with his boot and Andrew looked
down at old Februarie. A burst of machine-gun fire was stitched
across his chest. Heavy raindrops formed runnels in the dust on
his face.

'Do you know him?' Brock said, his eyes shining with victory.

'He worked for the Baron.' He looked about but could see no
further evidence to support Brock's claim of casualties.

'God in Heaven!' Brock burst out. 'I nearly forgot. You know
your friend, the one who lived at the castle? Southgate. I saw
him here, right here!' In spite of his excitement Andrew could
see a shrewd look in his eyes.

'Don't you think we should get out of this rain.' He turned
again towards the castle, hurrying slightly. 'Here? What do you
mean? What was he doing here? What did he want?'

'What do you think he wanted?'

'I wouldn't be asking if I knew.'

'He was their leader, Black! That's what he was doing here!'
Andrew did not fail to register the use of his surname.

'Rubbish!' he said. 'You imagined seeing him just as you
imagined twenty or thirty Hereros were a small army. There never
were a hundred here last night and you know it. And twelve or
twenty casualties, for Christ's sake! One old man!'

'I think you forget who I am.'

Andrew nodded. 'Sometimes I have a hard time remembering.'

'Come with me and I'll prove it.'

They hurried across the square to the fort. The rain was falling
in long streaks that seemed to come separately across the veld and
could be seen at a great distance.

Brock led him to one of the cells and an orderly unlocked the
door. Inside Andrew saw a Herero prisoner. He was manacled to
a ring-bolt fixed in the wall and one side of his body was crisp
with dried blood. 'We took him last night,' Brock said. 'One of
my men wounded him and instead of crawling away he came
right towards us. Have you asked him?'

The orderly prodded a naked black thigh with one of the huge
cell keys as though it were a joint of meat. The body swayed

slightly, causing the slack head to move from side to side where the bearded chin touched the chest. 'He's finished, sir.'

'He can't be dead!' Brock stepped forward and kicked the prisoner just above the ankle. Andrew looked at him with disgust, reminded of the gratuitous kick he had aimed at the baboon, and he realized that Brock had meant what he said; for him there was no difference between the species. The kick started the body swaying more violently, but there was still no sign of life. 'Damn him!' Brock said, wiping the rain from his face. 'But we'll find Southgate without him. I'm not worried.'

Just then the body swung slightly more to the left and Andrew was able to see the face. He was looking at Joseph. But at the same time he was seeing someone else. Perhaps it was the angle, or the dimness of the light, perhaps even the repose which death had cast on the features, for as he looked at the man he saw beyond the smallpox craters to the skin and bone beneath. He realized in that instant what had been nagging at his memory for so long : Joseph was Kaneena. It came back to him as a fully etched portrait superimposed on his mind and he remembered the Herero refugees in Bechuanaland and recalled, right up on the Okavango Marshes, the emaciated figure of their leader who had come to plead for sanctuary. Joseph and Kaneena were one, and now he was dead.

Unconsciously, Andrew stepped forward and looked more closely, seeing the arm shattered above the elbow where the bullet had struck.

'You know him?'

He shrugged. 'I think he worked at the castle.'

'Well, we'll string him up with the rest,' Brock said, moving towards the door.

For a moment Andrew was left alone in the cell and in that moment Kaneena opened his eyes. He looked directly at Andrew. The shock caused him to step backwards. He opened his mouth and closed it. There was no appeal in Kaneena's eyes, no fear, no regret. He looked steadily at Andrew for several seconds and then his eyes closed again as though two small shutters had been dropped. Andrew turned away. 'He's dead all right,' he said, following Brock from the cell.

'All right, bring him. We'll tie them to the wall.'

There was nothing he could do to stop them. They brought

204

ropes from a room at the end of the cell block and began to string up the bodies that had been cut down from the tree. Then they fetched old Februarie, and finally they carried Kaneena from his cell.

'Where must the ropes go?' one of the troopers asked. 'Here?' He pointed to his throat.

Brock thought for a moment. 'They'll rot too quickly and drop. Put them around the chest.' He turned to Andrew. 'I'll make this a warning they'll never forget.'

Ropes were looped around the chests and under the arms, and each body was swung out to hang from the embrasures. Andrew watched as they lowered Kaneena into place, wondering how soon he could get to him, how long he would last. The rain had stopped and the air was cool. In the hot sun he would have been dead inside an hour.

When they had finished Brock crossed to Andrew. 'I've had my suspicion about Southgate for a long time,' he said. 'How was it he was able to carry freight without ever being attacked? If we catch him that's where he'll hang.' He pointed to the row of corpses.

'We?'

'I'm ordering you to come with me. We'll take the Baron's Orlams. On horseback they'll have no chance against us.'

'I don't take orders from you, Brock. And you'll never get the Orlams.'

'We'll see about that. I'll speak to the Baron.'

As they walked up to the castle the rain came down again, making the square a bog. Neither spoke. Andrew's mind was at a fever pitch of impatience but he knew it would be impossible to act yet. There were probably half a dozen troopers around the post. He desperately probed various possibilities, trying first to see a pattern and then a course of action. He knew one thing; no matter what happened he was not riding with Brock. If he did he could never face Eva again, and in spite of what had happened it was vital to him that he did not lose her respect, affection, whatever it was, a second time. That, at least, was clear.

The scene on the battlements was precisely as he had left it the night before, as though all action had been suspended by his absence. The Orlams lay at the firing slits; the Baron sat majestically in his chair.

'Excellency,' Brock began. The Baron paid no attention. He was sighting along the heavy rifle, seeming to expect at any moment to see one of the raiders.

'Excellency. . . .' Brock touched him on the shoulder. Slowly the Baron moved. He leant forward against the rifle; the telescope stand on which it was balanced grated on the stone and canted to one side. He toppled forward and lay with head and arms lolling over the rampart. His rifle fell clear and they heard it rattle on the cliffs below. They examined him carefully, but there was not a mark on his body. By the stiffness of his limbs it appeared he must have died during the night.

'Well,' Brock said, the satisfaction apparent in his voice. 'Now I'm in charge.' He looked up at Andrew. 'I want you and these men saddled up and ready to ride at dusk. Do I make myself clear?'

'Perfectly.'

Jonker and Kraai, the Baron's two body-servants, tossed the last few clods of newly turned red earth onto the grave and patted the mound with the backs of their spades. They stood for a moment, uncertain whether their own part in the burial was over, and expressions of relief passed over their faces as Andrew indicated that they should leave the place. Only three figures were now left standing by the grave: Andrew, Eva and the Reverend Kaufmann. Around them the thunder still rumbled in the slate-grey clouds and the wind was cool, but the late summer storm had passed away to the east and the ground was drying rapidly. It was noon; by five or six o'clock in the afternoon there would be almost nothing left of the moisture that had soaked the garden. Some late desert flowers might give a show of colour for a few days but that would be all, and since Andrew would not be there to see them the thought did not affect him much.

They had done their duty. Dry eyed, stony faced and without emotion they had laid the Baron to rest. In a flat, expressionless voice the Reverend Kaufmann had read the burial service; mechanically Eva had placed a wreath of everlastings on the finished grave. Four of the Orlams had lowered the large packing-case into the ground and half a dozen others had fired a ragged salute over it as it lay there, cheap and glaring in the grey morn-

206

ing. That had been all. No tear had been shed, no expression of sympathy had been offered. They had done their duty.

Covertly Andrew watched the missionary as he read the service. There was no forgiveness in his tone, no weakening of his hate. In a sense Andrew was satisfied. Death had changed nothing. If they had expected some show of emotion from the Orlams they were disappointed. Not even the Baron's faithful servants seemed sad to see him go.

Andrew stood over the grave for a few more seconds then abruptly turned away towards the castle. 'Watch!' he shouted as he entered the hall. 'Where are you?'

During the service his half-formed thoughts had grouped themselves into a plan of action. Speed was the essential. If he didn't move fast enough Kaneena would be dead and without Kaneena it would take him longer to find Matthew. Nor did he want to see Eva again. He did not want his resolve shaken by the despair in her eyes, nor his own yearning to stay with her and share that despair. Nor did he want to see the Reverend Kaufmann, to explain what he was about to do when he could hardly explain it to himself. He did not want to see that face melt into softness and compassion. They had stood by the grave like people of iron and he needed that resolution.

He gave instructions to Watch. He was to see that Miss Eva packed her belongings, not too many, and he was to put her in the wagon. Then he was to go down to the mission and duplicate the procedure with the missionary. He was not to take no for an answer. He was then to go with them to the halt at Brakwater and they were to take the train to Windhuk, all three of them. Andrew handed him enough money for the fares. At Windhuk they were to go to the main Rhenish Mission and wait. Did Watch understand?

The old Nyasa nodded his head gloomily. 'And the Captain?'

'There's something I've to see to first. When I've finished I'll fetch you in Windhuk. Understand?'

'I go with the Captain,' Watch said.

'You go where you're told.'

'Too much,' Watch muttered. 'Too much.'

Half an hour later Andrew lay on the ramparts of Falkenberg, within feet of where they had found the dead Baron. He was hidden by the rise of the wall. Below him he could see Duke, loaded and ready for the journey. He was taking almost nothing, knowing that with luck the horse would be bearing a double weight. He let his eyes rove over the village for the last time, finally resting on the police post. The bodies still hung there but for the moment he was less interested in them than the courtyard. It was devoid of humanity. In the centre was the corrugated iron well-cover. He lifted the Jeffries and took careful aim, squeezing the trigger until he felt it begin to bite. He held the sights steady and fired. The heavy-grained bullet struck the tin and carommed off it with a loud whang. He fired two more shots in rapid succession then he sprinted along the wall, holding himself below the ramparts, and threw himself down the stairs.

As he ran out of the front door he could hear shouts from the fort. He sprinted down the hill. Brock and four of his men were erupting from the gate.

'Up there!' Andrew shouted, pointing to the far rim of the Falkenberg. 'Two of them! You go that way, I'll go round here!'

The pattern of action was already so advanced that in its context Brock did not seem to realize that it was Andrew and not he who was giving the orders. 'All right!' he yelled, and they disappeared around the far side of the castle's outer bailey.

Andrew ran for the horse. He knew that at least two men would have been left at the post and he was right. They crouched low over the Maxim. He galloped towards them and pulled Duke up harshly under the wall. 'The mission!' he shouted. 'They're attacking the mission!'

In the confusion the two troopers acted precisely as he had hoped. They lifted the machine-gun and staggered with it to the far corner of the fort where they had a clear field of fire towards the mission. In a matter of seconds he was standing up in the saddle, slashing the rope around Kaneena's chest. He lowered him onto the saddle. Less than five minutes after he had fired the original shots he was spurring the stallion into a gallop around the far side of the Falkenberg, hanging on to Kaneena's body and hoping with every second that life had not finally left him.

But he could not stop to find out and it was only when he saw the sweaty foam on Duke's shoulders and heard the labouring grunt of his breathing that he realized they would founder if he pressed the stallion too hard.

As the Falkenberg faded into the heat haze behind him he

began to feel a sudden sense of release. He knew it would take Brock hours to search every boulder and outcrop for attackers that were not there; nor would the machine-gun party move until Brock returned to the post. When he did it wouldn't take him more than a few minutes to understand what had caused the confusion, but that was in the future. And even when he did, things would not be easy for him. The last thing Andrew had done was to send the Orlams to the huts, allowing each man to take two bottles of brandy from the Baron's cellar. By the time Brock got to them they would be drunk past all caring.

He realized what it was that had given him this sudden sense of freedom : he was making decisions again. They might be the wrong ones, but they were decisions. For most of his adult life he had had to make a whole series of decisions each day, some trivial, some important. For the first time he realized how vital these simple acts were to his make-up. He could not, after all, live in a vacuum. What was not apparent to him was that now he was concerned with other people; this was something new.

About eight kilometres from Falkenberg he turned Duke up the side of a small hillock and searched the horizon behind him with the prismatic glasses. The plain stretched out on all sides and in the distance he could make out the dark line of the Tjirue Mountains. Then, and only then, he dismounted and lowered Kaneena to the ground. He began to bathe his face with water. After a few moments the eyes flickered open.

'Good,' Andrew said. 'Can you hear me?'

The other nodded. His good hand went automatically to his chest and began to rub at the livid weals which the rope had caused.

'We're going to find Matthew Southgate. And you must help. If we don't get to him first, Sergeant Brock will.' Andrew held out the water-bottle. 'Drink,' he said. 'Take as much as you want.'

He helped Kaneena on to the crupper and held him upright while he mounted. 'Right,' he said as he urged Duke forward. 'All you've got to do is stay alive until we get there.'

'I can offer you coffee,' Matthew Southgate said. 'It's one of the few commodities we did manage to get. Can you imagine anything more useless than coffee?'

Andrew was sitting on one side of a small open fire watching him make the coffee in a blackened fruit tin. He bent down and blew on the coals. The flames sprang up and for the first time since he had reached the Herero encampment that evening Andrew was able to see his face clearly—and he was shocked. It looked like an animal's face, fringed by coarse and matted hair, the jaw-bone angular and sharp, the eyes deep and glittering in their sockets. His clothes were in shreds and from what Andrew could see in the flickering light his wrists and ankles were as thin as a child's.

'There's no sugar or milk,' Matthew continued, 'but you couldn't expect that.' The voice, too, had changed. It was hoarse, and as bitter as the mixture of coffee and chicory he was brewing.

'Half a dozen bags of mealies, some tinned food and coffee—oh, yes, and a packet of digestive biscuits. Not very much for a well-planned raid, was it? Not very much on which to feed more than two hundred people. Not very much when you weigh it against four dead men.'

As they waited for the coffee to boil Andrew looked around at the pinpoints of light in the blackness of the defile which marked the other fires. The Hereros were all around him and he could hear their snufflings and voices as they settled down to sleep. He saw one of the guards pass close by the fire. He was the one who had brought Andrew and Kaneena to Matthew, and Andrew remembered how much noise he'd had to make to attract attention. He had done so purposely; he did not want to be shot by mistake. But Brock wasn't going to arrive with a song on his lips and his banners waving high. The Orlams would be in the middle of this camp before anyone knew it and if they went to work with their knives half would be dead in their places without knowing how they died. He estimated that Brock would ride through the night, rest up during the heat of the day, then attack the following night.

He accepted his coffee in what had once been a condensed-milk tin and sipped at the smoking surface. It was hot and smelt of wood ash and charcoal.

If they were attacked these people would simply fold up like wet sacking. He had noticed how terrified they seemed when he was brought into the encampment—terrified of one man! What would they do when the firing started? He knew what they'd do: run. Which was precisely what Brock wanted. Then he could ride after them at his leisure and pick them off one by one, starting with the women and children who would not be able to run far or fast, and ending with the strongest of the men. Natural selection, nature's way.

Matthew poured a second cup and moved out of the firelight to bend over a form that lay in the shadows. Andrew watched as he carefully raised Kaneena's head and helped him to take coffee. Kaneena. It was strange, he thought again, that he had never been able to see beyond the smallpox craters on the face of Joseph, the gardener, to the features below. Perhaps it was because one never did look closely at a black face.

They had inspected Kaneena's arm soon after they had arrived. The bone was splintered and pieces of it stuck out through the skin. Andrew had tried to fit the pieces back into some sort of pattern and then had splinted and bound the arm. All the time Kaneena had remained conscious, staring at him. They both knew that the arm would never set properly, if it ever set at all.

'We'd have got a lot more if the roof hadn't come down,' Matthew said, coming back to the fire. He seemed obsessed by the raid on Falkenberg.

After a long pause he looked up and Andrew could see the haggard expression on his face. 'How could I help it! How could I stop them? They're starving, they've been hunted like animals. Half of them will never recover! How could I have said, "Don't go there . . . leave the food where it is." Do you think I could have reasonably said that to them? I made them promise. Not the castle or the mission. I knew she'd be in one or other. I made Kaneena swear by all their old Gods. What else could I do?'

'She understands.'

'No one understands!'

'You'll have to believe me.'

'Why should I? Why should I believe anyone?'

'But that's why I've come. There's nothing more you can do. I've come to take you to her. She'll be waiting at the Rhenish Mission in Windhuk.'

Matthew stared at him for a moment, then said very slowly,

211

spacing his words: 'You've come to take me away? Who do you think you are? God?'

'Why the hell d'you think I troubled?'

'I don't know. Don't you understand anything? There's no question of me leaving them.'

'Listen, Brock will be here within twenty-four hours with his own and the Baron's men. They're on horseback; they'll cut you to pieces. They'll probably bring the Maxim.'

'And you suggest that I run?'

'I'm suggesting you do the only sensible thing. This is the *end*! It's finished, kaput, the war's over.'

'Your war may be over, mine's not,' Matthew said, savagely.

'Think of Eva, then. She wants you, can you understand that? She wants you and she's going to have you.' The sadly satisfying picture in Andrew's mind of reuniting Matthew with Eva, the dream of unspoken words—'There, you wanted him and I have brought him to you'—was fading, and he felt irritation turn to resentment. It had seemed hazardous, but essentially simple: he would ride to the Tjirue Mountains, collect Southgate, make a wide detour to the railway and take him, like some special treasure, to lay at Eva's feet. Now this.

Matthew threw the coffee-grounds onto the sand and shifted his position. After a moment he spoke again and his voice was less harsh.

'I'm obliged to you, but it's no use. As far as I'm concerned there can be no such thing as private happiness in the midst of public grief. It may be possible for you, it isn't for me.'

'You sound as if you despise happiness.'

'On the contrary.'

'Then you despise me.'

He shook his head. 'Words like despise don't mean anything any more. A crime has been committed; you as a policeman should understand that. It's a crime on a massive scale. What went before is insignificant. What comes after is important. What I did to Chik and what you did to me only have reality in terms of what can be done now. Otherwise they remain like petrified tumours in the mind. Perhaps they'll remain like that forever; perhaps one can chip away at them until they diminish in proportion so one can live with them. I don't know.' He rubbed his hand wearily over his face. 'I used to think of Chik a lot.

Now I don't. I'm trying not to believe this is only a matter of atonement. I want to believe it's something even more important than that.'

'I understand part of that because something similar has happened to me. But you've got to be a realist. As you've said yourself, this band of yours has acted like a magnet to every Herero man, woman and child on the run. You've fed them as best you could. You've done your duty. Now it's time to look after yourself. Tell these people what's going to happen. Let them split up again into small bands—they're a hell of a lot safer that way than cooped up here where a machine-gun can mow them down.'

'Where are they to go?'

'That's *their* business. Christ, why can't you see that!'

'Let me tell you a story. When you turned us back into German territory did you expect any of us to live? No, don't answer that, I don't want to know. I suppose if you'd known there was small-pox you might have acted differently.'

'Smallpox!'

'The man you threw into the water-pit had smallpox. So did one or two others. I wasn't sure at the time, but I tried to warn you. Anyway, that's not the point. What I'm saying is that we started that journey with smallpox among us. So we didn't go into the Sand Veld but waited until you were on your way and then turned south to the well at Rietfontein. Some of the refugees had had smallpox before so they were immune, and I had been inoculated; so we nursed the others. There wasn't much we could do. They were weak from hunger and they died like flies. As they died we burnt the bodies. A fortnight after we reached Rietfontein we had to keep the fires burning night and day, and all the time the water was getting lower in the pit. One day there was nothing but mud left and we got ready to move to another pit south-west of there. It was then that I got sick. Malaria. They could have gone on and left me but they didn't. They stayed for another week digging in the pit and squeezing the water from the mud until my crisis had passed, and then we went on. Now let me make the point : they *knew* it was because of me they'd been turned out of Bechuanaland; they *knew* that if I hadn't been there they would have been allowed to settle in a friendly country—and yet they stayed. And now you want me

213

to say, "Good-bye, the war's over." I'm telling you it can't be done.'

Andrew was tempted to give him the real reason why he had turned the Hereros out of British territory but something held him back; in any case, it was better for Matthew to believe what he did. 'And then?' he prompted.

'And then we came here. What was left of us. You know the rest.'

'You knew that Joseph Kaneena was taking work at the castle.'

'Of course. We had to find out its strength. We didn't want any part in the war. What we hoped to do was *exist*. We'd fought our war at the Rietfontein well and we were tired. But there was the question of food. The war helped us there. For every three wagon loads I fetched from the railway, one went to these people. There were only a handful then and it was easy; now there must be nearly three hundred. That's why we had to come out at last and attack.'

'So it was your people who stripped the Baron's armoury.'

Matthew nodded. 'How could I say no? How can you tell a dying race that one German woman is more precious than everything else on the face of the earth, when everyone here knows that a cupful of water and a handful of mealies are almost more precious than life itself?'

Andrew smoked in silence for a while, then said, 'What are you proposing, to stay and fight?'

'We'd never stand a chance against a machine-gun.'

'Well?'

'We'll go east. Try for Bechuanaland again. I'm told the British have settled nearly 5,000 Hereros at Lake Ngami; some even got their cattle through.'

'Across the Sand Veld! You must be insane.'

'Probably, but there's no other way. We'll go at first light.'

Andrew was unable to sleep that night. He lay on his kaross hearing the muffled sounds of the sleeping Hereros all around him. Occasionally a guard changed his station, or someone picked his way past the smouldering embers of a fire to urinate outside the perimeter of the camp. He knew one thing: Matthew Southgate was incapable of leading these people through the Sand Veld to safety.

He felt a wave of self-pity engulf him, for it was equally clear what had to be done. What, he wondered bitterly, had happened to that time when decisions were a means of making life easier? Now they seemed merely to confuse him, causing him to flounder in an area of morality of which he had no experience.

On some maps it is called the Sand Veld, on others the Omaheke Desert. On all maps it is simply an empty space. It lies in the north-west of the Kalahari, spreading out on either side of the border between German South-West and Bechuanaland. It is a desert within a desert, a private place of sand and scrub. No one lives there, no one goes there unless they're desperate.

On a day in March 1905, a fragment of the shattered Herero nation came out of hiding in the Tjirue Mountains and entered its western fringe. They were making for Lake Ngami in the Bechuanaland Protectorate. It would have been easier if they had circled the Omaheke either north or south, travelling from one water-pit to the next, but because of German patrols this was impossible. Their direction was through the bitter heart of the Omaheke to the Lake, more than four hundred kilometres away.

'Keep them tight! Keep them tight! Don't let them string out.' Andrew's voice was hoarse and weary. He had shouted this order hundreds of times in the past week without much permanent success. Nothing would suit Brock more than a long, straggling line of Hereros strung out over the desert for half a mile or a mile. All he'd have to do would be to ride up the line and by the time he reached the end there'd be no one left. They had to keep bunched. This way they could form up in a hollow square and use the Baron's guns to the best advantage.

But it was asking too much of them. How could you ask women with babies to keep up a pace which would log about twenty kilometres every twenty-four hours—for this was the pace he had set them. They had to move quickly or Brock would be up with them—they had already seen his fires—but moving quickly meant death from exhaustion. Either way death stared them in the face, but if Brock caught them now they would all die; the other way some of them, the stronger, might just battle through.

Andrew kept remembering the maxim he had lived by in the Kalahari : don't fight the desert let it fight for you. So he had been using desert tactics. His plan was to draw Brock further and further into the Omaheke, allowing him to believe he was closing the gap; then Andrew would drive the Hereros forward during the daytime when Brock would least expect it and the gap would widen again. In this way he hoped Brock would use up his water supply and be forced to turn back. One thing was clear to the simplest intelligence : Brock had to water his horses every day while the Hereros had no animals with them except Duke.

If Brock ever caught up with them Andrew knew that the mounted Orlams, with their greater mobility, would tear the heart out of the refugees within an hour.

Whenever they reached any sort of grazing he set it alight. He remembered Walter talking about a scorched-earth policy. It seemed worth trying.

All through the first days there had been evidence of other refugees. Such water-holes as there were on the western edge of the Omaheke were filled with the bloated corpses of cattle and men. The desert floor was littered with the symbols of lives drawing to a close : pots, pans, clothing, anything that could no longer be carried; and, everywhere, bones whitening in the terrible sun.

But now, as they approached the half-way mark, the very heart of the Thirstland itself, evidence of human passage became less apparent. There were occasional traces of Bushmen, but that was all. Of animal life there was nothing except snakes and scorpions. Once Matthew had seen a herd of wildebeeste in the distance but by the time he could tell Andrew they were gone.

'Are you sure you saw them?' Andrew asked.

'Yes. It wasn't a mirage. About eighty, all strung out in a line moving north.'

Andrew nodded. 'The autumn migration,' he said. 'They've been grazing in the Kalahari and now they're moving north b:cause of the dry season. They'll spend the winter up near the Okavango River and come down again next summer if they smell rain.'

216

But if the autumn migration had begun they saw no other sign of it. The wildebeest disappeared into the shimmering horizon and they were left alone to look after the living and the dying.

So far water had not been one of their problems, for they had filled gourds, leather water-bags, even empty ostrich eggs, at the well in the Tjirue Mountains before they left. But within ten minutes of starting the journey an old woman had died. She had simply lain down on the sand, folded her arms around he knees, lowered her head and died. There had been no time to bury her and they had left her there like a petrified foetus.

Exhaustion, starvation and a lack of hope had killed her and in the next week the same symptoms were to reduce the group of Herero refugees from nearly three hundred to just on two hundred. It would have been difficult even for a medical officer to tell the exact cause of their deaths; too much had happened to them; they had been driven too hard. They died in their blankets, they died whenever a rest was taken for water, they died on the march, simply dropping out of the column, dead before they hit the ground. And many, although they kept up, were ambulatory dead. Andrew could see it in their eyes. The indefinable something, which he knew of as spirit or soul, had fled from their bodies, leaving them automata. How long they continued before actual rigor overtook them depended on the mechanical memory of muscle and sinew. It was an easy path for Brock to follow : one corpse led to the next, for there was no chance of burial.

They didn't die without a fight, even though the fight wasn't their own. Matthew seemed determined that no one should be allowed to slip away without some effort and Andrew was staggered at his energy. He seemed to be everywhere, cajoling, driving, pleading, exhorting and sometimes abusing. Without him the death roll would have been greater, for he seemed impervious to the heat and the conditions. He helped women with their children, he helped the older people, he formed squads of young men to carry double loads and so relieve their weaker neighbours. In spite of him they died.

Kaneena was a problem on his own. His arm had become infected and he was hot with fever. Two days before he had been unable to rise after a rest period. Andrew had carefully removed the splints from his arm and had winced when he saw the purple swelling.

217

'The badness must come out,' Kaneena had said and Andrew knew he was right. He sharpened the soft steel of his O.I.O. knife on a piece of flat stone and heated the blade in a small fire. By the time he'd opened the swelling and allowed the yellow matter to drain he was surrounded by upwards of twenty men. They watched intently as he worked and finally, as he bound up the arm again, there was what sounded like a corporate sigh of relief.

In half an hour, using leather thongs, branches from thorn trees and cut-up blankets, the Hereros had built a stretcher. Andrew had never seen them do this for anyone else, nor, in spite of their exhaustion, was there any lack of volunteers to carry it.

If he had not realized it before, he now did in double measure : the love and respect which the people had for their chief.

He did not fully understand it, for it seemed to him that Kaneena had led them from one disaster to another. Nor did he understand a remark Kaneena made to him when, on the following day, he walked for some minutes beside the stretcher. Kaneena was weak but the fever had dropped. 'I must thank you,' he said, in German. 'Now, if I live, it is because of you.' He lay back on the skins for a moment then, lifting himself up on his elbow, said : 'At the mission school I once read a book which had in it an old Chinese proverb which said, "Why do you hate me, I have not helped you?" The Chinese were wrong, Inspector.'

And so they went on into the centre of the Omaheke, a dusty, pathetic little army of men, women and children, for whom death held little terror since nothing could be worse than life. All the while the fires burned, some lit by Andrew and some by Brock, who was always there behind them, a dark and menacing shadow.

At night, in the clear sky, Andrew was able to take accurate bearings by the stars. Each day he checked his compass bearing. They were moving ENE and he estimated that they had covered nearly 150 kilometres.

Lying in the morning shade of a mass of wait-a-bit thorn, he said to Matthew, 'He'll have to turn back soon. If he's going to attack it'll be in the next twenty-four hours. How's our water?'

'We're down to a cup a day. It'll probably last another four days, with luck.'

'You're not forgetting the horse.' He glanced at Duke's thin frame, the low-held head, the frosting of sand around the mouth.

'No. I'm not forgetting the horse.'

In the late afternoon they moved off again and marched until midnight. In those seven hours fourteen Hereros dropped by the way. They were relieved of their gourds and the water was shared out among the women with families. There had never been any need to guard the water supplies, for the Hereros were people of the semi-desert and they knew how long each mouthful had to last.

They camped that night in a thicket of thorn-scrub, a dense patch of dusty bush in one of the hollows formed by a broken eruption of low hillocks. Andrew filled his hat with water three times and allowed Duke to drink, then he stripped half a dozen acacia branches of their thorns and offered them to the stallion. Duke sniffed at them and turned his head away. They were too dry for mastication. Then Andrew saw to the guards. He usually posted six of the ablest men on the circumference of the camp and he and Matthew took it in hourly turns to patrol. Matthew had first watch and Andrew was asleep almost at once. It seemed that he had barely closed his eyes when he felt a rough hand on his shoulder.

'Already?' he said wearily.

'Inspector!' Kaneena was crouching over him, his voice thick with pain.

He came wide awake instantly. Near his feet lay a black figure, a young woman of about twenty. She was unconscious and obviously on the point of death. 'She came to warn us,' Kaneena whispered.

She had apparently dropped out some hours before, unable to keep up, unwilling even to try, one of the living dead. According to Kaneena, to whom she had gasped out her story some minutes before, she had lain on the desert floor until the coolness of evening had revived her. Some last vestige of animal instinct had caused her to fight her way forward, hoping to catch up with the refugees when they made camp. She had been staggering through the darkness when she had heard horses. She'd counted nearly thirty mounted men. Flattening herself on the sand, she had watched them dismount in a gully less than a thousand yards from where the Hereros were camped. She had come on to warn them, crawling for most of the way.

Andrew listened with growing apprehension. Just before dusk they had seen the smoke from Brock's fires a good ten kilometres away. He was certain of it. Later he had checked again, circling Duke behind the Hereros until he could make out the pinpoint of light against the dark hills. They *couldn't* be less than a kilometre away. Then he realized what a fool he'd been. He had been guilty of thinking like a German and assuming that Brock was thinking in the same way. He should have known that Brock would never attempt a frontal attack and he should not have allowed himself to be lulled into a false sense of security by the very regularity of the past few days' pattern. Each had watched the other's fires, each had assumed that the fire marked the other's position. Now Brock had out-thought him. He had lit a camp fire, big enough to be seen at a distance, then he and his men had come racing up through the darkness, squeezing the last drops of energy out of their horses. And why not? If they were successful they would capture the water supply of nearly two hundred people, enough and more to see them back to Falkenberg in comfort.

He tried to put himself in Brock's place. Thirty men against two hundred. What would he do? His racing thoughts checked, steadied, and ran smoothly. He knew precisely what he'd do.

'Get them up!' he said, springing to his feet. 'Every one of them. We're moving! As quiet as you can!'

It took them nearly half an hour to rouse the Hereros. Some, like the woman who had staggered and crawled to reach them, would never rise again. But Matthew had to make certain, shaking every figure three or four times before passing on to the next. In half an hour, with the help of the able-bodied men, Andrew had the entire band out of the thicket and huddling amid a sprawl of massive rocks about two thousand yards to the east. Then, with forty men who owned firearms, he and Matthew made their way back to the thicket. 'Why don't we just go on?' Matthew asked. 'They may turn back when they realize we're gone.'

'And they may not. They'll know we're not far.'

They hid behind the top of a limestone ridge and watched the empty thicket. It was an hour before they heard the faint noises of the approaching Orlams. They were dismounted and moved across the desert with the stealth of hunting dogs. Behind them Andrew could see Brock on horseback, his figure black and huge against the starlit skyline. It was a moonless night and Andrew had difficulty seeing exactly what was happening until Brock's arms began to semaphore the plan of attack. The circling movements of his arms gave Andrew a moment of satisfaction; it was precisely what he would have done himself.

The Orlams had now encircled the thicket and Brock's arms urged them forward. It was then that Andrew realized how fortunate it was there were corpses in the thicket. It would give them a few valuable minutes.

Brock was allowing his horse to find its way between the thorn bushes on the edge of the thicket and there was now no one in sight. Andrew could imagine the knives already going to work on the dead bodies, the grunting satisfaction of the Orlams. He wondered if they had been surprised to find no guards, but then Brock must have considered the whole band almost dead from exposure.

He turned to Matthew. 'You know what you've got to do?' Matthew nodded. 'Right then, quickly!'

Matthew and ten Hereros detached themselves from the main body and raced silently down towards the thicket, spreading out in a rough semi-circle on its western flank, the flank from which a night wind was blowing. Andrew saw the first flicker of flame as a match was lit and then another and another down the line of men. The flicker increased in volume as the brittle fronds of the fringe bush caught alight. There was a shout and a ragged volley of rifle fire and then—he found it difficult afterwards to explain what happened next.

His plan had been to fire the bush from the western flank and drive the Orlams and Brock onto the guns placed on the limestone outcrop. It had seemed an ideal tactic. But it was never executed, for he had not taken the dryness of the bush into consideration. No rain had fallen on that thorn scrub for nearly three years. Now it went up like a volcano. The light wind pushed the flames deeper into the thicket and all at once the whole area caught. As Andrew was to describe it later, it was a 'fire-storm'. It did not make the usual crackling of a bush fire. Instead it went up with a tremendous roaring noise. Even where he lay, fifty yards from it, the heat was almost unbearable.

The flames burnt incandescently, as though someone had thrown magnesium into the centre of the blaze. They burnt with white hot intensity for about five minutes, the roaring reaching a crescendo, and then as suddenly as it had flared the fire sank down to nothing, for there was nothing left to burn. The whole thicket had gone.

Andrew called the men and they ran down. Above the smell of wood ash and burnt gum was the sickly-sweet odour of roasted flesh. They found Matthew, his face and beard blackened by ash, his rifle hanging loose from one hand, his eyes wide and staring. 'Look!' he cried, and pointed to the middle of what had been thick scrub. There, sitting his horse like an equestrian statue in a city park, was Brock. Life must have exploded from his body with the intensity of the heat, leaving him, charred and rigid, his boots still smoking from their contact with the red-hot stirrups. Had the fire lasted longer it would have burnt away the thick branch that held both horse and rider upright, allowing them a decent funeral pyre. As it was it had blasted onto them a cara-pace of carbonized flesh and then had died itself.

Andrew heard Matthew vomiting beside him. He turned angrily. 'What d'you think would have happened if he'd caught us? There'd have been no quick death with a bullet. Make no mistake about that. We'd have gone back to Falkenberg to hang in his tree!'

'Even so . . .' Matthew said shakily.

'You want these people to get through, don't you?'

He seemed to gather himself. 'Yes,' he said. 'Don't you?'

Andrew felt the excitement of the past fifteen minutes fading. A sense of depression settled on his shoulders. 'Why should I care about them? They've no future. It's you I'm taking through. You!'

Matthew looked closely at him. 'You say things like that when you don't mean them. You seem to take pleasure in diminishing yourself.'

Later the following day he caught up with Andrew and said, 'Why didn't he do the same thing? Burn us out, I mean.'

222

'Still queasy? I'll put your mind at rest. He would have except for one thing. He wanted our water.'

It was only then that he remembered the horses, but nothing would have induced him to go back for them.

The long column split the landscape. It wound in and out of the dusty camelthorns, up the sides of hillocks, through the dry beds of streams that had not seen water for five years and might not see any for a further five. The long straggling column was the only thing that moved. It made its painful progress under a sky crowded with slate-blue clouds and rumbling with thunder. The scene was like a steel engraving.

There was no pretence now of being a unified body. The strongest plodded out in front, the weakest trailed off behind until despair and exhaustion claimed them. Less than half the original number now survived.

Andrew walked at the head of the column, leading Duke, feeling the stallion's weight on the bridle as it paced unwillingly forward. Every now and then he jerked on the bit, bringing Duke up level with his shoulder. For two days he had not been in the saddle, because there was perhaps only one effort remaining in Duke and he was hoarding it against—he did not know what, only that he might need the horse's final reserve of strength.

Some time in the past twenty-four hours they must have crossed Longitude 21 East, which marked the border between German South-West and Bechuanaland, if his calculations were correct. He had tried to keep an exact tally of hours travelled and tried to keep up the pace, but it was difficult to tell. Perhaps they weren't across the border. He watched for beacons and told Matthew to do the same, but they had seen nothing. Perhaps there were no beacons in this part of the desert. He tried to visualize it on the maps he'd used but as far as he could remember this whole area had been overprinted with one phrase only: 'Open grass veld (waterless)'. He drew to one side of the column and brought the prismatic glasses up to his eyes, but under the lowering sky the plain was featureless; limestone outcrops, stunted trees, dusty bush, patches of yellow grass; no range of mountains in the distance to give a bearing, not even the sun to cast a pointing shadow. They were travelling solely by compass.

He glanced at his watch. They'd been moving now for an hour. He held up his hand. 'Halt!' Those at the front of the column threw themselves down on the stony ground, placing their heads on their arms. This was the only way, walk for an hour, rest for fifteen minutes, walk for another hour, rest again, walk, rest. As long as the sun kept behind the clouds they could use daylight as well as night. The rest periods allowed those at the rear to catch up but in turn it gave them less rest than those in front, so that at the next rest period they took longer to catch up. Finally, of course, those in the far rear did not catch up at all. Some managed to reach the main body when they camped for a few hours, but many did not. Andrew wondered whether they might not be the lucky ones.

'What do you think?' Matthew had come up the line from his job of harrying the stragglers and now lowered himself onto the ground. There seemed no flesh left on him, just bone and sinew and a storehouse of energy and will.

Andrew shook his head. 'Dry storm,' he said, confining himself to the two words. His mouth was limey with scum and talking made him thirstier.

'There's only about half a cup left for each of them.' Matthew spoke with difficulty and Andrew noticed the dry scum around his lips. His thoughts went back to that day on Kela Pan when he and Chik had had to peel those same lips apart and force in the water drop by drop, and in spite of his own condition he felt an unfamiliar sensation of pity. The poor bugger, he thought, it's happening again and there's no one to help this time.

He looked past Matthew and suddenly noticed that the Hereros had unconsciously grouped themselves around them. Their faces were turned to him, the black skins hanging loose and dusty, the eyes blank and expressionless. Or were they? Was it his imagination or was there a corporate look of accusation. Christ! The ungrateful bastards! He glanced at them again, viciously angry. Without thinking he reached for his water-bottle and put it to his lips. A slight trickle wet his tongue and that was all. Savagely he hurled the water-bottle over his shoulder. His rage was that of a small boy, wild, unreasoning, unable to focus on any valid point; a childish mixture of self-pity and exasperation overlaid by a sudden and frightening feeling of panic.

He felt a touch on his arm and looked around into the face of

224

a young girl. She couldn't have been more than eighteen yet she seemed older. He didn't realize what she wanted until he saw the ostrich egg in her hand.

All the bitter anger in him boiled up. 'I don't want your bloody water!' he shouted. A moment later he was aware of a feeling of sick shame and also of contempt in Matthew's eyes. He struggled to his feet. 'Come on,' he muttered. 'It's time.'

They plodded on into the Thirstland, a company of dusty ghosts, the only thing keeping them together the deep-felt herd instinct of the animal.

At noon they halted again and drank the last of the water. Andrew had none and asked for none; the girl's gesture was not repeated. This time as the Hereros lay on the ground they did not look at him. A decision was forced on him. He got to his feet and went to Duke, pulling the girth tight.

'What are you doing?' Matthew said.

'Don't worry, I'm not leaving,' he said, thickly. 'I'm going ahead, there must be a bloody water-pit somewhere in this God-forsaken place.'

He was alone. He'd given the compass to Matthew and now he travelled by instinct. The desert swallowed him up.

All that day the heavy clouds sailed through the sky leaching the land of colour. At first the thunder had been distant, but now as the centre of the electric storm passed over western Bechuana-land the thunder grew louder and forked lightning crackled through the sky and hissed down to strike the desert floor. By mid-afternoon the atmosphere was charged and brittle, the light gloomy.

He did not glance at the sky. When he had first come to the Kalahari he had thought that storms meant rain. That was a fallacy he had soon put behind him. For every hundred storms that had crossed the desert, only one had shed its rain. Now, as the thunder crackled and the lightning flashed, he rode, head down in the saddle, weak from loss of fluid in the dry, burning atmosphere, already past remembering why he was there and what he was seeking. So, late in the afternoon, when Duke's weary steps began to pick up, it was some minutes before he realized it. He raised his red-rimmed eyes and saw the pan about five hundred yards ahead of him. With a wild surge of hope he let Duke take him forward at a canter.

The pan was small, about one hundred yards in diameter and shaped like the top of a miniature volcano. It was circular and completely surrounded by a four-foot lip of limestone.

On its southern side it was heavily flanked by thick bush and as he drew up with it he could see that the bush was greener than anything they had passed since entering the desert. He was sure this was the result of a freak cloudburst. The point was, how long ago had the rain fallen? He urged Duke down the side of the pan and the stallion's hooves broke through the crusty surface and he sank past the fetlocks in gluey mud.

Andrew held him there, every sense alert. 'Careful now,' he said, 'we don't want to be sucked down.' Gently he eased Duke forward towards the middle of the pan. The stallion took each step with caution and Andrew could hear the sucking noise as his hooves came out one after another. They went forward ten yards and stopped. As far as he could tell the bottom was firm about eighteen inches below the crust. They went on, Duke eager now with the smell of wet mud, making towards the centre of the pan where the last of the water would have collected. In parts the crust was firmer and in others Duke sank away, once almost to his belly, before pulling free. Andrew kept him going, a mixture of fear and nervous excitement dominating the part of his mind that called for caution.

The pan's centre was hidden by a stand of feathery rushes. About twenty yards away he stopped Duke and tied his bridle to a mud-covered rock. 'Don't worry, you'll have yours,' he said as the stallion wrenched at the bit.

He went forward on foot, his boots crushing through the surface. He parted the fronds of papyrus and looked down at a shining pool. He stood transfixed for a moment then gave a cry of terror and stumbled backwards. Something was lying half in and half out of the water. It looked like a body and in Andrew's imagination it had seemed to move, to turn slightly like a giant salamander and look up at him.

How long he stood among the papyrus stems he was never able to tell. It might only have been seconds, perhaps it was as long as ten minutes. He was in a state of catalepsy and was only brought back to his senses by the restless whickering of the horse.

Trembling, he went forward again. In the gloomy half-light the pit seemed to him the embodiment of everything evil, everything phantasmagoric, and yet his thirst drove him on.

What had frightened him was a log of wood about six feet long. It lay in a basin of ooze, one end half buried. There was no water in the pool at all, only glistening mud.

He threw himself down into it and began to dig furiously with his hands. He could hear his breath coming in sobs. He dug like an animal, scooping out handfuls of mud and throwing them backwards between his legs. The deeper he dug the dryer became the ground. He tore off his shirt and packed it with mud and began to squeeze . . . and then he stopped. In his mind was suddenly the picture of Matthew's blackened face and lips at Kela. Some primitive instinct held him back. If I suck mud, he thought, I'm done.

He sat on the rim of the pan with his head on his arms. He could do no more. He and Duke had covered every inch of the surface, ploughing through the mud, sometimes up to their knees, but they had found no water. And now there was nothing else to do. He had taken the Jeffries from his saddle holster and it lay across his lap, curiously comforting. He would not die like that traveller in the southern Kalahari, without his boots, without his stock and servants, abandoned in the desert. He would not die like that. He would leave no note, seek no pity. One shot for Duke, another for himself, and that would be that. The very thought that he could end everything in one split second gave him a slight surge of confidence and in that moment he seemed to see again the faces of the Hereros turned towards him and the girl with the water and he realized that the look in their eyes had not been accusation but simple, child-like trust. And he was reminded of the same expression in the eyes of the young German soldiers, that had said he would look after them, he would cope. Wearily he pushed himself to his feet. The lightning played around the sky, the thunder boomed and rolled. 'Come,' he said to Duke.

They hadn't gone ten yards when he heard a noise, a hard crack like a rifle shot. He heard a second and a third. They sounded as though they were coming from the heavy bush on the southern slope of the pan. He rode at a tangent for half a mile before he suddenly dragged Duke to a halt and flung himself from the saddle. In a second he had the glasses to his eyes. He was just in time to see the last of a great herd of elephants come out of the southern desert and enter the bush. He knew what had made those cracking noises. The first arrivals were feeding.

He crouched quietly, thinking out this unexpected turn in events. The herd would have been feeding in the Kalahari during the rainy season and now would be migrating towards the Okavango swamps. That meant they would have drunk heavily before starting their journey and would be carrying their water with them. Softly he remounted and turned westward. He rode for an hour before he began to fire shots at regular intervals. Thirty minutes later he heard the boom of a Martini-Henry in reply.

They lay well to the south, those that remained, for he had harried them unmercifully, bringing them across the desert at a shambling trot. It was dusk but the threatening sky made it seem darker. The centre of the storm had passed and the thunder was low on the horizon. Sheet lightning flared briefly giving sudden patches of white light. They could not see the elephants, but they could hear them.

They moved forward in a sickle-shaped line and as they closed with the area of bush Andrew fired a signal shot. The Hereros broke into a frenzy of screaming and shouting, guns exploded, gourds and watercans were rattled together. The noise was appalling and with it came the frightened trumpeting of the elephants. They crashed through the bush to get away from the noise, up over the lip of the pan and down, flailing and roiling in the soft ooze of the bottom. They were trapped. The armed Hereros raced to the raised bank and began to pour a tremendous fire into the plunging herd.

Andrew lay on the eastern ridge pumping bullet after bullet into the animals nearest him. Some went down, others plunged their way across the gluey surface only to find themselves under fire from the far side. The pan was now completely encircled by guns and the elephants had no chance. Screaming cows tried to mount the lip only to stick there, half-way, their back feet embedded in what had now become a bog. It was slaughter on a gigantic scale, nightmarish, horrifying, a primitive cataclysm of blood and noise that drowned out even the thunder.

Andrew watched two bulls try to raise a wounded cow with their tusks. She struggled, slipping and slithering, to regain her feet and then one of the bulls went down and Andrew shot the second.

In less than half an hour it was all over. The lightning, when it came, illuminated fitfully the mud-torn graveyard of an entire herd of 138 bulls, cows and calves. Not a single animal survived.

The first Hereros moved cautiously onto the pan. Now the shots came singly as they finished off dying animals. Finally there was only silence. But it was a silence that presaged an avalanche, for the Hereros literally fell on the corpses of the beasts, hacking open their still-warm paunches and drinking the hot blood as it spurted out. They pulled out entrails, sucked on wet, partially digested food, opened up the udders of cows in milk and drained them into their gourds and finally, once their initial thirst was somewhat assuaged, they entered the gaping bellies and siphoned out the oily water that lay in the water sacs under the last rib. Andrew had ordered them to be careful in handling these sacs but some were beyond care and a few of the sacs were broken and the water wasted. Andrew saw one which had been accidentally punctured. A spout of blood and water, about an inch thick, was shooting from the elephant's stomach.

He was offered a calabash and put it to his lips. The mixture of water and blood and herbs was bitter to the palate but it was liquid and as it coursed down his throat and was sucked into his dehydrated tissues he felt it renew his body like a life-force itself.

He stood, looking down at the greater transfer of life taking place in the torn mud of the pan; looking but not really seeing. At one time, had the question ever arisen, he would have put the life of an elephant above that of any black-skinned man in the world; he would have considered what he had just organized and executed a criminal waste. Now he watched as the stronger Hereros brought up water to those lying close to death outside the pan. He saw Kaneena, with the last of his strength, stagger from one near-corpse to the next; he saw others go back along the track they had earlier covered with such murderous speed, to save

229

as many as they could. And as he watched a sense of wonder and of pity rose in him; but above all a sense of respect. His thoughts went back to the Waterberg, to the last battle under its great red wall. He saw again the stampeding flight of a nation; he saw clearly in his mind's eye the woman who had said, 'I thank you' just before the bullet had ended her life; and he realized that though the Hereros had been vanquished, possibly more so than any other race in history, they had still to be defeated. He felt a sudden lift of hope.

He went in search of Matthew. He had assumed he would be found helping to give water to those unable to help themselves. Instead he discovered him sitting some way away from the pan with his back to a small thorn tree.

He sat down beside him, aware that Matthew was near the end of whatever storehouse of energy and determination had brought him this far and aware, for the first time, how much he himself had depended on it. They remained in silence for a long while. Eventually Matthew said : 'We had to do it. We *had* to.' It was part statement, part query and spoken as much to himself as to Andrew and Andrew knew he was referring to the slaughter of the herd.

A week ago, only a few hours ago, he might have felt a surge of the old irritation in the face of a quality he had mistakenly construed as weakness. Instead he now experienced a feeling of sympathy; for what he saw in Matthew he had ultimately been able to identify in himself.

'Yes,' he said. 'We had to.'

And so, two days later, they came to Lake Ngami, all that was left of them, seventy-eight Hereros and two white men. The war was finally over.

SOME SOURCE BOOKS

Andersson, Charles John. *Lake Ngami*. Hurst and Blackett, London 1856

Auer, G. *In Sudwestafrika gegen die Hereros*. Ernst Hofmann and Co., Berlin 1911

Bridgman and Clarke. *German Africa*. A select annotated bibliography. Hoover Institution, Stanford University, 1965

Calvert, Albert F. *The German African Empire*. T. Werner Laurie, London 1916

Frenssen, Gustav. *Peter Moor's Journey to South West Africa* (Trans. by Margaret May Ward). Constable and Co., London 1908

Galton, Francis. *Narratives of an Explorer in Tropical Africa*. Ward Lock and Co., London 1889

Green, Lawrence G. *Lords of the Last Frontier*. Stanley Paul and Co., London 1953

Hodson, Arnold W. *Trekking the Great Thirst*. T. Fisher Unwin, London 1912

Kerremans, A. *Strategie des Allemands dans leur guerre contre les Hereros*. Librarie Chapelot, Paris 1913

Mossolow, Dr N. *This was Old Windhoek*. Distribution by Author. Windhuk 1965

Steer, G. L. *Judgement on German Africa*. Hodder and Stoughton, London 1939

Vedder, Heinrich. *South West Africa in Early Times*. Oxford University Press, 1938

OFFICIAL DOCUMENTS

'Report on the Natives of South West Africa and their treatment by Germany.' (Cd. 9146 of 1918)

'South West Africa.' Foreign Office Handbook (Hist. Sec.) No. 112 Vol. 18

'Treatment of Natives in the German Colonies.' Foreign Office Handbook (Hist. Sec.) No. 114 Vol. 18

Time is running out for the savage splendour of Imperial China . . .

MANDARIN

Robert Elegant

Creator of DYNASTY and MANCHU

After the First Opium War of 1840, China is in turmoil. In the South, insurrection threatens; in Shanghai, 'barbaric' Western influence is spreading – and on all sides, the dazzling old world of the Orient faces the onslaught of the new . . .

Against the gorgeous and turbulent panorama of Imperial China under the Great Pure Dynasty of the Manchus, MANDARIN unfolds an epic adventure of revolution and romance, peopled by a glorious cast of characters – warriors and lovers, concubines and courtiers, seekers of fortune in war and in trade . . . the merchant Saul Haleevie, bidding for power alongside the great European trading houses; Fronah his daughter, torn between love and virtue; and the unscrupulous Yehenala, whose destiny would one day be inextricably linked with that of China itself.

MANDARIN magnificently recreates China at a momentous turning point in its colourful history: a sweeping, spectacular drama – vast yet intimately human – of an exotic world that was to vanish forever.

'A huge tale . . . full of romance, exoticism and danger.' *Good Housekeeping.*

FICTION/GENERAL   0 7221 3275 1   £2.95

THE VEGAS LEGACY

OVID DEMARIS

Bestselling author of THE LAST MAFIOSO

Ruthless multi-billionaire Rufus Boutwell made
his fortune in the wild days of the Nevada gold
rush. He bought up land and politicians, then
promoted gambling and prostitution for his own
profit – while trumpeting the virtues of personal
freedom. Now, as head of Nevada Consolidated
Mines, he is about to launch the mightiest
political coup of his long career which will make
or break him forever. . . .

From the barren sands of the Nevada desert to
the razzamatazz of a Vegas-style Republican
convention, THE VEGAS LEGACY is a
whirlwind-paced saga of greed, drugs, sex,
ambition and corruption . . . in the blockbusting
tradition of Harold Robbins and Mario Puzo.

GENERAL FICTION   0 7221 30163   £2.50

A selection of bestsellers from **SPHERE**

FICTION

CHANGES	Danielle Steel	£1.95 ☐
FEVRE DREAM	George R. R. Martin	£2.25 ☐
LADY OF FORTUNE	· Graham Masterton	£2.75 ☐
POMEROY	Gordon Williams	£1.95 ☐
FIREFOX DOWN	Craig Thomas	£2.25 ☐

FILM & TV TIE-INS

THE DUNE STORYBOOK	Joan Vinge	£2.50 ☐
SUPERGIRL	Norma Fox Mazer	£1.75 ☐
WHAT DO DOOZERS DO?	Michaela Muntean	£1.50 ☐
MINDER – BACK AGAIN	Anthony Masters	£1.50 ☐
ONCE UPON A TIME IN AMERICA	Lee Hays	£1.75 ☐

NON-FICTION

BACHELOR BOYS – THE YOUNG ONES' BOOK	Rik Mayall, Ben Elton and Lise Mayer	£2.95 ☐
THE BOOK OF SPORTS LISTS	Craig and David Brown	£2.50 ☐
THE HYPOCHONDRIAC'S HANDBOOK	Dr. Lee Schreiner and Dr. George Thomas	£1.50 ☐
WORST MOVIE POSTERS OF ALL TIME	Greg Edwards and Robin Cross	£4.95 ☐
THE FASTEST DIET	Rosie Boycott	£1.25 ☐

All Sphere books are available at your local bookshop or newsagent, or can be ordered direct from the publisher. Just tick the titles you want and fill in the form below.

Name _____

Address _____

_____

Write to Sphere Books, Cash Sales Department, P.O. Box 11, Falmouth, Cornwall TR10 9EN

Please enclose a cheque or postal order to the value of the cover price plus:

UK: 55p for the first book, 22p for the second book and 14p for each additional book ordered to a maximum charge of £1.75.

OVERSEAS: £1.00 for the first book plus 25p per copy for each additional book.

BFPO & EIRE: 55p for the first book, 22p for the second book plus 14p per copy for the next 7 books, thereafter 8p per book.

Sphere Books reserve the right to show new retail prices on covers which may differ from those previously advertised in the text or elsewhere, and to increase postal rates in accordance with the PO.